M000198312

waiting *for* december

other titles by riley costello

waiting at hayden's

waiting *for* december

a novel

riley costello

Sullivan & Shea
Publishing

Waiting for December is a work of fiction. Names, characters, places, and incidents are the products of the author's imagination or are used fictitiously. Any resemblance to actual events, locales, or persons, living or dead, is entirely coincidental.

Copyright © 2022 Riley Costello
All rights reserved
Published in the United States by Sullivan & Shea Publishing

Costello, Riley, author.
Waiting for December: a novel / Riley Costello
Oregon: Sullivan & Shea Publishing
ISBN 978-1-7323033-4-8

sincerelyriley.com

Cover Illustration by Lindsey Kath
Cover Design by Danielle Christopher
Typesetting by FormattingExperts.com
Author Photo by Ryan Selewicz

First Edition: September 2022

To Jordyn McCoy, for being my first reader
&
To Aunt Stephanie, the original reader in our family

one

I'm shaking as I board the plane from Atlanta to Vermont.

It's hard to tell if my nerves are coming from my fear of flying or from the realization that I'm heading to a state where I've never been, to work a job I have no experience in.

The image of the Cape Cod-style bed-and-breakfast where I'll be employed for the next three months flashes into my head, and for a moment I question if I'm losing my mind to take such a risk, to overhaul my entire life.

But, no, I'm not—I need the fresh start.

When I spot my row, I nearly smile when I realize that I've been seated next to a pilot dressed in uniform. Something about being near someone trained to know what to do in case of an emergency reassures me. Plus, given his experience, I imagine he'd be one of the first to pick up on a potential problem in the air and I like knowing that I'd have more of a heads-up than the rest of the passengers if something bad were about to happen.

Over the past six months I've been broken up with the day before my wedding and unexpectedly let go from my job, so I'm terrified of being blindsided again.

As I settle in, the pilot—not the one sitting beside me, but the one flying this plane—announces final checks for the flight crew.

We'll take off soon, then. I shut my eyes and press back into my seat. I'm not naïve enough to believe that flying away from your problems makes them go away, but I'm hoping it at least makes dealing with them a tiny bit easier.

—

Once we're at cruising altitude, I open my eyes again and notice that the pilot—not the one flying this plane, but the one sitting beside me—is fidgeting with his hands. His forehead is also wrinkled with concern, and he keeps looking out the window, then back to his hands, then out the window again.

Oh, come on.

There can't be something wrong with this plane. Well, I suppose there could be. But right now, my brain wants to rationalize that enough bad things have happened to me lately and the universe should cut me some slack. I know the world doesn't work this way, but damn if it doesn't feel like it *should*.

I clear my throat. "Is everything all right?"

The pilot stares at me, which gives me a chance to stare at him and notice that he looks more like a pilot you'd expect to see on TV than in a cockpit. Even if I weren't sitting here waiting on him to tell me whether or not this flight is going down, it'd be hard for me to turn my attention away from his green eyes and sandy blond hair.

"That depends on what you mean by *okay*," he says. Although his answer was not at all reassuring, I somehow feel as if he just told me good news. His voice is warm and deep like an audiobook narrator's. On the bright side, maybe he'll tell me a good story as we crash-land.

I *can't* believe I just tried to find a bright side.

Seriously, Harper, what's wrong with you?

"Are we going down or not?" I ask him point-blank, right as the drink cart rolls by. They wouldn't be getting ready to serve refreshments if something bad were about to happen, right? Or maybe that *is* the protocol before announcing engine failure. Now that I think about it, gin sounds good. And vodka. Maybe some tequila too.

The man hesitates before answering, "Are you close with your family?"

That . . . wasn't a response to my question. Or was it? Is he asking me because he's about to tell me I should call them for the last time?

"Yes," I respond. "With my parents especially. I'm an only child. But my two best friends feel like sisters."

He nods and says, "We're not going down. We're going to Vermont. Where *my* family is. And we are not close."

"Oh." That's all I say, because I get it now. He's not anxious about the flight, he's anxious about what happens after we land, when he has to see his family.

I feel my entire body relax.

He still looks on edge, though.

I realize I don't know the guy, but I do know what it's like to need cheering up, so I lean in a little closer and say, "Is there any chance you could avoid them? Even though Vermont is the second smallest state in the country, I've been researching things to do, and maybe you could hide out at a maple syrup factory like Morse Farm," I suggest. "Or at Cabot Cheese Factory. Do you know they have a dozen different cheeses you can sample daily? That could eat up some time."

He smiles. I like that I made him smile. It somehow makes me feel like I won a prize. Maybe because I get the sense this man doesn't smile all that often. Or at least he doesn't when he's heading to Vermont to see his family.

"I avoid them more than I don't," he tells me. "They're miserable to be around. But this is my mom's seventieth birthday, so it's sort of a command performance, if you will."

"Well, in that case, do you want to vent about your family? Maybe if you get it all out of your system before you see them, it will make it easier to be nice to their faces when you get there."

He smiles again, and this time it sends my stomach into flutter mode.

Oh no.

3

This is *not* good.

I am *just* talking to this guy. I am *not*—under any circumstances—going to become interested in him.

I am taking the next three months to find myself. And to figure out what I want next out of life after everything that's happened over the past six months. That is the whole point of this trip. I am not about to get sidetracked by a guy.

"If we're going to talk about my family, I'm going to need a drink," he tells me. "Have you ever had a gin and tonic in the sky?"

"Can't say I have."

"Ah, you've got to try it. It tastes so much better than it does on the ground."

The corners of my mouth curl up. "Should I be worried that you're a pilot and you know this?"

He grins again. "I fly even when I'm not flying. I love to travel."

"I hate to travel," I admit. "Or rather, I hate flying. It terrifies me."

"It's safer than driving, you know. And I presume you get in a car daily." He leans his head back against the headrest, getting comfortable. I don't know if he's trying to prove a point or put me at ease. I get the sense it's the latter.

"But driving, I feel I have some control," I counter.

He closes his eyes before he speaks. "We don't really have that much control over anything. We just like to think we do."

I sigh and lean my head back against my own headrest. "You don't have to tell me that. I was recently dumped the day before my wedding. And then I got laid off from my job. I'm heading to Vermont to try and start over."

I'm not sure why I just admitted this, other than that he confessed he's afraid of going home and it feels like a fair trade: vulnerable confession for vulnerable confession. Or maybe it's that I'm not looking to date him, so I don't care if he finds me pathetic.

4

His eyes are open now and he's looking at me again. "Someone stood you up the day before your wedding?"

He sounds pissed, as if he'd want to have a word if that someone were here. It's sort of sweet that he seems to feel protective of me even though he barely knows me. Most people react with some shock or awkwardness, but this is much nicer.

When I nod, he whistles and sits back in his seat. "What a dick," he says.

Jake's not a dick. Not even close. But it was a dick move, so I don't correct him.

He waited until the morning of our rehearsal dinner to break the news that he was in love with someone else: his first love, Anna. Apparently, the two of them bumped into one another four months earlier, when they returned to their hometown for the funeral of a high school friend who passed away unexpectedly. According to the story he told me that morning in the gardens of the hotel where our wedding was to take place, seeing her again stirred up unexpected feelings. Feelings that he'd been trying for the past several months to push away. But his attempts had been unsuccessful. Teary-eyed, he shared that his heart was being pulled in two directions and that he couldn't walk down the aisle with me, feeling the way he was about her.

If it weren't for my best friends, Zoe and Grace, whose arms I crumpled into right after, I'm not sure how I would have gotten through that heartache, or the setbacks that followed.

For starters, when I got home from my canceled wedding, I lost my job in marketing during a round of layoffs.

While I didn't love the job, it was hard to suddenly have tons of time on my hands to think of nothing but Jake and my absent career. I tried to find another job, but I had no success—I neither wanted any of the available roles nor was offered a position. I was lucky I had my severance package and savings to get me through. But the lack of any path forward drove me a little crazy.

That's probably why I caved and did what you're not—under any circumstances—supposed to do after a breakup: I checked Jake's Instagram page. It was four months later and I thought it'd be safe.

Instead, I learned he and Anna had gotten *married*.

He hadn't posted the wedding photo I saw, which I had to give him credit for. He wasn't trying to stick his happiness in my face, or anyone else's face, for that matter. I saw that Anna's mother simply had tagged him in a photo with the caption, "Congrats to my beautiful daughter and new son-in-law."

To be honest, if I weren't the casualty to their plot, I would have been inspired by the picture. Jake had on a beige sport jacket and jeans, and Anna wore a knee-length white dress and held a bouquet of daisies. They were walking down a cobblestoned street at sunset hand in hand and smiling at one another as if there was nowhere else they'd rather be.

"Ugh." That's what my broken heart had to say about it. "Ugh."

I don't hate Jake for following his heart, which is *clearly* with Anna. And he did apologize to me in a letter. And a voicemail. And an email. And a second and third email—because I couldn't bring myself to respond to any of his previous apologies.

See? Not a dick.

But I wish he had handled the situation differently. For instance, ending things with me sooner than the day before our wedding.

"That idiot—he'd fit in well with my family," the pilot next to me adds, breaking through my thoughts.

"They're really that bad?"

Sometimes looks can answer questions better than any verbal response can. This stranger gives me a look that tells me they're way worse than I can even imagine.

I tilt my head slightly, answering his look with a questioning one.

He sighs as he eyes the drink cart that hasn't quite reached us yet, like he's debating whether to hold out responding for a little longer. "You know how some people talk behind other people's backs and say really judgmental things they'd never say to someone directly?"

When I nod, he says, "That's basically my family, only they say those really judgmental things right to your face. Or to my face, at least."

I shiver because that *does* sound bad. "What do they have to judge you about?"

"That's the thing. It's not like I've made a bunch of bad choices. I've just made different choices than my parents, and they make me feel terrible about those choices every time I come home."

"Do you have siblings? To be a buffer between you and your parents?"

"I have three sisters and a brother, but they are part of it too. At least, three out of four of them. They tend to jump right on the same criticism train. See, we all grew up in Vermont. Each of my siblings stayed nearby for college, three married people from high school, and all opted to live right near my parents, who were also both born and raised in Vermont. I was the only one that moved away—to Boston for college, then to Chicago, then Los Angeles, and finally to Atlanta, where I'm based now. And I'm not married." He sighs. "My family would be easier to face if I had a girlfriend or a wife to mollify them, I think, but the thing is, I'm never going to get married. I don't want to."

I like that he's so clear on this, and it also makes me feel more comfortable around him. While there's attraction here, this admission—and that I don't want to get distracted by a crush—helps keep my interest in check because I *do* want to get married. I believe in marriage wholeheartedly. I'm really looking forward to spending my life with someone. At least *after* I take these next three months to find myself.

7

"What *do* you want?" I ask.

"To be free," he says, shooting a glance out the window, which he's seated beside. I'm in the middle. There's another woman in the aisle seat, but she has her earbuds in and appears to be asleep. "Free to explore, to change course if something isn't working, to go where the wind blows me. It's why I became a pilot."

"Where have you felt the freest?"

He pauses for a minute. "2013, Lagos, Portugal."

I think to ask why, but he's already turned the question back to me. "What about you?"

"Right now, I guess," I say. "I mean, I know where I'm going. I got a job at an inn for the fall-foliage and holiday season. But I have no idea what to expect when I get there. I'm not sure I like this feeling. I guess I don't want to be free so much as I want to belong—to myself, to a place in the world, to a community. I don't think I've ever felt any of that."

The drink cart finally arrives. "We'll have two gin and tonics in the sky," I tell the flight attendant, winking at my seatmate.

When she hands our cups and mixers over, I pass him his, then set mine down on my tray table and pull out my Vermont Bucket List from my backpack beneath the seat in front of me. I made a list of twenty-five things I wanted to try during the three months I'm there. I thought discovering more of my likes and dislikes would help me better understand myself and find my passion. Despite being twenty-nine years old, I've never really understood what makes me tick. I'm hopeful my time in Vermont will help me get more clarity. The list includes silly things like "go on a road trip with no destination in mind," along with more challenging items like "learn the art of patience" and "try thirty days straight of yoga." I add "sip a gin and tonic in the sky" to the list, then cross it off.

I'm about to slip it back in my backpack when the pilot glances over my shoulder and says, "What's that?"

"Just a list of things I want to try while in Vermont."

"Can I see it?"

I shake my head. I haven't shown this list to anyone—not even to Zoe and Grace. I think I want to keep it that way.

"I really like that," he says, as I put it away.

"Like what?"

"How decisive you were just then, not letting me see your list. Most people wouldn't do that—they'd cave easily to the pressure of other people."

"You say that like someone who doesn't cave easily either."

He smiles as he mixes his cocktail. "I generally do what I want, yes."

His comment sends my stomach straight back to flutter mode. I brush it off, then change the subject.

"I'm Harper, by the way. What's your name?"

He shakes his head and smiles again. "You're going to laugh when I tell you."

"Why?"

"Because you know I'm a pilot and that I love to fly."

When I raise a brow, he drops his head down toward his drink and says, "Skyler. But I go by Sky."

He's right. I do laugh. "Well, your parents are to blame, then, for you not wanting to stay in Vermont. They shouldn't have named you after the thing that would one day take you away. Try hitting them with that logic."

He laughs and then holds up his cup. "To starting over," he says.

"To surviving your family," I say, clinking my glass against his.

We both take a sip. "So you're going to be working at an inn, Harper?"

When I nod, he says, "Isn't that the plot of a lot of romantic comedy movies?"

I laugh because I can't believe he knows this. How *does* he know this?

9

"I grew up with three sisters. We had one television," he says, as if he read my mind.

I stare down at my cup. "It's stupid, I know," I say, biting the inside of my lip.

"I don't think it's stupid," he replies. "I think it sounds fun."

Fun. I hadn't thought of that. I'd thought this adventure might be scary, unexpected, a decision I might one day come to regret or look back on as a great learning experience. But I'd never thought it'd be fun. Maybe it *will be* fun. I could use some fun.

I look back up. "How long are you in town for?"

"Less than twenty-four hours," he says. "The party is tonight. We land at four, I'll be at my parents' house by five. And I fly out at eleven o'clock tomorrow morning."

"They didn't have a red-eye?" I tease.

He laughs and I feel warm.

It would have been nice if he were staying longer so I'd have a friend to show me around. But I guess it's a good thing he's only in town for one night. I don't think this is the kind of guy I could ever just be friends with.

He shifts and sets his arm on the armrest between us. I don't mind that he does this. But the thing is, my arm is already resting there, so we're sharing it now, which means we're touching. And I feel his touch everywhere. Even in places I didn't know it was possible to feel someone's touch, like in the back of my throat and all the way down in my toes.

I take another long sip of my drink. So long that I almost finish it. "You're right," I say. "A gin and tonic in the sky does taste way better than on the ground."

Sky smiles and takes a sip of his drink too. Then another. After he's finished, he leans his head against his headrest again and closes his eyes. I take a little more time to finish my drink, but once I do, I close my eyes too.

As I start to drift off, I realize Sky hasn't moved his arm.
I don't move mine either.

—

When I wake, my head is on Sky's shoulder. I must have really conked out because the flight attendant is announcing our descent.

Sky, on the other hand, is up and staring out the window. I'm surprised he let me sleep on him like this. All my life I've been told I'm not a pretty sleeper. I toss and turn, I drool, I often talk out loud.

When I sit up, I check for a drool stain on his shirt. Surprisingly, I don't find one.

"You were so peaceful," he says.

I'm about to tell him I don't believe it, but I'm distracted by how *not* peaceful he looks. As nervous as he seemed when we were taking off, he looks ten times more stressed now that we're about to land. I get the sense he didn't sleep at all.

"I never asked. What town are you headed to? What inn?"

It takes me a second to register that he's asked me a question. I'm too preoccupied feeling bad for him and wishing there were something I could do to help.

"Hudson Lane in Stowe," I say.

My answer makes him look my way. "Stowe? That's where I grew up, where I'm headed now."

"Oh, wow." I knew Vermont was small, but that coincidence sends a burst of heat through my stomach.

"Hudson Lane—it's a nice place," he nods, turning his gaze back out the window. "Nice couple that owns it too. Will you be staying there?"

"There's a private cottage for me, but it's not ready until tomorrow, so I'm staying at a hotel tonight."

"Which one?" I don't get the sense he really cares. I think he wants to make conversation so he doesn't think about where he's headed after this. My heart hurts for him. And then it gets an idea. An idea that it blurts out before consulting with my head.

"What if I join you tonight?"

That pulls Sky's gaze away from the window. He's looking right at me. "What do you mean?"

Too late to turn back now.

"You said it would be easier for you to face your family if you showed up with a wife or a girlfriend. What if I come along and pretend to be your plus one?"

He just stares. "You'd do that for me?" he finally asks.

Admittedly, I'm second-guessing the idea. I have from the moment I said it. I can't get distracted by this guy. And pretending to be his girlfriend for a night is definitely not the best way to avoid that. But I can't backtrack now. I'm the one who plunged ahead and proposed the entire thing. Besides, he's leaving in the morning. How hard could I really fall for him in one night, anyway?

"I know what it's like to be in a tough spot," I say. "If I can help you out, I'd like to be able to do that."

His smile is different now—bigger than when I saw it last and filled with relief.

"Thanks, Harper," he says, clasping his hand over mine. "You have no idea how much this means to me. This might actually end up being an enjoyable evening."

Or a dangerous one, I think, looking down at his hand on top of mine.

Either way, so far starting over is certainly interesting.

two

"**You** didn't tell me you were bringing someone!"

Sky's mom answered the door and looked right past Sky, the son she hasn't seen in a year, to me. Sky mentioned it's been that long since he'd been home on the forty-five minute car ride over. I don't say anything, expecting her attention to shift back to Sky for a hello.

"Mom," Sky says, but his mother's eyes stay on me. "Right. Mom, meet my girlfriend, Harper. Harper, meet my—"

"Oh, honey!" I'm wrapped in a hug before Sky can finish his introduction.

I was noticed before Sky, and now I'm getting a hug before him. My heart fractures a little for him, and I have a feeling it's going to be broken further over the next couple of hours. I feel even better about my decision to join him tonight. If Sky's mom is this happy he brought someone home, maybe it'll make the night easier. I try not to think about her reaction had he shown up alone—she still hasn't really looked at him.

"Happy birthday!" I say, as she releases me. She doesn't say thank you. She's too busy eyeing me up and down.

"She's so pretty," she finally says, as if I'm not standing right here and as if that alone makes me A-okay in her book.

To be fair, a lot of people comment on my looks when they meet me. I was incredibly relieved that Sky didn't mention anything about that when we met. I've always wanted people to see me for me, and my looks have nothing to do with who I am. They're just something we're born with. In the genetic lottery, I happened to

13

get thick blonde hair, a petite frame, blue eyes, and symmetrical bone structure. I know that's considered beautiful by a lot of people, and I'm not blind to that. But people tend to see that and ignore everything else about me. They make all sorts of assumptions about my personality and how likable I am. And that's what gets to me. People don't really bother to get to know me.

"You're so pretty too," I respond because even though I never know what to say to compliments on my looks, I've learned most people seem to enjoy hearing this about themselves. It's also not a lie. Sky's mom has the same green eyes and sandy blonde hair Sky does, which she's pinned back for the party.

She also has a nice sense of style. She's dressed rather chicly in black heels, a fitted ivory dress, and pearl earrings, making me feel understated in my flats, dark-washed jeans, and beige blouse—although I was pretty impressed I was able to put something semi-party-appropriate together considering that an hour ago I didn't know my time in Vermont would include a seventieth birthday celebration with a fake boyfriend whose judgmental family I was going to have to impress.

Sky's mom doesn't seem to care what I'm wearing, though. She's just happy I'm here. I know this because she tells me at least five times as she ushers me inside.

"We were all beginning to really worry about Sky," she whispers, as Sky wheels our luggage in and my eyes sweep the living room, taking in the generously overstuffed couch and the silver birthday balloons beside it, as well as the crackling fire that's loud but not loud enough to drown out the sound of the commotion coming from the back of the house where I assume everyone else is gathered.

"He spends his time gallivanting around the world completely shunning the notion of settling down. Not that you two are settling down. But at least he's brought you home, which suggests he's thinking about it. He's thirty-six years old. He should be thinking about marriage and a family, don't you think?"

I shoot a glance over my shoulder. Sky is pretending he hasn't heard anything, but his mom was talking loud enough that I know she wanted him to hear her. She got her wish.

"His independence was actually one of the things I was most attracted to," I say. "I like that he knows himself well enough to know what he wants, even if it isn't what society thinks he should want."

I realize I'm treading a fine line between starting a fight with his mother and standing up for Sky. But that's what a good girlfriend would do, right? It's also how I feel, and I think it will be easier to pretend to be his girlfriend tonight if I'm as honest as I can be.

Fortunately, this doesn't seem to piss her off. There's also a chance she didn't hear me because she's busy calling out that Sky and "his girlfriend" are here.

Sky heard what I said, though. "Thank you," he whispers, coming up beside me and slipping his hand through mine as if holding hands is something we do all the time.

Surprisingly, it feels that natural. I swallow, because while that might be a good thing for the show we're putting on, it's definitely not a good thing that I like it as much as I do.

The room fills with people, and Sky's mom starts showing me off as if I'm a shiny new toy Sky brought just for her. Technically, I was brought with her in mind, and with everyone else in his family in mind—which, by the way, is a lot of people. Sky and I should have done flash cards or something on the way here because theoretically I should be able to tell one sibling from the next and know the names of their spouses and children. I'm sweating by the time I get to the silver-haired man in the corner, but at least he's easy to identify: this must be Sky's dad.

I hold out my hand. "Nice to meet you Mr. . . ." I begin, but my voice falters.

I don't know Sky's last name. His girlfriend would know his last name.

"Babe," Sky says, coming up behind me and wrapping an arm around my waist. "I'm sure he wants you to call him Cal."

"Of course, please call me Cal," his dad says.

I nod, trying to commit it to memory, but I'm not sure it's going to stick because I'm preoccupied by the fact that Sky just called me babe.

I've never had a guy call me a pet name before. I didn't think I would like it. I do like it. Or maybe I just like it because Sky used it.

"Are my eyes deceiving me or is my knucklehead of a son finally getting his life together?"

Did Cal seriously just say that? I guess his name did stick. And that might not be a good thing since I'm tempted to use it in a not-so-nice sentence. Why is he making it seem like his son is returning from prison or rehab instead of from Atlanta where he has a full-time job and a full life he's built for himself?

"Looks like it takes a milestone birthday to get you to leave Atlanta and grace us with your presence," chimes in one of his sisters. I'm blanking on which. Two of them look near identical, with dark curly hair, and this is one of those two. I do remember the name of Sky's blonde sister. It's Andrea. Sky mentioned on the car ride here that she's not as bad as everyone else because it took her the longest to meet someone and get married. She was given a hard time for a while because of this and understands to some extent what Sky has to deal with.

"I don't know what you like about Atlanta, Sky," Curly Haired Sister continues. "The crime rate is so much higher than here. Plus, it's so crowded. And is a big city really a good place to raise children? You are planning on having children at some point, aren't you?"

Sky circles his hand around mine. "I guess you never know what the future holds," he says calmly, as if his family wasn't just firing insults at him like bullets.

16

I doubt I would have responded with half as much class if our roles were reversed and this were my family. It makes me respect him, and when his eyes meet mine, I can't help but smile. He smiles back and reaches up with his free hand, gently brushing my hair off my cheek and tucking it back behind my ear as if it's a maneuver he's done a million times.

"As for why I like Atlanta," he says, circling back to his sister's first question, "I can think of one damn good reason it's got a hold on me."

Holy shit.

Sky is one good actor. And he's turning me into Actress of the Year because I don't even have to act when he delivers that line. My body just reacts to his comment the way it would if we really were in love. My heart has taken off racing so fast it feels as if it's trying to run right into Sky's arms—or into another room where Sky and I can be alone, without the rest of his family. And then my lips get a mind of their own and plant a kiss right on Sky's cheek. They want more, but fortunately my *actual* mind jumps in and puts a stop to that.

"Excuse us," Sky says, pulling me by the hand into the kitchen. He breaks out into a wide grin when the door swings shut behind us.

"Wow," I say. "Are you sure piloting is your true calling, not acting?"

He laughs and casually hops up on the counter as if he hadn't just managed to convince his family and me that we're head over heels for each other, while covertly telling them to go to hell.

"Are you thinking about planning an escape yet?" he asks.

I laugh as I hop up beside him. "Surprisingly not." *Although I should*, I think. *I already like him.*

"I wouldn't blame you if you wanted to fake a stomachache."

"I could if you want me to," I say. "Then you could pretend to have to take care of me. They're *a lot*, Sky."

17

"I told you," he says, sitting back on his hands and letting out a deep exhale. "My last name is Alder, by the way," he offers. "If that comes up again."

I'm about to ask him to refresh me on his sisters' names when his mom barges in.

"Mrs. Alder," I say, winking at Sky as I hop down from the counter, "can I help you with anything?"

"Darling, call me Maryann, please. And yes, you can start by bringing this cheese platter into the living room." She pulls it out of the fridge and hands it to me, then snaps her fingers at Sky. "Off the counter, honey. That might fly in your apartment, but not in this household. Speaking of your apartment, please tell me you're at least considering moving into a house. Even Drake Evans has a house now, Sky."

Maryann turns to me. "Drake Evans was a high school dropout. Now he is married to a wonderful gal and has a kid in addition to a house. His mother is in my bridge club, so every week I hear Suzy Evans go on and on about Drake's fabulous accomplishments, and I feel like I have to lie to her when she asks me about Sky's whereabouts."

"You could just be honest and tell her I'm happy," Sky offers.

Maryann looks to me as if she's expecting my sympathy. I'm not sure why. At this point, the only thing I want to give this woman is my middle finger.

I lean in toward Sky while Maryann turns away to retrieve something from the pantry. "I might not have to fake that stomachache," I whisper.

He laughs. "Code word is *vanilla*."

"What?" I raise a brow.

"If I need you to pretend to be sick, the code word I'll use is *vanilla*."

"Why *vanilla*?"

He gives me a mischievous grin. Yet another of his smiles for me to catalog. And, not that I'm ranking them or anything, but if I were, this particular one would be my current favorite. "It's the scent of your perfume," he whispers. "I like it. Actually, I more than like it. It kind of drives me crazy."

I look from Sky to his mom, then back at Sky. Maryann is not within earshot and seems quite distracted by her search for serving bowls. So this was just a conversation between the two of us. Meaning Sky didn't need to pretend to flirt with me. He just *was* flirting with me. Because he *wanted to.*

Yep. I should probably excuse myself right now. Otherwise, I might start flirting back.

But I don't.

"Vanilla," I repeat. "Got it."

—

I spend the next half hour or so in the kitchen sipping red wine while I help Maryann and Sky's sisters get dinner ready. The men are in the living room watching football and drinking beer. I find it odd that it's Maryann's birthday and she's having to make her own birthday dinner. But traditional gender roles are clearly present in this household, which I suppose isn't all that surprising, given what I know about Sky's family so far.

The only person who isn't doing what's expected of him is Sky.

As I carry two bottles of wine into the dining room, I spy him sitting on the floor with the kids, letting the girls put clips in his hair and—in between beauty treatments—wrestling with the boys. The kids clearly love him, and the feeling appears to be mutual. Watching him interact with all six of his nieces and nephews, ranging in age from two to eight, might be the cutest thing I've seen in a while.

The kids' laughter is also a nice auditory break from the gossip I've been listening to in the kitchen. It's been a while since I've been around women who have so much to say about their supposed "friends" that they could fill an entire issue of *US Weekly* with stories. No wonder they're up in Sky's business all the time. They seem to enjoy bad-mouthing others.

I'm grateful once dinner is served and I'm by Sky's side again.

"Everything good, babe?" Sky asks, as the food is passed around the table.

There's the pet name again. I still like it.

"Everything's great, babe," I say, trying it out myself. I like that too. *Dammit.*

"So, Harper, Sky, how did you two meet?" Cal is looking at us from one head of the table, and I immediately look at Sky because— *crap!*—we didn't rehearse our story. I'm not sure why not, since of course we knew this question was coming. It's *the* most asked question a new couple gets.

I contemplate mentioning a dating app, although it's been a while since I've been single, and I'm not sure which ones are still in existence. I suppose I could also say we met through a mutual friend, but then I'd need to make up a person and come up with another lie.

As I'm filtering through more ideas, Sky rests his hand on my knee and says, "We met on a plane."

At least, I think that's what he said. My entire focus shifted to his hand the moment he touched me. It's burning my skin even through my jeans. It's difficult to pay attention to anything else.

"She's scared of flying, so I tried to calm her nerves by talking to her."

The context clue lets me know he did say *plane*. An honest response. Why didn't I think of that?

"Actually, that's not entirely true," he continues. I'm not sure why he does. His family collectively let out an "aww" after his last statement, meaning they bought it and were satisfied. It would have been easy to stop there.

"I didn't realize until we started talking that she was nervous to fly. But I was so happy when I found out she *was* scared because I realized she'd probably want to continue talking to me. I knew I wanted to talk to her the second she walked on the plane. Actually, that's not entirely true either. I saw her walking through airport security, and that's when the thought first popped into my head."

I set my hand on top of Sky's, and ignoring the tingles in my palm, I squeeze. I'm trying to let him know he doesn't need to take this act further. His family gets it. *He wanted to talk to me.* But he doesn't take my cue. Or maybe he misinterprets it. Either way, he draws in a breath and continues.

"I had already gone through security and was about to walk to my flight, but then I saw her. There was something familiar about her, despite her being a stranger, and as I watched her smile at a security guard, I felt warmed by it, even though it wasn't directed at me. In that moment, I didn't care where my destination was anymore. I told myself that wherever that woman was headed, I might just have to buy a ticket."

Okay, Sky. Tone it down. While it's great acting, he doesn't need to make up more stuff for us to remember.

"I kept trying to think of ways I could casually strike up a conversation with her—first as she was repacking her suitcase after a security check and then as she was buying a pack of Mentos at the Atlanta Made store. But then I lost sight of her. I couldn't believe I lost sight of her."

Wait, wait. I *did* have a security check. I did buy Mentos at Atlanta Made.

My heart starts pounding, and I turn toward Sky, hanging on to every word, along with the rest of the table.

"I was crushed," he continues. "Because I knew I'd probably never be able to get her out of my head. So I'm sitting on the plane kicking myself, and then I see her walk on. And not only that, but

21

she sits down right next to me. I was struggling to come up with an opening line, afraid I would say something stupid and blow my shot. She picked up on my nerves and asked me what I was so nervous about. I didn't want to tell her I was nervous about talking to *her*, so I mentioned something else I was equally nervous about, and the conversation went from there. I realized after we shared a drink together that this must be what happens when your path is meant to cross with someone else's. It just does. You don't miss each other."

I took an acting class in college. One of the lessons was on monologues. I remember the teacher telling us they're hard to deliver because people tend to get bored easily, so to combat this, her advice was to speak as much as we could from the heart. That pops into my head now because that was *definitely* a monologue, and at no point was I bored, which makes me think Sky gave his heart a megaphone and let everything inside of it out.

It shouldn't matter if Sky likes me. I'm not interested in developing anything—not feelings, not attraction, and definitely not the start of something.

The problem is my mind doesn't seem to be falling for that denial anymore.

I'm still in my own head when I become aware of the silence and notice everyone looking at me as if they're waiting for my response.

Oh, no.

For one, I can't top that speech. And two, I don't think I can even speak. Not for at least another solid minute. I'm still trying to catch my breath, to calm my racing heart.

I'd also prefer not to lay my feelings out in front of Sky's family. I'd rather talk to him one-on-one. But as the silence stretches, with no one volunteering to end it, I decide that because I'm not going to see his family after this evening anyway, it doesn't matter what they think of me. "I was actually disappointed when I met him," I announce.

22

Out of my peripheral vision I see Sky turn his head toward me. I bet he wasn't expecting me to say that. Well, I wasn't expecting his speech either. Now that I think about it, I'm kind of mad at him for delivering it. I didn't want to know all that. That wasn't the plan here.

"I told myself I wasn't going to open up my heart for at least three months," I press on. "I had just gone through a big breakup, you see, and it was really important to me to spend some time alone, finding myself. But from the moment I sat down beside Sky on the plane, he started testing how committed I was to that. Just being near him tested that. And then we started talking and I was tested more. Against my better judgment I agreed to spend the rest of the evening with him once we landed, and he *kept* testing my resolve with every touch and every conversation."

I realize now that it's not Sky I'm mad at. He didn't know this part of my story until now, so he couldn't have realized his speech would bother me. I'm upset with the lesson I seem to just now be learning: It's pretty hard—if not downright impossible—to control your heart.

I know this is a strange moment for Jake to cross my mind, but he does, because it strikes me that this must have been how he felt around Anna. The realization makes me forgive him a little bit more, because chemistry like this is hard to fight. I didn't realize how hard until now; I didn't know chemistry as strong as this even existed until a couple of hours ago. Jake and I had a version of this, but not *this*.

"And now, here we are." I wrap things up just as Sky's hand finds my knee again under the table. This time he seems to be passing along a silent apology. Ironically, this only makes me like him more, because now I can add *considerate* to his list of attractive qualities.

"Harper?"

"Hm?" I'm nervous to look up from my plate and meet Sky's eyes, knowing they're going to pull me right in. Can't Sky's family start passing the food around again? Or change the subject? Heck, I'd take listening to them bad-mouth anyone—including me—right now if it would break the silence.

Sky says my name again but whispers it this time. His voice is so soft it lures me into looking up. I feel my face heat at the intensity I find there.

"Is it just me or are you picking up some hints of vanilla in the wine?" he whispers next.

"Vanilla?" I repeat. *Oh!* We're back to acting. *Thank God!*

I take my napkin off my lap and set it on the table. "You know, I think I need some air."

It doesn't occur to me until after I get up from the table and hear Sky do the same that he didn't use the code word to get away from his family. He used it because he wants to continue this conversation somewhere where it's just the two of us.

Just the two of us.

That has a dangerous ring to it if you ask me.

three

I'd been looking forward to coming to Vermont for three reasons. One was to get out of Atlanta since it reminds me so much of Jake. Frequenting all the places the two of us used to go to together wasn't helping me move on as fast as I thought I would be able to somewhere else.

Reason number two was that I thought it would be easier to focus on myself in a place where I knew fewer people. Zoe and Grace stopping by my apartment every night proved they were the best friends a girl could have, but it meant I rarely sat alone with my thoughts, and while I know too much of that is unhealthy, I need to do it enough to find out who I am and what I want from life.

And, finally, because Vermont this time of year is supposed to be breathtaking. Who hasn't seen the magazine and Instagram photos of tourists visiting the state when the trees are morphing from normal green forests into art-exhibit-worthy yellow, red, and orange masterpieces? I was thrilled at the idea of being someone who has been to the state during the time of year when seemingly everyone hopes to visit one day.

It occurs to me, though, as Sky and I are walking down the street outside his parents' house, that I haven't yet taken in Vermont at all. On the forty-five minute drive from the airport to here, I was sitting next to Sky, and—as much as I don't want to admit it—it's pretty hard to focus on anything *but* Sky when he's near me. This is exactly the derailment I wanted to avoid. Now I'm with Sky and it's dark, so I wouldn't be able to check out my surroundings even if I forced

25

myself to. Instead, I'm looking ahead of me toward a cul-de-sac. Neither Sky nor I seem to know what to say to each other.

"Do you remember on the plane when you asked me when I felt the freest?" he finally says once we reach the end of the cul-de-sac.

I've got to admit, as I was imagining ways this conversation might go, I wasn't expecting him to bring up that, or anything we talked about on the plane. At least not until we discussed what all that talk at dinner was about.

But, okay. At least it's conversation.

"Lagos, Portugal, 2013," I say, recalling what he told me.

He nods and blows out a breath. It's cold enough that I can see it in the space between us, and the amount of space it takes up makes me think there's a big story here.

He has a seat on the curb. Apparently, this is one of those conversations we need to be sitting down for. *Great, not nervous at all here.*

I take a seat beside him, sitting close because I'm cold. Okay, because I'm cold and because it feels really good to be next to him.

I'm annoyed with myself but can't really deny it anymore. I'm pulled to Sky in a magnetic way, and I don't know what to do about it.

I watch Sky look down at his hands.

"I had just broken things off with someone," he says. "Someone who meant a lot to me. We were about to move in together, but I told her I wanted to break up instead because I thought I wanted freedom more. I bought a ticket to Portugal to celebrate my decision, and there I was on the beaches of Lagos, the freest I'd ever felt, and . . . the most unhappy."

He looks up at me now. One of the things that draws me to Sky is how his face so clearly shows his emotions. So many people make you guess what they're feeling—myself included, at times. It's refreshing to be around someone who's the opposite. But I don't like seeing the emotion he's wearing right now. Regret isn't a good look on anyone.

"I know I fed you that stuff on the plane about wanting to be free, but I think that's an old story. It's what I wanted for so long, so I tend to act like it's still true. But ever since that trip to Portugal, I've realized that what I really want is to never make that same mistake again—and that's hard to admit to just anyone, let alone . . . someone like you. But it's the truth. If someone comes into my life who I think there could be something with, I want to explore it."

I nod, processing. "And just to be clear, I'm the someone in this scenario, correct?"

He laughs on his exhale and I chuckle too. It feels nice to laugh after the intensity of this evening. Under the chuckle, I'm a little irked, though. Because while Sky might have been feeding me a line on the plane, everything I've told him so far is true.

"I'm sorry I wasn't honest from the start."

I like that I didn't have to call it out. "It's okay," I say, and I mean it.

He wraps an arm around me and I lean right into him. I'm not sure how it's possible to feel this comfortable with someone I just met. I've heard people talk about this, but I have never experienced it until now. I guess it's yet another thing I can add to my Vermont Bucket List, then check off. The problem is I'm here to make a dent in the things I wrote down before I arrived here.

With this in mind, I force myself to sit up and scoot back a bit. "I like you, Sky. At least, everything I know about you so far. Except for your family. They suck." He laughs again. I pause, then continue. "I meant what I said at the table, though. I came to Vermont to find myself. I don't plan to fall for someone."

He nods as if he hears me, briefly looks down, then meets my eyes again. "What about just a little?"

I'm sorry, did he just ask if I'd be open to *falling for him a little*? It's a good thing it's dark out, because color is working its way up my neck.

I want to tell him that his ability to make comments that affect me as much as this is an answer to that question. Sky isn't the kind of guy I could ever fall halfway for. He's the kind of guy I could potentially lose myself in, if I'm not careful.

Then again, I don't *really* know him. Maybe I'm overthinking this. What if he's only affecting me so much because we have great chemistry and we haven't kissed yet? Perhaps all I need to do is get him out of my system.

His mouth is inches from mine now, as if he's ready to put my theory to the test. A beat later, he does.

His lips connect with mine briefly at first, as if they're saying a quick hello, and then longer, as if they'd very much like to wear out their welcome. The contact shoots down my spine, and as the kiss stretches on even longer, that electric desire buzzes higher, crackling and snapping on my skin. When he pulls back, I feel a flash of loss.

He brings his hands to his lips right after. "Dammit," he says.

I'm shocked by his response. And confused. "What?"

He lets out a deep breath and leans back on his hands. "I was hoping that wouldn't be so good. Because I want to respect your wishes, Harper. But now . . . I'm not sure how I'm going to do that."

I blink. "What were my wishes? I forgot."

"I hope you're being serious." He comes closer. "Because I'd really like to continue."

I am being serious.

But, seriously, Harper! I shake my head once. Then again. *What am I doing? What am I saying?*

"No, don't snap out of it," Sky begs, seeming to read my mind again while taking my hands in his.

It's too late. I already have. I should have never let it get this far.

"Sky, I'm not looking to get into a relationship," I reiterate. "Plus, how would a relationship between us even work right now? I'm going to be here for the next three months, and you'll be in Atlanta."

"I could visit," he retaliates.

"You hate Vermont."

"I have a reason to like it now."

"We barely know each other. What's the point?"

"We know each other enough to know we want to find out more. That's what dating is all about."

"You don't want to get married."

"Whoa." A smile creeps onto his lips. "You're already thinking about marriage? So you definitely *do* want to date."

I sigh. "That didn't come out right. I just mean at some point in my life, I want to get married. You said on the plane that you didn't want that, so there's no point in dating in the first place when our long-term goals aren't aligned."

He lets out a sigh even deeper than mine. I'm not sure if he's frustrated with what I said or upset with himself for confessing his opposition to marriage. "That's part of my old story too," he tells me. "If I met the right person, well . . . let's just say I'd be open to it."

Before I can say anything back, he squeezes my hands, then brings them up to his lips and blows. At first, I think he's trying to be seductive, but then I realize he's trying to warm me up because I'm shivering. I somehow only just realized this.

"Come on." Sky pulls me up with him as he gets to his feet, then takes off his jacket and drapes it around my shoulders. "Let's argue more inside."

"If we're already arguing this much on our first date, isn't that an indication of the future?"

"So you agree we're going to have a future?" he asks as we start back.

"Don't be funny. This is serious." I reach out and smack his stomach.

He pretends to be wounded, but there's no way he even registered that because all my hand felt were abs. Plural. Of course, he has to have more than one of them.

29

"I am being serious," he says. "I seriously want to date you, Harper."

Ugh! He makes it seriously hard to protest when he says sweet things like that.

———

Once we get back inside, I'm relieved that Sky doesn't make us rejoin the dinner table. He tells me to go upstairs to his bedroom while he goes back into the dining room to tell his family I'm still not feeling well. He'll bring up some plates for us to share.

Before we part ways, though, he pulls me toward him and gives me a peck on the lips. This isn't your average peck, though. Sky's lips are pressed to mine as if he's trying to make me dizzy. He succeeds.

"Last door at the end of the hall," he says, nodding to the stairwell, then giving my ass a pat.

Pet names I didn't think I liked. Butt pats I didn't think I liked either. Sky is making me rethink a lot of things.

When I enter Sky's childhood room, I find that it doesn't resemble a teenage boy's bedroom at all. Sky's parents must have repurposed it as a guest room when he moved out. There is one bookshelf that appears to still have some of his high school paraphernalia, though, and I'm drawn toward it.

I pick up a picture of him posing in a green-and-white football uniform. Should have figured he was a star athlete back in the day, given the abs I felt earlier.

When I set that down, I spy several trophies that I'm expecting to be for football or another sport, but upon closer examination I see that they're for math and spelling bee competitions. Athletic and smart. Even my teenage self would have struggled not to develop a crush on the guy.

When he walks in with our food a second later, I hold up a folded Taylor Swift poster that was on the shelf with his other things. "Taylor Swift was your high school crush, huh?"

"Taylor who?" Sky sets the plates down on his desk and pulls a blanket off the edge of the bed. He lays the blanket on the floor, then brings our food over, setting up a picnic.

Athletic, smart, and romantic. I'm guessing I'm not the only woman who's been quick to develop feelings for him.

"I have a one-track mind, Harper. When I'm focused on someone I like, I forget everyone else. Including celebrity crushes."

"Does this mean you've never cheated?" I ask, as we both take a seat on the floor. Sky is using his bed as a backrest and pats the spot beside him, but I shake my head, deciding it's probably best if I avoid the general vicinity of his bed altogether. At least for now. I do realize we have to sleep in here together.

"Nope. Never have. Never will." He hands me a fork. "I don't believe in being with someone you'd be tempted to cheat on. I would end the relationship if I felt that way, or more likely not be in the relationship to begin with."

I haven't cheated either because I've always thought of it as generally wrong. I like that he's put thought into exactly *why* he'd never cheat. Spoken like someone who knows himself. I feel a pang of jealousy that he's already at that place in his life but remind myself that I'm taking the necessary steps to get to that place too.

"What's been your longest relationship?" I ask.

Sky deflects. "How long were you with the idiot who stood you up?"

"Touché, we don't have to talk about exes."

"Never a fun topic," he says, as we both dig into our lasagna. "Why don't you tell me about your younger years instead?" he tries. "You're getting a glimpse into mine by looking around here. It's only fair that I get to hear about the younger you."

I shake my head. "That's date talk and we're not dating."

"It's conversation and we're eating."

I sigh because he's impossible in so many ways, and then he sighs too and sets his fork down, running a hand through his hair.

31

"I'm sorry. I don't want to frustrate you or make your life more complicated. I don't normally go around begging women to date me. But how I feel around you isn't normal. When I was downstairs just now, I kept trying to chalk up my feelings to chemistry, but I liked our conversations on the plane, Harper. And the way you stood up for me in front of my mom. And how being here with you has made this town not only bearable, but actually a place I'm now going to miss. I wouldn't be pressing this issue if it didn't somehow feel like a mistake to walk away from something that has so much potential."

I'm surprised there aren't awards for the speech and debate team in here, because if I didn't know any better, I'd say Sky could have been a captain.

As much as I wish I could argue with what he's saying, I can't. I feel the same. But I also can't change my entire plan—not when it's so important to me.

When I reiterate this, he nods as if he's trying to accept our fate. I can tell how much he's disappointed by it, though. I am too—so I throw out an idea.

"What if we try to figure out all our incompatibilities? Then we might realize that we're not losing something as special as we think we are."

Sky nods, willing to play along.

"Are you more of an introvert or extrovert?" I begin.

"Extrovert," he says.

"I'm an introvert," I confess.

"I once read an article that said introverts are better off with extroverts. And vice versa."

Yep, he definitely could have been debate team captain.

"Send me the study or I'm not buying it."

"Do you really need the study? Opposites attract, haven't you heard?" He scoots in closer, possibly to reinforce his words with a kiss, but I jump to the next question.

"What's your love language?" I figure that with three sisters, he's likely taken this test.

"Physical touch. Did you really have to ask?"

He's right. I could have guessed that.

"Mine is quality time."

"I like that second," he adds.

"What about religion?" I continue. "Do you believe in God?"

Sky gets a faraway look in his eyes. "When I'm flying planes and I'm up there in the clouds—especially during sunrise or sunset—there are times I get so overwhelmed by all that's around me that I tear up. There's so much about the universe we don't know. So much we don't understand. I don't know what's out there, but I know it's something so much bigger than us."

His answer is not the same as mine here either, but it's beautiful. So beautiful it makes me want to give looking out the window a shot next time I'm in the air.

"How about you?" He goes back to forking his lasagna.

"I grew up Christian, and I go to church on the major holidays, but I realize I go more because I'd like to believe in something rather than because I'm sure I do. Maybe I'll find more faith while I'm here."

"Pretty sure you don't find faith, it finds you. It's a lot like love in that respect."

And here we are, on *that* topic again.

"I think this game sucks," I announce.

Sky chuckles. "Me too. Luckily, I've got a better idea for handling this predicament than trying to convince ourselves that we don't want what we want."

I set my plate down and fold my hands together. "Explain."

"What if I wait for you?"

I wrinkle my brows.

"You said you want to take these three months for you, right?"

"Yes."

"Then take them. Three months from now is right around Christmas Eve, correct?"

It's September 17 now. "About that, yeah."

"I'll be back Christmas Eve." He sits up taller. "We could have our second date then."

I blink. "You'd wait for me?"

He shrugs as if to say it'd be no big deal. "You're going to be on my mind for the next three months whether we make this pact or not. It'd be nice if I knew that on the other side of missing you, I'd get to see you."

No doubt Sky will be on my mind for a while too. And now that I think about it, trying to get him out of my mind might end up detracting from my ability to focus on my goals while I'm here. But if I did agree to this, I wouldn't have to work to stop thinking about him. He could just stay in my head until I see him again.

"I could maybe be convinced of this. Keep talking."

"We should keep talking." He snaps his fingers, liking that idea, but I cut him off before he gets too excited.

"I don't want to hear your voice during our time apart."

"What's wrong with my voice?"

How can I possibly express to him that his voice alone practically heats me up? "It's . . . distracting."

"Fine. What if we email?"

"Once a week," I agree.

"Once a week until Christmas Eve. Then a date?"

I nod.

"I'll take it," he says.

"Wait." I suddenly remember my job description on Christmas Eve. "The inn hosts an annual Christmas Eve party with sleigh rides and Santa and everything. It's apparently the busiest day of the year, and I'll be working late."

"The whole town goes to that party every year," Sky says. "Including me and my family. It'll be perfect. We can reunite then."

I nod, feeling a flicker of excitement in my stomach. I realize I haven't been this excited for Christmas since I was a kid.

"All right, it's a date," I say.

"So you're really in?"

"I'm in." I reach across the blanket for Sky's hand to shake on it. After our shake, he tugs on my hand, pulling me into his lap. I let him. It's the kind of pact that should be sealed with a kiss.

Or maybe I just want to kiss him again.

Either way, a minute or so later, I'm flushed as I get to my feet.

"Where are you going?" he asks.

"If we're eventually going to have a second date—one where your family is going to be present, no less—I think we should rejoin the party."

Sky gives me another one of his grins that I feel everywhere. That's another reason I'm getting us out of his bedroom. I don't need to resist him completely now that we have our plan, but I'm also not sure I'm ready for everything yet. And it'll be a lot easier for me to contemplate it all if we don't spend the rest of tonight in these close, private quarters.

four

The only positive thing I can pin down about Sky's family so far—other than Sky, of course—is that they like their alcohol. I'm not a big drinker, but they're the kind of people who drive you to drink, so it's helpful that they like to keep the wine flowing.

Dinner was over by the time Sky and I rejoined the table, but we were just in time for dessert. Cal carried out a chocolate pound cake with candles from the kitchen, and Andrea trailed behind him with plates.

Once everyone was served, I found myself wondering who brought the pound cake and why, because Maryann criticized it at least nineteen times. Leave it to her to figure out how to make a dessert feel bad about itself.

You'd think by the woman's seventieth birthday, her husband and kids would know what she likes and serve that instead. But when I whispered this to Sky, he said chocolate pound cake *is* her favorite dessert. "Imagine how much she'd complain if this were a dessert she *didn't* like," he replied.

It was then that I realized it had been a terrible mistake to leave Sky's room. But we couldn't exactly head right back upstairs.

So now we are in the living room, trying to make it through gifts. Luckily, I'm seated beside Andrea on the couch. She's the only nice one. Sky's other siblings scare me almost as much as Maryann and Cal. At the table, I overheard Sky's brother, Owen, getting upset with Sky about the declining stock price of the airline Sky works for, as if Sky were in control of the ticker. And his other sisters,

Olivia and Michelle, (I've finally gotten everyone's names down) keep glaring at me.

"I know it's a lot to walk into," Andrea says as she bounces her two-year-old daughter, Emily, on her lap. We're all having side conversations as we watch Sky's mom unwrap a sweater. "You seem really good for Sky, though. I'm glad he met you."

"How did you and Edward meet?" I shoot a glance at her husband, sitting over near Sky and Maryann in chairs near the fire.

"We met on a plane too. I've only flown three times in my life, and Edward was on one of the flights. We've been going strong six years now. So I'm a big believer in romances that start in the air."

"Romances that start in the air," I repeat. "That has a nice ring to it."

She smiles and sets Emily down on the floor, then twists her blonde hair back into a low bun. "You're the first girl Sky's brought home since Julie, so he must really like you."

Julie. That must be the name of the woman Sky was about to move in with. The one he regrets dumping.

"Well, I really like Sky too," I say. Sky catches my gaze and gives me a flirtatious smile even though he couldn't have heard what I said amid all the commotion. Maybe he read my lips. Or maybe, like me, he's had a little too much wine.

I have no idea what glass I'm on. Every time I set my glass down it seems like someone fills it right back up. I better slow down. I imagine everyone will leave soon, and then it will be just Sky and me again, upstairs.

Too much wine coupled with what his smile does to me, and I might end up leaping into something I usually approach much more slowly.

"This next gift is from Sky and Harper," Maryann announces. Oh, boy. I have no idea what it is, but that was sweet and smart of Sky to add my name to the package.

37

As she begins to unwrap it, Sky walks over to join me on the couch. I cuddle up next to him, hoping for his sake that Maryann is nice no matter what he picked out.

After she gets the big package unwrapped, there's a smaller one inside it. In the smaller package is an even smaller box. And inside that, an even *smaller* one. The kids are having fun with all the packages and suspense, and I must admit, so am I.

Once she finally opens the last box, she's left with a black velvet one.

"Oh my gosh," she gasps, spinning it around after she's popped it open to show us a pair of diamond earrings.

For the first time, Maryann appears to be without words. It makes me wonder if Sky chose this gift because he knew it would leave her speechless, and a speechless person can't complain. Her hand is covering her mouth as she stares at the earrings.

I'm a bit speechless myself. I know Sky's love language is physical touch and his second is quality time, but now I've just learned he's *also* a good gift giver.

He kisses the top of my head as Maryann continues to shake hers.

Yep, I should definitely slow down on the wine before we go back upstairs.

—

It's ten o'clock by the time the dishes are done, Sky's siblings and their kids have all headed home, and Maryann and Cal have retired for the evening into their room on the main level. Ten o'clock is late, but not late enough that Sky and I are going to pass out once we get back into his room, so I contemplate my game plan as we climb the stairs.

I know I need some kind of strategy before we walk back in there because while I did slow down on the wine, ever since Sky joined me on the couch, we haven't been able to keep our hands off each other. I can only imagine how handsy we're going to get once it's just us. So I block the doorway with my back before Sky can grab the handle.

"We need another code word," I say.

"For what?"

"So I don't have sex with you."

He nods, processing this. "You don't want to have sex with me?"

His question, his voice, and his proximity are making it really hard for me to remember that "no" is supposed to be my answer to that question.

"I *do* want to. But I generally don't have sex with men I've just met. I like sex. But it needs to be combined with a connection and familiarity for me. I like being comfortable with someone."

Sky nods again and stuffs his hands in his pockets. "I like having sex that way too," he says. He strikes me as the kind of guy that likes having sex *every* way. Then again, just because he exudes sex appeal doesn't mean he sleeps around every chance he gets.

"The thing is," he goes on, "I do feel comfortable with you, Harper. And you do feel familiar to me. But if you don't feel the same way, I totally understand."

I do feel the same way. I'm just not used to experiencing those feelings with someone I just met, and I don't know what to do with that. Sky is blurring the lines of all my categories. And I need a minute to figure it out.

"It's not that I don't. It's just that I haven't completely made up my mind about what I want to do here."

"Okay, then code word it is," he says this with a smile, and I know he's honestly respecting what I've said. Ironically, this makes me even more comfortable with him and in less need of a code word, but I don't say that.

"Halt?" he suggests.

I smile. "Perfect."

I open the door and walk in, Sky trailing in behind me.

39

"So I take it you've never had a one-night stand?"

"I got close once in college," I say as I take a seat on his bed. Sky sits down beside me but leaves a respectful amount of space between us so that we're close, but not touching.

I find myself wishing we were touching.

"Freshman year I left a party with a guy I'd just met who seemed nice and whom I found attractive. We got as far as naked in his bed before I realized I didn't want to sleep with him. So I put a hand to his chest and told him I wanted to go home. He didn't seem bummed out about my decision at all, which was nice. But I think that's also why I wasn't into it. I could tell it didn't matter to him one way or the other whether we hooked up or not, or whether it was me in his room or some other random girl from the party, which made the whole thing feel meaningless. And that wasn't what I wanted."

I look from my hands up to him. "How about you? Any one-night stands?"

Sky doesn't respond. He looks as if he's still thinking about my story.

"I hate that someone made you feel interchangeable with any other girl, Harper. You aren't, and you shouldn't ever be made to feel like you are. I know when I look back on this crazy fake date we've had, it will be meaningful. One of those nights that sticks in my head and plays on a constant loop when I'm daydreaming or pops up randomly months later and puts a smile on my face."

If I were to repeat everything Sky has said to me tonight to Zoe and Grace, I bet they would think some of his lines are cheesy. But they don't sound cheesy when Sky says them. They sound sincere. Maybe it's because I'm seeing the sincerity in his eyes when he delivers them.

I like how sincere Sky seems. I like how he's making me feel.

I just like Sky.

I follow that thought with a kiss. Sky willingly receives it, and when I launch into another, something shifts, and he takes control then, smoothing down my hair and pulling me closer before lying me down and positioning himself over me. I hum my approval against his lips.

We keep kissing like this for a while. It's the most I've ever enjoyed a kiss, so I don't feel the need to rush it. Sky doesn't rush it either, but I'm pretty sure that's because in his mind there's nothing to rush *to*. I told him no sex. And he seems set to honor that. Although I can feel how much of a challenge this is for him by the way his jeans are pushing against me.

"Sky?" I breathe.

"Yeah?" His lips are on my neck now, leaving a trail of kisses.

"What's the opposite of *halt*?"

He pulls back a bit, looking at me. "Full speed?"

"Okay," I nod. "I'm ready for full speed, then."

His eyes light up and he grins before his lips meet mine again, fiercer than before. I feel the snap of that electric attraction tighten my stomach into a knot. He'd been holding back.

He only breaks off the kiss to reach down for my shirt and pull it over my head. I reach down for his in return, yanking it out of his jeans before starting to undo the buttons. He sits back, kneeling as he finishes the job himself.

Oh. He definitely has more than one ab. Closer to six. Possibly eight. I don't bother getting an exact count because he's back over me again, kissing my neck and my stomach. Then even lower.

Yeah.

Good call on opting for full speed ahead.

I grip the comforter with my hands as Sky tugs my pants off and starts planting little kisses on the soft skin between my thighs. After, he moves his mouth to my panty line and starts kissing me there.

Definitely good call.

I'm already more heated than I've ever been, and there's still a layer of lace between us. As I imagine what will happen once that lace is pulled back, my body begins to quiver.

Unreal.

Seriously, is this actually happening?

Some guys can't even get me to this place after a full night of foreplay and sex. Sky's managing to accomplish it just by me picturing his mouth reaching its next destination.

He holds my hips steady, continuing to kiss the same spot until a whimper escapes from the back of my throat. I guarantee that sound made it all the way down the hall, possibly even down the stairs. As Sky kisses his way back up my stomach, I apologize for not being able to keep that sound in. He doesn't seem the least bit concerned. He looks more pleased than anything.

"I like that sound," he whispers against my neck. "I want to hear you make it again."

He raises my hands above my head and runs his hands down my body, convincing me that he's going to not only pull more whimpers from me but also inspire sounds I've never even heard myself make.

It's not that I've had bad chemistry with men I've dated in the past. I wouldn't have gotten engaged without chemistry. It's more that this is next-level, mind-blowing chemistry—and apparently quite rare, because I'm twenty-nine years old and only now experiencing desire like this.

I reach down for the button on Sky's pants and start to undo it. "Condom," I breathe.

Sky lets out a groan against my neck. It's not the good kind, though.

He pushes himself up and looks down at me, panting. "Please tell me you have one in your luggage."

"Why would I have one?" I prop myself up on my elbows. "I wasn't planning to go out with anyone during my time here."

He drops his head and groans again.

"You don't have one in yours?" Not that I want to think about Sky with other women right now, but he's single and isn't on a three-month sabbatical to find himself like I am.

"I was coming to town for one night to see my family. And I don't normally sleep with women I just met." The part of me that's crushing on him likes this answer, but the part of me that wants to have sex with him is seriously crushed by it.

"What about in here?" I look around his room. At this point, I'm prepared to search every drawer top to bottom.

"I might, but nothing with a valid expiration date. The last time I brought a girl into this bedroom, I was eighteen."

I let out a groan too as Sky rolls off of me to stare up at the ceiling.

"Maybe it's for the best," I sigh, trying to convince myself. Unfortunately, no matter how many times I repeat the mantra in my head, I can't make myself believe it.

I want this.

I roll toward him and prop my head up with my hand. "How far is the nearest corner store?"

He exhales as he rolls toward me. "Everything here closes early. Small town."

"And here I thought I was going to like small towns. Now I've already got a problem with them."

He laughs as he lies back down, resting his hands behind his head. Then he yawns.

Not just a little yawn. A yawn so big it's immediately clear he's fighting off the deepest kind of sleep.

I'm not sure why this upsets me, but it does. Maybe I'm projecting my frustration with the situation onto him. Or maybe the insecure part of me that's still reeling from being left abruptly by someone I thought I was going to marry is worried that he was only feeding me lines, and that I mean less to him than I was originally thinking. Maybe not being able to find a condom was for the best, after all.

I get to my feet.

"Where are you going?" Sky asks.

I pause. I hadn't really thought about it. "The bathroom," I say. "I might as well get ready for bed."

Sky's on his feet now. I hear his footsteps behind me, then feel his arms circle my waist. He turns me around toward him.

"I'm sorry," he says, tilting my chin up.

"For what?" I try to play it cool because I realize I'm overreacting.

"For yawning." I like that he knows this is why I was upset. I wasn't expecting him to read my mind—I usually make a point to communicate well—but it's comforting to know he picked up on what bothered me.

"Do you know why I was wearing a pilot uniform on the plane that I *wasn't* flying?"

I shrug. I honestly hadn't thought about it. I guess I should have.

"I flew a plane that left Amsterdam at 2:00 a.m. Vermont time to Atlanta. Then caught the flight to Vermont after we landed."

"You mean you haven't slept in . . ."

"Almost twenty-four hours," he says, finishing the count.

I know Sky intended this to be reassuring news, but I'm not so sure it is.

"So you could be completely delusional right now?"

"Not a chance." He's already looking into my eyes, but now he brings a hand to my cheek. "I'm even more aware of everything when I'm sleep-deprived because I'm focused, not on autopilot. If I were on autopilot, I would have passed out a long time ago. That you managed to keep me so alert all night speaks to how into you—and into us—I am."

And there he goes, winning me over again.

"I'm bummed about not being able to have sex too, believe me," he says, pulling me closer to him so I can feel the truth of his statement. "But just think." He pulls back to look at me again. "The next time I see you, there will be even more of a buildup. And you know what that means, right?"

When I say nothing, he smiles. "You and I, lady, are going to have one very Merry Christmas."

"Oh, God." I press a hand to my head. "My date for the holidays is a total cheeseball."

He reaches down and scoops me up, throwing me over his shoulder. "Oh, yeah!" he says as he carries me toward the attached bathroom. "He's the cheesiest!"

I guess he's forgiven.

—

Once we return to Sky's bed, he pulls back the covers and tells me to pick whatever side I want. I slide into the covers on the side closest to the door, leaving Sky the window. I wasn't thinking about it when I made my choice, but now Sky has to climb over the top of . . .

Yep.

He's hovering right above me again.

Great.

We briefly glance at each other's lips, but Sky shakes his head and continues all the way across, letting out a loud grunt as his head hits the pillow.

"I'm going to pass out so hard," he says, sliding one arm under me and the other over my waist.

"Nope," I say, peeling his top arm off. "I can't sleep with you touching me."

"What?"

"Seriously," I say pushing him off. "I like the idea of cuddling during sleep, but in reality, I'll lie awake all night if your arms are wrapped around me like that."

He moans as he pulls his arms back. "I guess we found another thing we don't have in common."

"Is it a deal breaker?"

We're both on our sides now, facing each other.

"Nice try," he says, reaching out and tickling my chin. "You're not wiggling your way out of this pact."

I laugh again and push his hand back. "Luckily for you, I don't want to. You've officially sold me on it."

His grin grows wider, and he leans in and presses his lips to mine. His breath tastes like spearmint, and I smile remembering how he kept making funny faces in the mirror as we brushed our teeth together, trying to get me to laugh.

I'm starting to think I'd really enjoy sleepovers with Sky, despite the differing cuddling preferences.

Speaking of sleeping preferences . . .

"Do you snore?" I ask. I know I don't have a right to care about his answer, considering I snore quite loud. But I'm a light sleeper. And given how exhausted Sky is, I bet he's going to fall asleep first, so he probably won't hear me, but if he snores, I'll hear him.

"I do," he says. "But it's a cute snore."

"What the heck does that mean?"

He shrugs. "No idea, I've never heard it. I've just been told it's cute."

I try not to think about the other women who have slept beside him and let him know this.

"Only by my brother and sisters when we were kids, of course," he adds with a completely straight face. "No one else has ever slept in the same room as me."

I smile against my pillow. I'm not sure what's cuter—that he can read my mind or that he's trying to make me feel as if I'm the only woman he's ever been with.

"What time do you need to be at work?" Sky's eyes are closed, but he's still facing me, and I can tell he's listening by the curious expression on his face.

"I have to be there at eight. I set my alarm for six, just to be safe."

"Great. I'll drop you off on the way to the airport." He leans in and kisses me again without opening his eyes.

"Goodnight, Harper," he says against my lips.

"Goodnight, Sky," I say after we break apart.

—

Ten minutes later, I roll onto my back and stare up at the ceiling. It's always strange to sleep in an unfamiliar room, and it usually takes me some time to feel comfortable sleeping next to a new guy. Tonight seems different, though. I already feel so at ease with Sky. Maybe I'll pass out quickly too.

I close my eyes, then realize my body is still overheated from our interaction before. I open my eyes and kick my leg out from under the covers. There, that's better.

I close my eyes, take a deep breath, and then I hear it: Sky's snore.

I open my eyes and look at him, listening as he inhales and exhales. *Wow*, I smile, lying back down and closing my eyes for good.

It really is totally cute.

five

At the breakfast table the following morning, I text my parents and send a message in my group chat with Zoe and Grace. I forgot to let them know that I made it to Stowe safe last night. I decide to save details about what "safe" means for later (for one of those group chats, at least).

Went home with a hot, romantic pilot with major potential and we made a pact to reunite on Christmas Eve.

I also write a thank-you note to Sky's parents on stationery I had in my suitcase mentioning how wonderful (downright terrible) it was to meet them and how much I'm looking forward to (completely dreading) seeing them again on Christmas Eve.

I have time to do all this because Sky and I are the only ones up this early, and he's busy working on his computer. He was working when I woke up this morning too. I'm admittedly a little bummed that this is how he's choosing to spend our last bit of time together. But I get that he has a job and obligations he might have put off last night on account of me staying over.

My own job should be where my mind is this morning, anyway. I glance down at my phone to check the time, noting that I'll be an official employee of Hudson Lane in exactly thirty minutes.

Sky's aware of the time too, even though he's still typing. "One minute and then we'll leave," he tells me without looking up. "You feeling ready?"

I nod, though I'm more nervous than ready. I barely touched the bagel Sky toasted me. This is a big day in many ways. New job.

New responsibilities. The real beginning of my Vermont Bucket List. Not to mention I have to say goodbye to Sky, which I couldn't have imagined would be an item on my agenda when I left Atlanta yesterday morning.

Yesterday morning!

I can't believe it's only been one full day since I left. It seems so much longer than that. So much has happened.

Okay, one thing—a whirlwind romance—but still.

"Finished." Sky finally closes his laptop.

About time. I can't help the thought from popping into my head, but I know I'd be totally out of line to verbalize it.

—

Fortunately, on the car drive to the inn, Sky is much more talkative and present. The energy between us feels just as strong as it did yesterday, which fills me with relief because a part of me was starting to worry that maybe last night was a fluke.

Now I see that couldn't be further from the truth. He's holding my hand over the center console, asking me questions, and cracking jokes. When we pass by a park filled with trees flaunting their yellow and red leaves, he even shares a childhood memory, telling me about when the park once hosted a meet and greet with Santa and his reindeer. Apparently, Sky saw Santa leave and didn't realize he was only headed to the bathroom. Thinking the reindeer had been left behind, he unhooked them from the sleigh and each other and told them to go find Santa.

"I was so proud of myself," he says, "because I thought I was doing the right thing. But when they inevitably took off and disappeared, I felt like the whole town hated me for being the kid who lost Santa's reindeer." He laughs with a shake of his head, and I laugh too, even though it's kind of sad imagining little Sky being shunned for trying to do something so sweet.

49

The only problem with the way this is going is that the drive is not long enough.

We pull up to Hudson Lane before I feel ready to (a) meet my new bosses, Mr. and Mrs. Hudson, and (b) part ways with Sky.

He turns to me then. "Why an inn?"

"Sorry?"

"Why did you decide to work at an inn?"

Ah. I wondered when I'd get this question.

"A product of watching too many rom-coms following my failed engagement," I grin. "As you mentioned when we first met, many of those movies feature a character who inherits or is gifted an inn after hitting rock bottom. I don't have many deceased relatives, fortunately, nor rich relatives, unfortunately. But it got me thinking that if I wasn't going to magically inherit a bed-and-breakfast, maybe I could get a job working at one while I figured out what I wanted to do with the rest of my life. I didn't want the romance"—I glance at Sky a little apologetically—"but I wanted the quiet to figure myself out."

I wonder if Sky is about to judge me for my choices or my logic.

But he says, "I think it's great."

"You do?"

"Yeah. You've got an exciting adventure ahead of you," he says, waving a hand at the inn in front of us. I briefly take in the brick facade, white-painted cedar siding and black clapboard shutters, noting that it's even more charming in person than in the pictures, before unbuckling my seat belt and returning my attention to him.

"I do," I say. "But I'm also enjoying the adventure of meeting you."

Sky responds to my comment with a kiss. I can tell he meant for that one kiss to be it because he pulls right back after delivering it. But seconds later he comes in for a second, and I hear his seat belt unclick. I feel that sound in my stomach, the anticipation building. He scoots in even closer, placing his hands on my face as his lips find mine again and again—and again. I'm swept up in the sensation of his lips on mine and of his hands sliding into my hair but force myself to pull away and push Sky back, sticking out a hand to ensure we keep our distance. Messy hair and flushed cheeks won't be a good look for my first day.

"I can't get fired before I even start."

"You're right." Sky leans his head back against his headrest, trying to catch his breath. "I'm sorry. I can't seem to control myself when I'm around you."

I flush. I happen to feel the exact same way.

"I promise, hands off for good now." He holds them up with his palms out. I appreciate him listening to me, but now all I can think about is how much I want his hands touching me again. "At least until Christmas Eve."

"So you'll be here then?" I'm fishing for confirmation that we still stand where we did last night, because we haven't talked about our pact at all this morning.

"Oh, I'll definitely be here," he says. "And if you want to read about just how excited for it I am, check your email when you can."

"My email?"

"Yeah, for your first letter. I wrote it this morning, and it should have hit your inbox just before I closed my laptop. I found your email address on your LinkedIn page."

"That's what you were doing on your computer all morning?"

He nods.

He wasn't spending his time working. He was writing me.

"How many days is it until Christmas Eve, exactly?"

He laughs. "Ninety-seven." That was too fast for him to have just done the math. And I know he didn't make the number up because I too already counted this morning.

I smile a big, goofy grin. I can't help it. Who knew when I applied for this inn gig after watching too many romantic comedies that I'd end up living a rom-com of my very own?

51

It's about time, I think.

For the past six months, I've been a casualty to someone else's plot.

Now I'm finally in my own damn plot. And I like it much better.

"So I'll see you in ninety-seven days?"

"See you in ninety-seven days." Sky's hands are gripping the steering wheel so hard his knuckles are white. It's cute how hard he's trying to honor my wishes.

Really cute.

"Oh, kiss me one more time, already," I cave.

His hands are off the steering wheel in a millisecond. "I was sure hoping you'd say that."

six

No one is at the front desk when I walk inside. I can't say I'm surprised, since I know the inn is short-staffed. Apparently two of their longest-standing employees recently retired and another got married and relocated. I know all this from the email exchange I've had going the past few weeks with the sixtysomething couple who runs the place.

Manning the front desk is going to be one of my main tasks while I'm here, along with a handful of other duties, such as feeding the chickens in the barn near the rustic cottages and hosting the nightly happy hour in the parlor, which I presume is the room I've just wandered into.

"Hello?" I call out as I poke around, admiring the white brick wood-burning fireplace alight with a strong blaze, and the fine-dining bar and varied seating options. There is a mix of wooden two-seater tables, two cream-colored love seats with navy throw blankets draped over the arms, and several striped armchairs tucked into nooks near the wide-paned windows that look out over the back of the property.

"Anyone here?" I try again, as I wander over to a window and shoot a glance out at the view. From my online search, I know Hudson Lane sits on thirty-five acres, and from this vantage point I can see maple trees for miles. A handful of them have leaves that have already turned colors, and I can only imagine what the view will be like in the next couple of weeks as the rest of them change, let alone how things will look come winter, when the snow dusts the trees and blankets the ground.

After a quick glance over my shoulder to check that I'm still alone, I jump up and down, doing a silent freak-out because I can't believe I get to work and stay in such a breathtaking place for the next three months.

I'm pumping my fists in the sky for the final time when I hear a voice behind me say, "Hello?"

One second. That's how long it takes for me to drop my hands back down to my sides. It's fast, but not fast enough that I can guarantee whoever is behind me didn't just witness me having a dance party by myself.

"Hello." I turn around, trying to play it cool, although I realize it's a little late for that.

Whoa.

The man standing in front of me is the very definition of ruggedly handsome. Embarrassment heats my cheeks. Of course, it had to be a male guest that spotted my dance party.

At least it wasn't either of my bosses.

"You must be Harper," he says.

Okay, maybe not a guest.

"Yes? And you are?"

"Jesse. The guy you're going to be running this place with for the next three months."

I'm sorry, what? "I thought I was going to be helping out the owners: Mr. and Mrs. Hudson," I say.

Jesse stuffs his hands in his pockets. "That was the plan, yes. But Mr. and Mrs. Hudson have had a change of plans. I'll be filling in for them. I'm their son."

I swallow. Then swallow again when I shoot a quick glance at Jesse's ring finger and see he's not only ruggedly handsome but also unmarried.

Which is not good.

Not good *at all.*

It's not that I have something against ruggedly handsome unmarried men. Quite the opposite—which is the problem. Don't get me wrong. I'm not incapable of controlling myself just because a man is ruggedly handsome.

But he could end up being a distraction. And I don't want a distraction from my goal while I'm here. Look at the lengths I just went to in order to distance myself from Sky. There is absolutely no way I would have accepted the position at the inn if I knew *this* was who I'd be working with.

"But I've been emailing with Mr. and Mrs. Hudson," I explain. "Did they move to another inn of theirs?" Maybe I could transfer there instead.

Jesse scratches his head. "They don't own another inn, and you *have* been emailing them, yes. I'm sorry for the confusion. The change is recent. Really recent. Today is my first day, actually. My dad had an accident about a week ago. That's why they aren't here."

"An accident?"

"He fell off a ladder while hanging some string lights. He'll be fine, but he's in physical therapy for the next couple of months. I think it freaked my parents out more than anything. They realized they can't run the inn like they used to, that it's time to slow down. They didn't want to see it go downhill, so they were thinking of selling, but I encouraged them to let me try to step in and take it over. This holiday season is a test run to see how that goes. If it goes well, then we'll be co-owners, with me overseeing the place. But I'm not technically in charge yet, so I don't want you to view me as a boss. I hope you see me as a coworker and teammate since you and I are the primary staff for the next three months."

You and I. I'm trying to find words; I really am. I'm trying to transition into calm, cool, and collected. But those three words keep looping around in my head.

"I'm sorry, I know it's probably stressful to think about working with someone else who's new as well," Jesse says, misinterpreting my silence. "But I do have some experience. My parents have had this place since I was in high school, and I worked here in the summers all through college."

"I'm sure you're perfectly competent," I say. "It's me I'm worried about."

"Aw, come on." Jesse reaches out a hand and rests it on my shoulder. I know he's trying to be reassuring, but his touch has the opposite effect.

I feel that touch in ways I have no business feeling. For many reasons.

Breathe in, Harper. Now breathe out.

"Like I said, my parents have been doing this a long time. They wouldn't have picked you if they didn't see something in you."

Desperation, I think. That's what they saw. *Willing to relocate*, my application said. *Up for any task.* Just not the task that involves working alongside your handsome son. I should have specified that.

I draw in another deep breath, realizing I have two choices. I could quit on the spot and fly home to Atlanta where I don't have a job and where Sky will most definitely distract me from my goal. Or . . . I stay here and focus. I really want to stay here.

"I guess we're in this together," I say.

For all I know, Jesse could end up being a total jerk. Or in a serious relationship. Either would stop me from ever looking in his direction.

"Great! I'll show you to your room so you can get settled. Here, let me get your bags." He picks up the duffle and hoists it on top of the roller, then opens the front door for me before wheeling my luggage out.

Okay, not a jerk.

"You'll be staying in one of those cottages," he says, pointing ahead to six identical structures. They all have white cedar siding

56

and black shutters like the main building where most of the guest rooms are, and each has its own brick chimney. "I'll be staying in the one right next to yours."

I swallow. "You will?"

"Yep."

"On your own too?"

"Uh-huh."

Okay, apparently not in a serious relationship either.

I almost laugh because it's comical, really. Good thing I am a grown adult with self-control and goals. Goals that I'm not going to let get derailed—by a pilot or an innkeeper.

"I can take it from here," I say, once we reach my front door.

"You sure?" Jesse asks.

"Yep."

He nods, setting my bags down on my doorstep before stepping back. "Oh, here's your key."

He fishes it out of his pocket, and I take it from him and nod my head, waiting for him to leave.

"Right." He claps his hands together. "Take as much time as you want getting settled. I'll give you a tour after, and then we can get to work. If you need me, I'm going to be chopping wood by the barn until you're ready."

Of course he will be.

I hold up the A-okay sign with my fingers on one hand while crossing the fingers on my other hand behind my back because I don't want to lie to my new coworker. I wouldn't exactly say I'm peachy right now.

seven

Once I finish unpacking, I decide to FaceTime—not call or text—Zoe and Grace. For starters, I want to see their reactions when I share all that's happened on my journey so far. Also, they *need* a virtual tour of my cottage. Who gave Chip and Joanna Gaines the keys to this place? Though the bones are old, it looks styled to be photographed for the front cover of one of their magazine issues.

There's a wood-burning fireplace and bronze log rack beside it. A cream-colored rug covering most of the knotty pine floor. A queen-sized bed with a brown weather-stained headboard. And a snow-white sofa with pillows galore.

There's also a kitchenette with a forest-green fridge. A small oven and stove. And a rail of hanging brass pots and pans mounted to the wall. By the kitchenette, there's a small round farmhouse table with two chairs, perfect for when I want to eat in my room.

The best part of the entire place, though, is the bathroom. Right next to the shower—where I presume I'll spend very little time—is a claw foot tub where I now plan to spend every evening!

I'm thrilled I decided not to head home. So what if I have to work side by side with Jesse day in and day out? I can manage anything if I have this quiet, quaint place to return to at the end of each day. It's the perfect place to work on starting over.

I have no idea why I panicked before. Maybe I was still thrown from the past twenty-four hours: getting on a plane, starting a new life, meeting Sky. Maybe my pulse was still racing from Sky's goodbye kisses and that made me more susceptible to panic in reaction to unexpected changes. But Sky and I have a pact, this cabin and this property has my bucket list painted all over it, and everything is going to be fine.

I need to trust in that—in the idea that it will all work out.

The first thing on my Vermont Bucket List is to learn to trust again. And my whole experience in Vermont thus far has been a big step in that direction.

I nod to myself, determined to have faith.

Then I jump up onto my plush new bed and dial Zoe, with the plan to add Grace to the call right after.

That's odd. No ringtone. I check my cell phone's bars.

There's no service.

I climb down off the bed and pull out my computer from my duffle, thinking maybe I can reach them through Zoom if I can log onto the internet.

I check my connection, but nope, the Wi-Fi is down too.

Hmm . . . I'm pretty sure this is *my* problem to deal with since I work here now. Or Jesse's and my problem. Better to address it before guests start complaining.

I head outside and find Jesse by the barn with his axe raised in the air midswing. More notable than the axe position, though, is what he's wearing: a white cutoff t-shirt. Don't we have a dress code or something?

"Excuse me," I say, once he's split the wood in half. I hold up my phone. "There's no cell service. Or internet."

He picks up the axe to swing it again. "You're correct."

Why is he looking at me as if this isn't a problem? "Are we going to fix that?"

He shakes his head.

"Sorry, I mean who should we *call* to fix that? Obviously, I know *we* can't fix that. Or *I* can't, at least."

"No one is going to fix it, 'cause there's nothing to fix," he says, slicing another piece of wood down the middle. "It's part of the experience here. People come to Hudson Lane to get away from the noise. There's no cell service. And no internet. It's intentional."

It makes sense now: why I got the job. Surely this was mentioned somewhere in the fine print, and those who hadn't had a couple glasses of wine before applying probably read it and decided to apply elsewhere.

I stick my hands on my hips. "How was I emailing with your parents, then?"

"There's a bakery, a bar, and a few other shops with internet in the town about a mile that way." He points in the direction Sky and I drove in from.

Sky! This means I'm going to have to walk a mile to read his emails and to email him. That's fine for the time being, but what about when it gets colder and snows?

"I don't have a car here," I say.

"I can always drive you," Jesse offers.

I picture him sitting outside while I read Sky's letters and write him letters in reply. On second thought, maybe there's a taxi service. I'll look into that later.

"I take it there's no TV either?" I might as well ask while we're on the topic.

He shakes his head. "There's chess and cards and peace and quiet."

When I say nothing, he laughs. "I think you might come to like it." He sets the axe down and reaches for a plaid button-down beside the woodpile. He must have stripped it off when he started working. I turn away slightly as he starts to button it up. It's the polite thing to do. Once he's finished, I turn back. "What do you say? Ready for that tour?" he asks.

"Why not?" I shrug. "It's not as if I can get caught up on *How to Get Away with Murder*."

"What?"

"It's a show," I say, as we start walking. "Didn't you have a TV in your last place?"

"I spent a lot of time here growing up and I got used to not having one. I never felt the urge to change that when I moved away."

"Which was to where, exactly?"

"Just to Burlington, Vermont, for college and then to downtown Stowe in an apartment a few miles from here."

"You've never been tempted to move anywhere else?"

He hesitates. "Once." It's one word but sounds like an entire story. I think to ask, but he doesn't seem as if he wants to talk about it. Besides he's my coworker, not my best friend or love interest. It's not my business.

He's pointing out the pool and the hot tub, as well as the fire pit, all of which fall under his jurisdiction in terms of maintenance, he tells me. I just need to point guests in the general direction of the amenities and let them know the pool is eighty-five degrees Fahrenheit and everything opens at nine and closes at the same hour in the evening.

As we head back to the inn, he returns to the earlier topic. "How about you? I assume you've hopped around quite a bit more than I have."

I laugh because it's funny he sees me that way. I can't blame him, considering I relocated for a seasonal gig, but that impression couldn't be further from the truth.

"This is very uncharacteristic of me," I say. "Or, at least, I think it is. Maybe not anymore, I suppose. I don't know."

I'm rambling. Why am I rambling?

"I'm trying to start fresh," I continue.

"You kill someone or something?"

When I laugh again and say no, he shrugs and says, "Sorry, you mentioned that TV show about murders, and then you said you wanted to start fresh. I wasn't going to judge you or anything."

"You wouldn't judge me if I murdered someone?"

"Well . . ." he chuckles. "Maybe a little. But you're my right-hand woman now. We've got each other's backs."

"So there's no one else helping us out?" I look around as we approach the front desk. The inn is small, but it does seem like a lot of work for two people.

"There's us and then one other couple that does the daily housekeeping." As soon as he says it, he clears his throat. "I mean, there's one couple that does the daily housekeeping and then there's us. I wasn't implying that you and I are going to be a . . . you know."

"I figured as much." *I'm certain of it.*

"Right. Let's get you set up." Jesse doesn't strike me as the kind of guy who gets flustered easily, but his face and his neck appear flushed as he shifts his focus to the computer.

I'm not sure how I feel about him being thrown off by those words. Was it just the awkwardness of a new working relationship? Or is the thought of us as a couple pleasing to him? Maybe it's better I don't think too much on that answer.

"There will be two guests checking in later this afternoon, and you'll use this computer program to get that process started." He's all business now, and the flush has vanished, making me wonder if I imagined it.

"Doesn't a computer program require Wi-Fi?" I ask.

"Yes. There's a router connected to this computer. So if you really need to check your email or something, you can here. But it's used by me too, and the housekeeping staff, so don't go planning your next murder on it or anything."

"Right." It's probably not the best place to check Sky's letters. I wouldn't want to accidently leave one open for everyone else to read. But if I'm ever in a bind and can't get to town, I suppose I could.

Jesse goes through the check-in process, which is quite simple, thankfully, and then has me follow him into the kitchen behind the parlor. "Happy hour starts at five," he explains. "You'll want to put the baked brie in the oven around four-thirty. And then you can bring out the wine and the rest of the cheeses."

He shows me where everything is in the fridge, then pulls out the crackers from a cupboard and points to where I can find the serving trays before leading me back into the lobby.

"Oh, by the way." He spins around once we reach the doorway. "I stocked the fridge in your room with enough food to get you started for this week, but I can take you to town whenever you need more."

I nod and thank him.

"Any questions?" he asks.

I fold my arms over my chest. "Where will you be in case . . . you know . . . something goes wrong?"

"Around," he says. "Just holler. Or you can ring this." He walks me out to the porch and shows me a hanging triangular iron dinner bell.

"So old-fashioned."

Jesse leans against one of the porch pillars and scratches the couple days' worth of scruff on his face. I'm only staring because I'm waiting for him to speak—no reason other than that. "The world's moving forward at crazy speeds," he says, shooting a glance my way. "Sometimes it's nice to slow down so we don't miss all the great things in front of us."

I swallow. When did it get hot out here?

Jesse shifts his gaze and nods in the direction of the driveway. "Looks like that first guest just arrived. Remember, if you need me, just . . ."

"Holler," I cut in. "Got it."

———

I check in the new guests—a young couple from Idaho—without a single computer glitch. An hour or so after that, a family from Upstate New York arrives, and I get them situated with ease. Once that's squared away, I hurry to my room to make a sandwich for lunch, then return to the inn to get to work on the happy hour spread.

It takes some time, but when I emerge from the kitchen with the cheese platter, I must say it looks Instagram-worthy. Not that there's a way to upload a photo of it to social media or even to text a picture to my parents or Zoe or Grace. Still, I feel pretty good when a couple guests snap photos of it when they arrive, even though they know there's nothing they can do with the pictures at the moment either.

I'm feeling pretty proud of myself in general for acing all of my Day One duties. So proud that I pour myself half a glass of wine to celebrate once I finish filling glasses for everyone else. I'm just about to take a sip when one of the guests turns to me.

"Do you smell that?" she asks.

"Smell what?"

"Smoke," she replies at the same time the fire alarm starts to blare.

Oh God. Please tell me I did not leave the baked brie in the oven for more than an hour.

Only I did. I most certainly did.

"I'm so sorry," I say, addressing the room. "If you could all please head outside to the back patio for a couple of minutes." I'm trying to keep my voice calm when the voice in my head is screaming: *What the hell, Harper? How could you slip up this badly?*

I hurry into the kitchen, and the second I open the door I start to cough because smoke is spewing out of the oven.

I race over and turn the oven off, then step back. There might be an actual fire inside there rather than just a very burnt cheese—the smoke is black. I'm pretty sure you're not supposed to open an oven when there's a fire inside. I'm not totally inept in the kitchen, despite current evidence to the contrary. But you know who will surely doubt that? My new coworker. I'm going to get fired when he tells his parents about this. Who starts a fire less than twenty-four hours into her new gig? Certainly not a good employee.

I reach for a dish towel and start to wave it near the fire alarm so it will stop going off, but eventually I give up because I realize it's not a battle I'm going to win; it's one I have to wait out.

I open the window to let in fresh air, hoping it'll speed up the process. Still coughing, I turn to head back into the parlor and run right into Jesse.

He catches me. "You okay?"

I don't say anything because I'm crying. The tears started when I was futilely waving the dish towel at the fire alarm. I can't believe I'm crying in front of him, but I can't stop. It's been a big week. Coming here was a big change. And now I messed up, and I wish I hadn't because I don't want to go home. I *really* don't want to go home.

"Who said anything about you going home?"

It's not until Jesse speaks that I realize I said half those thoughts out loud in between coughs.

"Jesse, I'm not normally like this," I say, pulling back and wiping my eyes. "I don't want you to think I'm a crying, babbling arsonist."

He ushers me out of the kitchen and sits me down at a table in the parlor, bringing over a glass of water and waiting beside me until I stop coughing and my breathing settles down.

"What are you normally like?" he asks once it's quiet.

At first I think he's asked an interview question and my answer will determine whether or not he tells his parents to give me a second chance. But when I look up, I don't see judgment on his face. He's watching me with genuine curiosity. It takes the pressure off my response.

"Six months ago, my fiancé left me for his first love the day before our wedding, and then I got let go from my job a week later," I confess. "Prior to that, I'd say I was responsible, put together, fairly predictable, and routine. I mostly did what was expected of me. I'm

65

not sure who I thought expected me to be all those things—society, I guess. Maybe my parents, to some degree. But I came here because since that moment six months ago, everything has changed, and I want to try and figure out who I'm going to be going forward."

Jesse folds his hands on the table. A beat later, he looks up from his hands and meets my gaze. "I think that's brave."

I have a flashback to Sky's response after I told him a similar version of this story: "*I think that sounds fun.*"

I thought I liked the idea of seeing my time here as a fun adventure, but I like the idea of it being a brave one even more.

"Thank you."

I allow a second or two of silence before I blurt out, "So you're not going to tell your parents to fire me? Believe me, from now on I will be someone who puts out fires, not starts them. Figuratively speaking, of course."

I see a smile creep onto Jesse's lips. I can't quite believe it because he has every right to be pissed at me right now. The fire happened under his watch on his first day and so will make him look bad to his parents. But he seemingly couldn't care less that it happened.

"I get it now," he says.

"Get what?"

"Why my parents hired you." He still has a faint grin on his face when he gets to his feet.

"Why?"

"Nothing," he says, with a shake of his head.

"Seriously?" I get to my feet as well. "You can't say that and then say 'nothing.'"

I follow him out to the lobby, where he opens the door and welcomes the guests back in, assuring them that the space is safe and apologizing for the inconvenience. I nod to the guests and do the same, but rather than lead the guests back to the room, I stand in the doorway, waiting for him.

Once the last guest is inside, he drops his head, seeing that I'm not going to let him leave me hanging. When he looks back up, he meets my eyes.

"This place has been missing something for a while," he says.

I cross my arms, waiting to hear the rest. "And that would be . . .?"

"Life," he finishes. "And spunk. And passion." He pauses, then adds, "You changed your whole life because it wasn't enough to stay the same anymore. Whether you realize it or not yet . . . I'm pretty sure Harper 2.0 has enough determination to do anything."

The flush that worked its way up Jesse's face earlier is doing a number on my face now. That was quite the compliment. Especially since I'd been feeling so lifeless before I got on the plane yesterday morning. I do feel more lit up here. I'm glad Jesse can see that. It helps me see it even more in myself.

He starts down the stairs, then spins back. "Hey, next time you need help remember just ring this." He reaches up and sounds the dinner bell. "No need to be all dramatic and set off the fire alarm."

I laugh.

Ten minutes ago I was crying and convinced I was getting fired, and now I'm laughing and convinced I'm the perfect person for the job.

As far as who I'm going to be working alongside during my time here . . . maybe I did get lucky after all.

eight

As resistant as I was to the whole "no technology" aspect of this place earlier this morning, I'm starting to think that sitting here at ten o'clock at night wrapped in blankets in a rocker outside my cottage is exactly what I need.

It's the stars that seem to be convincing me. Sorry—stars are what I saw on clear nights in Atlanta. These are so much brighter; they deserve to be described as something else entirely. Stars 2.0.

I smile as I remember how Jesse referred to me earlier this evening: "Harper 2.0." I like that name for myself. We all probably have a 2.0 version of ourselves somewhere inside us. The trick is to figure out how to be that person more often.

Which is precisely why I'm out here reading this self-help book. It's my first of fifteen in this genre that I'm hoping to get through while I'm here. Reading them is on my Vermont Bucket List, and now that there's no TV at night to distract me, I might knock them off the list faster than I thought.

Then again, there's also a chance I won't be alone out here every night. I just heard Jesse's front door open and swing shut a moment ago. If I look over, he'll probably say something to me, so I don't.

It's not that I mind talking to Jesse. I'd go so far as to say I enjoy it. It's just that as an introvert, I often get in these moods of just wanting to *be*—I don't want to talk to or engage with anyone—and I happen to be in one of those moods right this moment.

Jesse must be an introvert too because he doesn't say anything for the first couple of minutes he's outside. When he does eventually look over and address me, I get the sense he's just trying to be polite.

"Not too cold out here for you?" he asks.

I regard him for a moment. He's in a sweater and jeans and his hands are seeking warmth inside his pockets.

"I took a bath before I came out, so I'm still nice and toasty."

"Ah," he replies, and the conversation drops. It drops because it's my turn to speak, and I'm not sure how to talk to Jesse when we're off duty and at our cottages. On the one hand, we're coworkers. On the other hand, he's my neighbor.

These different hats make our relationship confusing. At least to me. Jesse's not making it weird. Maybe it's *not* weird, and I'm just making it that way in my head. *Less thinking, Harper. More speaking.*

"How about you?" I ask. "Cold?"

"I run warm, so I'm fine," he says.

That explains why his shirt was off earlier when he was chopping wood.

Barely any emotion stirs in me when I think of that now. *Good.*

He nods to my book. "What are you reading?"

I hold it up to show him the cover.

He wrinkles his nose as if he doesn't approve.

"Do you have something against self-help books?" I ask.

"Not at all. I've read a few."

"Then what's with the look?"

He walks toward one of his porch pillars and leans his back against it, facing me.

"I just prefer novels. Someone spouting advice from the comfort of his or her home just doesn't do it for me. I think living teaches us the most about life. Followed by books about other people living."

I hadn't really thought of that before. But I see his point. I glance down at the book in my hand. I won't immediately rule it out as a tool that might help me, but I'll consider reading a novel or two while I'm here.

"Was your first day okay? Minus the fire, of course," he asks.

I smile. "It was great, thanks. I like it here."

"Good."

He turns, then, toward the view and gazes upward. I wait to see if he's going to say anything else, but he doesn't.

Definitely a fellow introvert. There's something comforting about that.

Since he seems content just taking in the night, I go back to reading and get through a few more pages before he turns back toward me and interrupts.

"Do you think we all go up there when we die?" He nods to the stars.

I study him, wondering if he was smoking weed in his cottage or if he just likes philosophical conversations. Either way, it doesn't matter to me. Though I don't smoke, I'm not against it, and I also don't mind going deep. In fact, I wish people wanted to have conversations about this kind of stuff more often.

"I don't know," I answer honestly. "I hope so. It sure would be a pretty place to hang out."

He smiles as if he likes my answer. I don't know why that makes me happy. I don't care what he thinks of me. Well, I care to some extent, of course. I need him to like me enough to tell his parents to keep me around and to operate the inn smoothly with me. But I'm pretty sure I have great job security if he didn't tell them they should fire me after the fire-in-the-kitchen mishap.

"What about you?" I ask as he sits on his porch step.

"I'm with you, I guess." He shrugs. "It doesn't look like a bad spot. Although sometimes I wish we had a choice between going up there and staying down here forever."

"It's nice you feel that way about life," I say. "Not everyone does."

He smiles but doesn't respond. He raises his eyes to the sky again instead. Then, after another minute or so, he gets back to his feet. "I should head in."

"Time for bed?"

"No. I have more work, actually."

"Anything I can help with?" I would have felt bad not offering, although I really hope he doesn't say yes. I'm enjoying being out here and don't want to head in yet.

"It's not for this job," he explains. "It's for the one I was working at prior to this."

"Where was that?"

"A consulting company in town. I didn't want to leave them hanging since I made the decision to jump ship so quick, so I'm finishing up some projects until they can find a replacement for me."

"That's nice of you."

"They were good to me. And I'm big on commitment. It matters to me to see things through."

Huh. I like that. It's so solid.

"See you in the morning?" he says.

"Yeah," I nod. We already discussed earlier that we're meeting at the barn at six to collect eggs from the chickens to make breakfast for the guests.

"Goodnight, Harper," he says.

"Goodnight," I reply.

Hearing the door swing shut behind him, I go back to reading, getting through another couple of chapters before I start to feel cold and decide to head back inside. My bed is calling.

Luckily, I've already brushed my teeth, and I'm wearing my pajamas, so I climb right in. Once I slip under the covers, I roll over onto my side, and when I close my eyes, the strangest thought pops into my head: *I miss Sky's snore.*

71

I almost laugh out loud because it's such an odd thing to miss. It's even odder that I miss it after only sleeping beside him for one night. I guess it means my crush is even bigger than I thought. I might have to mention this to him in the first email I send.

Which reminds me . . . I need to get to town tomorrow. It's killing me that I haven't been able to look at what he wrote me in the first email *he* sent.

Then again, I guess there's no need to rush things.

After all, I have a feeling our story is just getting started.

nine

"**What** do you mean they don't have names? We need to name them right now!"

Jesse laughs as he reaches into the nest box. He's collecting the chickens' eggs while I stand in the coop picking up one chicken after another.

"There are twenty-six chickens," he says. "Even if we can come up with that many good names, how would we keep them straight?"

"What if we each name three, then? Our favorite three! Oh, but then won't the others be sad? You're all our favorites," I coo as I set down the one I'm holding and pick up another who seems to want to be held.

Jesse laughs and shakes his head. "Maybe you were a farmer in a past life."

"You think?"

"You're good with the animals."

"Well, they make it easy. They're all so cute." We fed the goats before we came over to the chickens, and they were just as endearing.

"What else is on the agenda for today?" I ask as I follow Jesse out of the barn.

"Two guests are checking out at eleven today. But after that, the next two aren't supposed to arrive until tomorrow afternoon. Which means you'll be free to do as you please from eleven till happy hour."

That should give me enough time to walk into town this afternoon. I smile at the thought of getting to read Sky's letter.

"Perfect," I say as I spy the rising sun start to pinken the sky behind the golden trees. Last night I was convinced the evening was going to be my favorite time of day here, but morning is giving it a serious run for its money.

"What are we doing with all these eggs?" I ask as Jesse opens the door to the inn for me.

"What do people come to Vermont for?" he replies, trailing behind me.

"Maple syrup?"

"Correct. This morning, we're going to give these folks the best thing to pour it on: pancakes."

——

Jesse tells me I've officially redeemed myself in the kitchen for my fiasco yesterday evening as we carry the first tray of golden brown pancakes to the parlor at seven-thirty, along with bowls of fruit and six varieties of syrup.

"I told you I'm not normally an arsonist," I say. "I do know how to cook."

He steals a pancake right off the top of the stack and takes a bite. "These validate your statement."

"Hey, I thought those were for the guests."

"You snooze you lose," he says, just as a couple of early risers walk in. "Oops," he whispers, gobbling up the rest of his pancake before smoothing down his shirt and shifting back into professional mode.

"What do we do now?" I ask, examining my shirt to make sure there's no flour on it.

"We pour coffee and mingle," he says. "Replenish the pancakes as needed and answer any questions guests may have about Vermont in general, Stowe in particular, or the inn."

"I did some research, but I don't know that I'm enough of an expert yet."

"Just hang by me. You'll catch on quick."

I *do* hang by Jesse, following him around the entire morning as we talk to the guests that stop in. The whole time I make mental notes of recommendations he gives for places to eat and attractions to visit so I can refer the next round of visitors to the same spots. Not that I'm going to be able to sound as enthusiastic as Jesse when I'm giving the recommendations. He's really selling guests on the places he mentions. And not in a salesy way. It's just clear that he's passionate about his hometown and Vermont on the whole. Strike that—*passionate* doesn't seem to be a strong enough word to describe how he feels about this state. *Love* is a better one.

Jesse loves Vermont. *A lot.*

It's really something to watch a man talk about a subject he loves in this fashion. Turns out, it does weird things to your body. It makes your palms clam up and your heart pound fast. It even causes strange thoughts to pop into your head. Like, if this man is talking about loving *a place* with this much enthusiasm, how much does his heart expand when he's in love with *a woman*?

I have no idea why I just asked myself that. The last thing I care about is the mechanics of Jesse's heart. I care about how my own heart works. And, if I did think about a heart besides mine, I'd care about learning how Sky's heart works. No space for more hearts than that in this girl's head.

You see? Strange thoughts.

"Hey." Jesse reaches out for my arm as soon as he wraps up the conversation. "I don't mean to leave you with cleanup. But I've got to run out and take the cover off the hot tub and the pool, then check the temperatures of each."

"Of course," I swallow, a little relieved he's leaving so I can refocus.

And I *will* refocus. Those strange thoughts were just passing. They won't come back.

I become surer and surer of that statement as breakfast wraps up and I check out the guests who are leaving today, because my excitement to read Sky's email overtakes my thoughts.

I head straight to town to find that bakery with internet access Jesse mentioned, and the speed with which I walk there is a testament to how much I can't wait to see what's waiting for me in my inbox. Though Jesse said town was a mile away, I swear I make it there in ten minutes—maybe less.

I'm relieved when I spot the bakery, Milk & Maple, right on the corner, and even more relieved when I see it's not crowded inside. I hurry to the counter and ask for the internet password in a rushed breath, as if I'm a marathon runner demanding water after crossing the finish line.

"*Creamandsugar*, all lowercased, all one word," the college-aged girl behind the counter says as she twirls a strand of her curly red hair with her finger.

"Great, thanks!" I turn to find a spot to sit, then spin back, remembering I need to order.

"I'll have a pumpkin spice latte," I say.

The girl looks annoyed; perhaps she's sick of making pumpkin spice drinks for tourists. I want to tell her I'm not a tourist—I live here now—but I don't want to waste time either, so I make a mental note to order something else next time before rushing to claim a table that just freed up by the window.

I scan the room as I pull my computer out of my bag, noticing details I missed in my dash to get internet access: a display case with yummy pastries, a fireplace with two tables beside it, a bookcase in the back filled with novels.

I'm glad it's so cute, since I plan to spend quite a bit of time here. And equally as glad, once I join the Wi-Fi network, to see that the internet connection is strong. I pull up my email, and I'm surprised to see, amid all the junk mail cluttering my inbox, not one but *two* new emails from Sky.

The first was sent yesterday morning when we were still together and has a subject line that reads *Letter Number One*.

The second was sent this morning and has no subject.

My stomach instantly drops, fearing the worst: maybe he's written to tell me this arrangement was a mistake, that it's not a good idea to meet up on Christmas Eve after all. I hate how quickly I jump to the worst-case scenario. But I can't help it. In the past six months it's become my new default.

Of course, the second email could just as likely be Sky reiterating how much he's looking forward to seeing me again. In fact, this seems much *more* likely. Still, I feel sick to my stomach as I open it.

To: Harper

From: Sky

Subject: no subject

Date: September 19

Harper,

I'm embarrassed by how many times I've checked my email to see if you'd responded since my flight back to Atlanta. Since you still haven't replied, I just wanted to say I'm sorry if I came across too strong. If I freaked you out, I can tone it down.

Okay?

Hope you got settled all right.

Best regards,

Sky

P.S. I realize this is two emails in one week. I promise to only send one going forward.

I let out the deepest sigh, relieved on two counts: (1) the email isn't negative; (2) it appears I'm not the only one who's nervous.

Then I sit up straight and lean in because if Sky was worried he came across too strong in his first email, I'm dying to read what it says.

I click it open, breathing much easier this go-round.

To: Harper

From: Sky

Subject: Letter Number One

Date: September 18

Dear Harper,

Since we're only emailing each other once a week, bear with me, because I'm about to use up all the space I can get.

I'm up early, sitting at my desk while you're still sleeping, because I can't stop thinking about something. Don't judge me when I tell you what it is, okay?

Rom-coms. Yep.

Remember when you said you wouldn't judge?

Specifically, I can't stop thinking about those *scenes* in rom-coms that I used to roll my eyes at when I'd watch them with my sisters. You know, the ones when the main characters bump into each other and form this instant connection? Like in *Serendipity*, for instance. Or *The Wedding Planner*. (See, I wasn't lying. I know this genre well.)

Well, I don't think I'll be rolling my eyes from this point onward. Because I get that it's possible now. Meeting you has made me believe that a guy actually can meet a girl and get a feeling and just know that he wants to be with her.

And you know what that got me thinking? I wonder how many other things are possible that I've written off my whole life as ridiculous. That's a big extrapolation, but I like that our chance encounter has me wondering about all the other ways my universe might expand.

Isn't that what a good connection is supposed to do? Open up our worlds? Make us think *more* is possible?

What more do you wish were possible, Harper, if the sky were the limit? (See what I did there? I used my own name in a pun. That's a total dad joke if you ask me. Not that I'm thinking about becoming a dad. But I guess it's in my "someday maybe" category.)

Do you want to be a mom? Have kids? What would you love your life to look like if it could look like anything? What are your dreams for the future?

You're waking up now, and I like that you just rolled over to my side of the bed to try and cuddle up next to me. You look disappointed that I'm not there, and it makes me want to crawl back into bed beside you. But then you might not get to work on time, and I might not catch my flight and . . . condoms. We still don't have any damn condoms.

I thought about running out this morning to pick some up, but I think you and I could do better for our first time than a morning when we both have places to rush off to. We *will* do better than that. I promise.

I'm picking up writing this again now that we're down at the kitchen table. You're currently looking at me like you're pissed I'm still typing. I want to laugh because I think even your pissed-off face looks cute, Harper. It makes me think you and I are going to be able to resolve any future conflicts quickly. I know I couldn't stay mad at that face longer than a minute. Maybe two. We'll have short fights and lots of make-up sex. How does that sound?

I only have a few more minutes now, so typing fast. Share with me your fantasies, Harper. All of them.

(Did your mind just go where mine went after I typed that statement? I didn't mean *those* kinds of fantasies, although I wouldn't mind at all if you did want to share them . . .)

I've got to get you to work now, but I wish I didn't have to. I wish we had more time. That's my dream right now.

Until next time,

Sky

This barista must think I *really* like pumpkin spice lattes. Because she happens to be setting my drink down at the exact moment I'm looking up from Sky's letter, and although I can't see my expression, I can feel that I'm beaming. I've never received a letter like this before. I want to print it out and frame it so I can read it over and over again.

It's definitely safe to tell Sky I missed his cute snore when I write him back. Which I should. Right now, before he sends a third email. I take a sip of my pumpkin spice latte and begin.

To: Sky

From: Harper

Subject: Re: Letter Number One

Date: September 19

Dear Sky,

My first dream would be for the inn where I'm working to have Wi-Fi so I could read your emails right when you send them and email you back in a timely manner. I found out when I arrived that the inn doesn't have internet or even cell service.

Please know I'd never ghost you. Or intentionally leave you hanging. Also, please never sign an email ending in "regards" to me ever again. The formality of your second letter made me sad, and so did the context. You didn't come across as too strong in your first email. Please keep flattering me.

I'll come on strong myself for a minute and admit that I missed your cute snore last night. I also might have had a few fantasies when I woke up this morning. But I'm not going into detail on those. At least not yet. ;)

As for my fantasies about the future . . . yes, I do want kids one day, and I'd like a great love too. I'd also like to spend my time doing some activity or a career that's personally meaningful. I've never had that and have always been envious of people who proclaim they have a passion and know what they're "meant to be doing." Like how you described feeling when you're traveling and flying.

That's what I'm working on figuring out while I'm here. I'm going to pick up some paint while I'm in town today to give an art project a shot. Maybe I have hidden artistic abilities that I haven't tapped into yet. I know, I know, it's unlikely. But you never know until you try, right? I'm also working through a list in a book I'm reading that's supposed to help me figure out what I'm "naturally drawn to."

Should I add you to this list? (See what I did there? I made a cheesy dad joke. By the way, why aren't mom jokes a thing?

Are moms not funny? Or are moms actually funny and dads are just corny funny? That was a tangent, but I am curious if you know the answer to this.)

What about you, Sky? What other big dreams did this big revelation provoke? I want to hear yours too. I also want to hear what your life is like in Atlanta. Fill me in so I feel like I'm there with you.

Vermont, I must say, is working its way into my heart. I got to feed goats and chickens this morning, and the maple syrup on the pancakes is everything I ever dreamed it would be. I will probably dream about it tonight. And possibly you. In a separate dream, of course. Because maple syrup in that context isn't a go for me.

Do anti-fantasies give you hints to my actual fantasies? I suppose you'll have to guess.

Until Letter Number Two,

Harper

I'm blushing when I press send. I probably should have proofread it and maybe cut out the part about maple syrup. But if I reread it, I would have nitpicked it, and I don't have time to rewrite it. I still have to find a place to get those art supplies I mentioned to Sky. And then I need to race back to the inn and shower before giving the ole happy hour another try. And, oh, my phone!

I pull it out from my purse and find so many messages.

Mom: Glad you made it safe. Next time text us as soon as you get off the plane. Your father and I were worried, dear. Okay, honey, hope your first day is going okay.

Dad: Did your first day go okay?

Mom: Did you get your dad's text?

I respond to their messages first because Mom is right. I should have texted her and Dad right when I got off the plane. As parents, they naturally worry, and since I'm their only kid, they worry more than most parents. I know this and I left them hanging. It doesn't matter how old I am. That wasn't cool.

After I apologize, I let them know about the Wi-Fi situation and cell phone service, so they know not to expect to hear from me in a timely fashion from here on out.

Then, I move onto the conversation with my friends.

> **Zoe: Please expand on that smiley face next to "safe." I'm thinking there's more to the story of your arrival there!**
>
> **Grace: Um . . . saw online there's a new innkeeper at your inn. Judging from the looks of him, my money is on THAT being why you haven't responded!!**

I pause. Grace's comment hits me the wrong way. I don't like the insinuation, and I really don't want my friends framing Jesse that way. I want them talking about Sky. Then again, they don't know about Sky. Of course! They'll love the sound of him when I fill them in. And, okay, I did have the same gut reaction Grace did when I first met Jesse. He's an objectively good-looking guy. So the leap makes sense. I just have to correct the assumption.

I type a long text message to fill them in about Sky and the pact we made. I'd call, but they're both at work now.

I also let them know about the Wi-Fi and cell service. Then I feel the need to send along a photo of Sky to really drive it home that he's the one to focus on. Sky said he found my email on LinkedIn, so he must be on there. I search for *Sky Alder* and find him in seconds.

Wow, this picture is . . . wow. He's even wearing his pilot's hat. It's a good thing I'm just now seeing him in it. If I'd seen it before, it would have made parting ways even more of a challenge.

I screenshot it and send it to my friends. Within seconds I have responses.

Zoe: !!!!

Grace: OMG!

Zoe: That's some serious willpower on your end to make him wait for you! How adorable he's waiting for you!!

Grace: Seriously adorable! I mean, THE PACT is adorable. Sky is not adorable . . . he's HOT! And sounds swoon-worthy. We like him!!!

I close my eyes and let their excitement further stoke mine. Is there anything better than sharing details about a crush with your friends? Then I respond.

Me: Yeah, guys . . . I really like him too!

ten

It's crazy all the things a new crush can do to you, like make you:

1. Smile incessantly. Half the people at this happy hour I'm hosting have asked me what I'm so happy about.

2. Forget things. I completely spaced on grabbing art supplies when I was in town and will have to go back tomorrow.

3. Gush about everything. While chatting to the guests about the cheeses, the wine, the town, and the inn, I sound almost as passionate about Vermont as Jesse did this morning.

4. Not notice things you normally would. Like someone calling your name.

"Harper?" Jesse tries again. I only know it's not the first time he's tried to get my attention because he laughs when I finally spin around and spot him sitting by the fire outside the inn. "What kind of daze were you just in? A good one, I hope."

I grin and nod but don't elaborate. As *if* I want to tell Jesse all about my crush.

"How did happy hour go?" he asks. It's pitch-black out, but Jesse's face is well lit from the outdoor fire and the string lights hanging high above that run from the porch pillars to two evergreen trees in the distance and back.

"Better than yesterday," I reply. "But I suppose that's not saying much."

"You're being modest. Sounds like you're becoming quite the spokeswoman for Vermont. I heard you talking to some guests when I popped in there to make this." He holds up his drink.

"What do you have there?"

"A hot toddy," he says, taking another sip from his mug. "Want one?"

I was just making conversation. But I don't say so aloud. "That's okay," I say. "I don't want to bother you to make another."

"It's no problem at all. Wait here." He's on his feet before I can protest and throws me his blanket.

Oh. Okay. I guess we're having cocktails.

I wrap the blanket around my shoulders and take a seat in an Adirondack chair on the opposite side of the fire. Because Jesse and I work together, a little physical distance seems the most appropriate right now. Although there's also a chance I just made things weird. If Jesse thinks it's weird, he doesn't let on when he rejoins me. He simply hands me my drink, then fetches another blanket out of a basket near his chair and sits down where he was before.

"Good?" he asks as I take my first sip.

"Delicious." It is.

My answer makes him smile. "How was town today?"

How does he know I went to town? Before I can ask, he explains. "I saw you heading that way when I was chopping wood."

Didn't he just chop wood yesterday? I guess there *is* a fireplace in every room. Wood chopping must be part of his daily routine. Noted.

"Town was really nice," I respond. "That bakery you mentioned is quite charming."

"Everything in town is quite charming," he says.

I grin because he's right and because he's doing it again: selling me on this place and making me fall for it a little more.

"Do you miss living off of Main Street?" I remember him telling me he lived near there last night.

"A little," he says. "But this place is pretty hard to beat. I'm not complaining."

"Me either," I say, shooting a glance up at the stars that are out in full force again.

"What was Atlanta like?" he asks.

"You've never been?"

"In the South, I've only been to South Carolina."

I take another sip of my drink. Between the fire, my blanket, and the alcohol, I'm feeling much toastier than I thought was possible to feel out here. It can't be more than forty-five degrees tonight. "Atlanta is a thriving city with great food and lots of young professionals. I like it. But I don't love it the way you seem to love Vermont . . . and the way I'm starting to."

"I'm glad it's making such an impression on you," he responds.

I shift my focus from him to the stars, circling my thumb around the top of my mug and thinking again how beautiful it is here. I eventually break the silence. Not because it's uncomfortable, but because a question pops into my head.

"Can I ask you something?"

"Yeah, of course."

He angles himself toward me a little more. I like the way Jesse gives his full attention to whomever he's talking to. He's been this way with me since I arrived, and I noticed this morning that he does the same with the guests. I'm not sure if he's always been this intentional of a guy or if he's this intentional because he doesn't have a cell phone to check. Either way, it's nice.

"Last night you asked me what I think happens after we die. And yesterday afternoon you mentioned that the inn has been missing some life for a while. It made me wonder if you've lost somebody."

When Jesse doesn't respond, I backtrack. "You don't have to tell me or talk about it. I'm sorry, I shouldn't have pried."

87

When he still doesn't speak up, I wonder if I should apologize again and leave. Clearly, I've made him uncomfortable. That wasn't my intention. I am only curious and trying to get to know him better because he seems to have an interest in getting to know me.

"I'm sorry," I reiterate. "I shouldn't have brought it up." I start to get to my feet, but his voice stops me.

"I'm surprised you put that together, that's all." He's looking directly at me, and the *way* he's looking at me makes me think he does want to talk about it. I settle back down and watch as he shifts his gaze to the fire like he's searching for the words or trying to muster up the strength to say them.

Watching this makes me think the loss must have been recent. Or else it was someone he was really close with.

When he finally speaks, his voice is low. "My brother."

So it was someone who was close. A heaviness fills my chest.

"And his wife," he adds a beat later.

Two people who were close. Oh, Jesse.

I'm on my feet the next second, moving to sit in the chair right beside him. When he bows his head, I rest my hand on his back. I haven't lost anyone that close to me. I imagine there aren't words that make it any less painful. So I don't try to find any. I just stay beside him so he knows I'm here—whether he wants to share more with me or sit in silence.

His voice cracks when he finally finds it. "It happened eleven months ago," he shares. "A car accident as they were driving here. There was a bad rainstorm. They hydroplaned and hit a tree. Both of them died on impact."

I close my eyes and shake my head. *So it was semi-recent too.*

I honestly wasn't expecting such a sad story. My guess had been that a grandparent might have passed, or a distant friend—because Jesse doesn't seem altogether unhappy, and after losing a sibling *and* a sister-in-law in the same instant, some people might struggle to even get out of bed eleven months later. Then again, people deal with grief in different ways. Maybe staying busy has helped him. Or maybe he's good at putting on a brave face. Or perhaps he's processing his grief in pieces.

When Jesse speaks again, I open my eyes and remove my hand from his back, resting it in my lap. "This was their dream," he says, motioning to the property. "To take this place over once my parents stepped down. If you think I love Vermont . . ." He stops to whistle. "Brendan loved it ten times more. And so did his wife, Molly."

"How long were they married?" I reach up to wipe away a tear that's made its way down my cheek. I'm not sure when I started crying.

"Only a year," he says. "But they'd been together since high school. They'd driven the road from town to this property a million times. They knew it so well. Sometimes I still can't believe it happened."

I blow out a breath and shake my head, continuing to listen as Jesse goes on. "As hard as it's been for me, my parents have taken it even harder. I think it's another reason they were okay stepping down when they did. Knowing how much this place meant to Brendan has made it difficult for them to be here. It makes them miss him too much. I feel the opposite. I feel *more* of a connection to him when I'm here. Which is why I really want to keep this property in our family. I know hanging on to this place is what Brendan would want. As crazy as it sounds, sometimes I feel like he's still here. Or his soul is, at least."

This is the longest Jesse's ever spoken to me without looking at me. I get it. It can be easier to say hard things when we pretend we're just talking out loud to ourselves.

"I don't think that sounds crazy at all," I chime in.

Jesse's eyes find mine. "Thank you," he says.

It's the sincerest thank-you I've ever received. And I didn't do anything but sit here and listen.

"Brendan and I were really close," he continues, still looking at me. "We're only two years apart. He was older than me. He always ran in a bigger circle than I did, so I was just one of his best friends. But he was my only best friend."

I think this is Jesse's way of explaining why his thank-you was so sincere. Normally, he'd be sitting here sharing this tragedy with Brendan. Only Brendan isn't here. I am.

"Do you have siblings?" he asks.

"No, but I've had the same best friends since high school, and they're like siblings." I shudder at the thought of losing either of them. "Grace is a therapist who has always given the best advice. Zoe owns a yoga studio and is super free-spirited. They're both fiercely loyal."

Jesse takes another sip of his drink. "Will they visit while you're here?"

"I think they plan to around Thanksgiving."

"I look forward to meeting them."

"What were Brendan and Molly like? Besides passionate about this place," I ask, pulling my blanket tighter around me. It's getting colder, but I'll be damned if I can't sit here long enough to hear Jesse talk more about the most important people to him.

"Brendan was a big jokester," he explains. "He was always pulling pranks and trying to make whatever room he was in more fun. And Molly . . . she was both sweet and ambitious. The way she laughed at Brendan's jokes always made them seem funnier than they ever really were. They both studied hospitality in college and were really looking forward to being in the shoes we're in right now."

"I wish they could take our places," I say.

"Me too." We both sit in silence. I'm not sure what's going through Jesse's head, but I can't stop thinking about how unfair life can be. I wish there were more I could do to ease the pain he's feeling.

"It's getting cold," Jesse says eventually. "Here, let me take that." He reaches for my mug as we both get to our feet.

I hand it over and fold up my blanket, then his, tossing them back in the basket.

"Thanks again," he says.

"Thank *you* for the drink. And for trusting me enough to share all that."

He gives me a bashful glance before he starts to head in.

I've just taken a step toward my cabin when I turn back. "Hey, Jesse?" I call out.

"Yeah?" He faces me and meets my eyes, giving me his full attention again.

"Zoe and Grace may still be around, but it's not like I have them with me for the next three months while I'm here."

As soon as I say it, a silent understanding passes between us.

"Thanks," he grins.

And with that one word, I think we just went from coworkers to friends.

eleven

After last night, I wasn't quite sure what mood I'd find Jesse in this morning. As I dressed to meet him at the barn, I wondered if he'd have an emotional hangover. Or at least be a little subdued. I even prepared myself for more teary conversation. Never once did it cross my mind that he'd be in good spirits.

And not just run-of-the-mill good spirits, but the kind of good spirits that had him suggesting we name the chickens. *All of them.* Forget just the six I proposed we name yesterday morning.

Given that there are a total of twenty-six, Jesse thought it would be a good idea to give each chicken a name that starts with a different letter of the alphabet, beginning with A and working our way to Z.

We're currently stuck on X.

We would have called this one Xander—the only X name either of us seems to know—if I had picked up a boy. But I have a girl in my hands. Jesse thought it would be fun if I had to close my eyes before picking up the next chicken to be named so that the sex would be a mystery.

Jesse thought it would be fun.

I'm still shocked by his mood, even though we've been out here a full half hour. I'm certainly happy about it, though. Last night I left the fire worried I hadn't said or done enough for him. But it seems Jesse just needed someone to listen.

"What about just X?" Jesse tries.

"No," I veto. "We can do better than that."

I woke up feeling determined to do better on all counts while I'm here. Not that I thought I was slacking on the job. But now that I know how much this season means to Jesse, I'm even more motivated to ensure everything is done at its best—including naming the chickens.

I study the one I'm holding more seriously.

"You doing all right?" Jesse asks.

When I look up, I see Jesse is studying me.

"Yeah, why?"

"You just look a little more intense than usual."

I'm surprised he picked up on this subtle shift in my demeanor.

"Is there something specific we need to do to make sure you keep the inn past this holiday season?" I ask.

"That's what you're thinking about right now? I thought we were naming chickens."

I sigh and share what's on my mind and why I'm taking the chicken naming so seriously.

"As long as we keep the place running as well as my parents did, I think they'll let me step in and co-own it," he reassures me. "They just don't want to see it fall apart. Brendan and Molly both had the hospitality background, as my parents do, so they wouldn't have doubted their abilities. But I think they are questioning mine."

"I don't have a hospitality background either," I point out.

"Yeah, but you studied business like me. I think as long as we keep the guests happy and the oven fires to a minimum, we should be good."

"Was that a dig?"

"Just a suggestion." His smirk tells me he's only teasing, and I can't help but laugh. Last night Jesse mentioned Brendan was the one in their family who always made everything more fun. But he seems to have that skill set too.

"How about Xylophone?" I say, contemplating the chicken again.

"You mean like the instrument?"

93

"It keeps popping into my head when I think of words that start with X. We can call her Xylo for short."

"Xylo," Jesse echoes. "That's cute."

"And unforgettable. We certainly won't forget you, Xylo," I say, stroking her feathers before setting her down.

"Xylo won't forget you either," Jesse says. I think he's just being sweet, but then he tells me that chickens don't forget faces.

"Seriously?"

"Yeah. All of these guys and girls will remember you forever. Even once you head back to Atlanta."

As soon as Jesse says this, my stomach clenches. I'm already dreading leaving the inn, and it's only my third day here. I suppose that speaks to how much I'm liking it. But it freaks me out a little bit for what's to come. Then again, Sky is waiting for me at the end of my time here. Maybe the good times are just getting started.

—

Jesse and I make fried eggs this morning for the guests. And toast and bagels and of course waffles because Jesse says we must serve the guests something that goes with maple syrup every morning.

After, I get the two new arrivals checked in and then head to town to grab the art supplies I forgot about yesterday. I feel a little guilty when I leave the inn. Part of me thinks I should stick around in case the new guests have questions. But then I remember that Jesse told me not to stress. Also, I can't forget about my Vermont Bucket List. That has to remain a priority on par with helping Jesse save the inn.

While I'm in town picking out my supplies at Stowe Crafts, a few doors down from Milk & Maple, I can't help but check my email to see if Sky has written me back.

He hasn't.

It's a little disappointing but makes complete sense. I told him I wouldn't check my email often. He probably figured there's no point in rushing to get back to me. I was just hoping he'd shot me something fast because I'm so curious to see what his next one says.

After leaving the store, I wander down the street. Last time I was here I was in such a rush that I didn't fully take in all the details of the delightful downtown, so I do so now, snapping pictures as I go to send to Zoe, Grace, and my parents.

Downtown Stowe is an idyllic New England town punctuated with charming storefronts that dare you to walk by without stepping inside, and a tall white church steeple watching over everything. I pass by The Country Store on Main, which sells home goods including candles and cookware, linens and seasonal décor. And Shaw's General Store, where a variety of jackets, boots, scarves, and hats are on display in the front window. A little further ahead, I run into a cozy tavern called Harrison's, whose menu is pinned up outside. I steal a peek and the items listed make my stomach growl, including crab cakes and mussels, chicken piccata, and butternut squash soup. There's even a delightful bookstore—Bear Pond Books—with a giant teddy bear sitting out front in a white rocker holding a novel.

As I continue meandering, I pass another charming inn, as well as a handful of other shops, cafés, and fine-dining establishments. My eyes are constantly torn between wanting to check out what's inside and wanting to admire the building exteriors set against the backdrop of the vibrant trees in autumn colors. At first, I think the red treetops are the most stunning, but then a minute later I'm convinced it's the orange ones I like best, and a beat after that I've fallen just as in love with the yellows. I've never seen trees blush like this—in so many shades of color.

When I stop to send along the photos, I see the pictures don't do this place justice. But I'm glad I'm able to send a few home. And that I have some on my phone to show any inquiring guests. Speaking of guests . . . I should probably get back to them now.

I bring my painting supplies with me straight to the inn's kitchen, since I make it back just in time to start happy hour prep.

After happy hour ends, I decide to spread my things out in the parlor on a table with a view outside for inspiration. Though all the guest rooms have kitchenettes, everyone tonight seems to have either called an Uber or driven into town for dinner. I'm grateful the place cleared out so that I can have some quiet and focus on my craft project without interruption.

I'm not expecting to be the next Picasso or Warhol or anything. Other than an elective art class or two that I took in high school, I don't have any painting experience. I just want to see if I *like* to paint. And if I can get into a meditative zone while doing it. I've heard people talk about getting "lost in their work." I keep hoping one day I'll experience some version of that.

Though the sun has set, it's still light enough when I sit down that I can see some of the trees out the window as well as the flames from the fire outside that Jesse must have gotten going.

I set the canvas I picked out from the craft store right in front of me. Then I get to work.

———

An hour later, I step outside with my panting in hand and spot Jesse by the fire, sipping another warm drink. He looks so relaxed he could be mistaken for a guest. I try to think of another job that makes being on the clock look this good on somebody, but I'm drawing a blank right now.

"Is this your nightly routine?" I ask with a grin as I approach.

"I don't know," he says, cupping his mug with both his hands. "It's only my third day on the job too, remember? I'm still trying to nail my routine down." He nods to my painting. "Are you an artist?"

"Not exactly. Just was giving it a shot." I hold it up for him to assess.

"Looks like Hudson Lane," he says.

"An *abstract* version of Hudson Lane, maybe." Saying it looks like the inn is giving me way too much credit. It's safe to say that art is not my hidden talent. And I wouldn't say I loved painting either. It didn't put me in any kind of mental zone, though I did feel a sense of accomplishment when I crossed the activity off my Vermont Bucket List. So at least there's that.

"I think abstract is in," Jesse says.

"Not this level of abstract," I laugh as I take a seat in the Adirondack chair beside him. I'm not sure why I just made myself at home. For one, Jesse didn't invite me to join him. And two, it's cold out here. But it just felt so natural to sit.

"Can I get you a drink?" Jesse asks.

"Sure."

It felt natural to accept that too.

It's not like I have other plans—and even if I did have other plans, I'd cancel them right now to hang out with Jesse. We're in that beginning phase of our friendship when there's still so much to learn and it's exciting to find out more.

Just as he did last night, he tosses me his blanket before he heads in, and I wrap it around my shoulders. Unlike I did last night, I don't feel the urge to move to the opposite end of the fire. I actually laugh when I look at the spot where I originally sat down yesterday. Only twenty-four hours have passed since I decided to stop thinking of Jesse as my coworker and instead view him as my friend, but it seems like a lot longer than that. Putting five chairs between us strikes me as ridiculous now.

Jesse returns a few moments later and hands me a mug before retrieving another blanket out of the basket for himself.

"What are we drinking tonight?" I ask.

We. When did I decide Jesse and I were a unit? Last night, I guess. I suppose we are the innkeepers—at least, until I head home. I wonder what Jesse will do then, assuming his parents agree to let him take over running the inn. Will he hire someone else? Jealousy flashes through me. I wonder why I'm already jealous of my replacement. It's not as if my forever dream is to run an inn. Well, I don't think it is. I suppose anything is possible in my life at the moment.

"We've got spiced cider tonight," Jesse says.

I bring it to my nose, inhaling the scent of apples and cinnamon before taking a sip.

"Good?" he asks.

It tastes like fall in a cup. "I wouldn't complain if part of your nightly routine included making me this. Although I don't know if I can sit out here every night and drink it," I confess. It feels colder out here tonight than it did last night. And the temperature is only going to drop. In another month or so, the average low will be below freezing.

"Here." Jesse stands and sets the blanket that was on his lap on top of mine. He kneels down then, tucking it in on both sides of me so that it's snug.

I assume he's going to grab another one for himself, but he sits back down. When I peek at the basket, I see why. There aren't any more blankets left. Some of the guests must have taken the others off to their rooms or abandoned them inside after sitting out here earlier when it was warmer.

"I can't hog the only two blankets," I say, starting to take off the one around my shoulders, but Jesse stops me.

"I'm fine," he says. "Honestly."

I do remember him saying he runs warm, but there's no way he's warm right now. He's just being nice.

"When Brendan and I were younger," he says, "he and I would see how late in the year we could make it sitting out by the fire at night. The rule was we had to be out here for at least fifteen minutes for it to count."

Picturing this makes me smile. "How far into the season did you get?" I ask, thinking I probably wouldn't make it past mid-October.

"December 2. But we didn't have alcohol." He lifts up his mug before bringing it to his lips.

"Are you thinking that with it you could beat the record?" I ask.

"I'd be willing to try." His eyes land on mine like he's trying to gauge whether I'd be up for joining the challenge.

"What do you say?" he asks a second later, confirming that I read him right.

I surprise myself with my answer. "I'm in."

"Really?"

Apparently, I surprised Jesse with my answer too.

"Why not?" It wasn't on my Vermont Bucket List, but it sure sounds like a bucket-list item. "As long as you buy more blankets. And promise to always make stiff drinks."

"Anything you want." I get the sense he means this. I know I haven't been friends with Jesse for long, but I'm starting to think he's the kind of friend who goes above and beyond for those in his inner circle. I recognize that devotion in him because it's the same way I operate. I've never been popular or had a lot of friends, but the friends I do have, I'd do anything to help them.

He scoots in closer to the fire and gazes into the flames, apparently thinking seriously about something.

"What's on your mind?" I ask eventually.

He shrugs. "Nothing."

"Come on." I too scoot in closer to the fire with the aim to nudge him to open up. After last night, he should know I'm a good listener.

"No, seriously," he says. "I was thinking about nothing."

I raise a brow. "People do that?"

He nods and grins. "Sometimes it's nice to just enjoy the moment. Isn't there a lesson on how to do that in one of those self-help books?"

I grunt and wrinkle my nose. "I'm starting to think those books are only going to teach me how to overthink everything."

"You see my problem with them. Oh, which reminds me." He reaches into his jacket pocket and pulls out a worn paperback. "I brought this in case I ran into you."

He brought this in case he ran into me. Even more confirmation that he's the kind of friend I thought he was.

When he hands it over, I take it, running my thumb over the bent and faded cover.

"*East of Eden*," I read.

"It's one of my favorites," he says.

"And this book will teach me how not to think?"

"It will help you get lost in a moment. Reading a good novel does that to you. And I think once you learn how to do that, you'll get better at appreciating the good moments rather than overthinking them."

I'm willing to give it a shot. "Thank you, Jesse."

"No problem." He takes another sip of his drink and I do the same.

"Now I feel like a bad friend. I don't have something up my sleeve for you," I say. "I'd give you my painting if it were better."

"I'd hang that."

"You would?"

"Heck yeah." I'd set the painting down beside my chair earlier, and Jesse now picks it up. "I wasn't lying when I said I liked it."

The way he's looking at it is convincing. *Okay, then.*

"Look at us, exchanging gifts way before Christmas."

Jesse sets the painting down on the opposite side of his chair before cupping his mug with both hands again. "Trust me," he says. "I'll get you something way better than a book for Christmas."

I'm not sure what he means, but I make a mental note to get him something really good too.

twelve

After we wrap up at the fire, Jesse walks me to my room. Part of me wants to invite him in for dinner because I'd like to keep hanging out, but we already spent the better part of the day together. He might want some time to himself. So I just say goodnight.

I toss my purse on my bed as well as my bucket list and run a bath, thinking I'll enjoy dinner more after a quick soak. Once I get out, I pull on a cozy sweater and leggings and brush my hair. I'm just about to start the stove to warm up some soup when there's a knock on my door.

I open it and see Jesse holding a bowl of soup *and* a grilled cheese sandwich. "I had extra," he says.

I wonder if that's true or if he purposefully made extra because he too was bummed we ended the night early and was looking for an excuse to come by. I suppose the reason doesn't matter. I'm just glad he's here.

"Thanks," I say, opening the door wider to let him in. "Did you already eat?"

"No, mine's in my room."

"Do you want to get it and join me?"

"Sure." The speed at which he accepts my offer lets me know he came knocking because he wants to spend more time together. I take back what I said about the reason not mattering—it does. I'm happy to know he's been enjoying my company as much as I'm enjoying his.

There's a two-seater table by the window in the corner. Jesse sets the soup and the sandwich down, heads back to his place, then reemerges a minute later with his soup, grilled cheese, and a deck of cards.

"Any interest in playing a round?" he asks as he joins me at the table.

"Sure, what game?"

"Do you know gin rummy?"

I nod and tell him I used to play with my parents growing up.

"Great." He deals us both in, and we get the game going as we start our meal.

I'm rusty, so Jesse has to remind me of some of the rules the first few rounds, but he doesn't seem to mind. He also doesn't seem to mind when I end up winning both rounds, thanks to his help. I appreciate that he's a good sport. I've never been overly competitive and find games more fun when the goal is enjoyment. By round three, we're both focused and quiet as we study our new cards.

As much as I like talking to Jesse, sitting quietly with him feels just as comfortable—which is not the case with everyone.

"So is it helping?" Jesse asks, finally breaking the silence.

I give him a blank stare. "Is what helping what?"

I know we're becoming good friends fast, but we're not quite at the point that I know what he's saying when he speaks completely out of context.

"Sorry." He shakes his head—I guess he was half-focused on his hand and half-focused on his question. "Is being here helping you get over the job you got let go from and the guy?"

The guy. How does he know about Sky?

He doesn't. Oh, he must be referring to Jake!

It's nuts that when I now hear "guy," my mind goes right to Sky. I guess that means I really am over my breakup with Jake.

"That I'm loving this job so much makes it easy to not look back on the one I lost," I tell him, and it's an easy truth to share. "And, yeah, I'm over the guy. As soon as I got on the plane, I pretty much knew that."

Because I met this other guy, you see. But I don't say that out loud. Maybe I should mention Sky. But the window to share passes before I have the chance.

"Good," Jesse responds as he lays down a hand. "You don't want to waste time working for a company that doesn't make you a top priority."

"Amen," I chime in.

"You also don't want to waste time on a *person* who doesn't prioritize you." He says this with so much conviction, it makes me wonder if he's speaking from experience.

I'm about to ask him about it when he sets his cards down and says, "Are you cold?"

Before I can reply, he gets to his feet. "I can get the fire going."

"Okay." I watch as he wanders over to the wood rack and pulls out a few logs, then sets them down on the grate before turning on the gas and lighting it with a match from the box on top of the mantle. When he goes to turn off the gas, I refocus on my cards to determine what hand to play next.

"What's this?" he asks a moment later.

"What's what?" When I raise my head, I see he's pointing to my Vermont Bucket List. I can't believe I forgot I left it on my bed. I also can't believe it doesn't bother me all that much that Jesse spotted it.

"I came up with a list of things I want to accomplish while I'm here," I explain.

"May I take a look?"

"Okay." I hadn't wanted anyone else to see it, but now that he's holding it, I'm kind of glad he is. Since we'll be spending so much time together over the next couple of months, it might be nice if he knows what I'm up to.

"This is really neat," he says. I can tell by the look on his face that he's being sincere. Feeling confident that Jesse isn't the kind of person who would make fun of my bucket list is another reason I didn't care he found it.

103

I suddenly remember I didn't show the list to Sky. I feel a little bad about that now. It's not that I thought Sky *would* make fun of it. It's just that, on the plane, I didn't know him well enough to be *sure* he wouldn't. Yes, some of the items are silly—but I still don't want to be laughed at.

Jesse doesn't laugh once as he scans it. When he rejoins me at the table and I explain my reason for creating it, he doesn't laugh about that either.

"I really like that you're carving out time to figure out what matters to you," he says, folding up the list and handing it back.

I reach up and tuck a strand of hair behind my ear. I've never been great at receiving compliments. "I'm trying," I say.

"A lot of people don't even get that far. You should feel good about that."

I smooth back a strand on the other side. "Thanks."

"You know," Jesse says, "if you need help with any of these items, I'd be happy to assist. I can loan you my car for the road trip with no destination. And there's a soup kitchen I know of that I could recommend for volunteering. Oh, and I'm happy to teach you to ski or snowshoe. I know it says here you want to learn how."

I'm overwhelmed by his support and am not sure what to say.

Jesse misinterprets my silence. "Of course, I can also stay out of it completely," he says, reaching for his cards and shifting his focus back to his hand. "I didn't mean to insert myself into something so personal."

"No, no," I rush to explain. "I appreciate the help, Jesse. It just means a lot to me—both your offer and my list."

"As it should." He peeks over the top of his cards, meeting my eyes again. "Life's short. If you don't start doing the things now that you've always thought about, you might never have the chance."

—

I think about what Jesse said throughout the rest of our game. *If you don't start doing the things you've always thought about, you might never have the chance.*

It makes me even more glad that I'm here. And, as soon as we wrap up, it makes me want to do something spontaneous.

"Will you read item number seven on the list?" I say, holding it out to Jesse once we've done the dishes.

Jesse takes it and unfolds it, scanning down the page and reading the item out loud.

"What do you think?" I ask.

"You want to do this *now*?" he replies. To be honest, I was thinking this item would take me until the very end of my trip to cross off because I'm afraid to do it. But right now I feel brave, so why not jump on that wave and see if I can ride it?

"No time like the present, right? Do you know anywhere that might still be open?"

Jesse checks his watch. My guess is it's around nine o'clock. "Yeah, I think I do," he says, running a hand through his hair.

"Could you take me there?"

He hesitates before responding. "I'm not doing this *with* you," he clarifies.

"I didn't expect you to. I just need a ride."

I press my palms together.

"All right," he says. "I'm in."

thirteen

Spontaneity isn't all it's cracked up to be. I'm learning this lesson now. And it's a *painful* one. "How much longer?" I ask.

"It would be over a lot faster if you'd calm down," the tattoo artist replies. I glance at my wrist and see that I'm bleeding again. Apparently, this happens when you're nervous. This whole process was only supposed to take a couple of minutes, but because I'm nervous, the tattooist has to keep stopping and blotting up blood so the ink doesn't smear.

Jesse squeezes my hand even tighter, which was something I did not think was possible. He's already gripping it so firmly, you'd think the needle was being driven into *his* wrist, not mine.

"Tell me a story," I say. Maybe if Jesse talks to me, I'll calm down and we can speed things up.

"This one time," he says, "I let a girl convince me to take her to get a tattoo, and it was the worst decision I'd ever made."

I smack his arm. "Come on. A real story."

"I can't think of a real story right now. I'm too preoccupied thinking about how much I want this to be over for you." It's sweet how concerned he is. I try to focus on that rather than on the incessant needle, which feels like a hundred bees stinging me at once.

"Why are you doing this?" he clarifies. "I mean, I get that you're doing it because it's on the list. But why is it on the list?"

"All of my bucket-list items are supposed to challenge me in some way."

"What's the point of this challenge?" he asks. "To see how much pain you can endure?"

"To do something I'm afraid of."

I must start bleeding again because the woman gives me a look as if to say "calm down." Jesse returns her look with a glare that says "back off."

I can't help but smile. I'm so glad I told Jesse about the list. And I'm so glad he's here. This is not something I would have relished doing alone.

"What was the challenge behind the painting you did earlier?" he asks.

"I was trying to discover my passion. Do you have a passion?"

"I'm passionate about wanting this to be over soon."

"You and me both," I say as I shoot a glance at the tattoo gun. Why am I looking at the tattoo gun?

Jesse reaches out and turns my chin. "Eyes right here," he says, pointing to his own.

I do what he says because I know he's looking out for my best interest. Jesse's eyes also aren't a bad place to have to stare. I had thought they were brown, but now I can see flecks of blue too. More noticeable than the color of his eyes, though, is the way they make me feel: *seen*. This is equal amounts nice and unnerving, but I concentrate on how nice it is given that I can't afford to feel any more unnerved than I already do.

"Seriously, though," I say, circling back to our earlier conversation. "Do you have a passion?"

"I like to think I'm a passionate guy," he says.

"That's not what I meant."

"What did you mean?"

"I mean are you passionate about something specific, like a skill or a hobby?"

He narrows his eyes at me. "Is this something the self-help books have convinced you that you need to find?"

I sigh and explain that everyone seems to have a passion except for me.

107

He narrows his eyes even more. "Who cares what everyone else has? That seems like a bad reason to want something."

"You know, for someone who doesn't read self-help books, you know a lot of self-help speak."

He shrugs. "I just think everyone's journey is different. Read a few novels and you'll see that. There's no point in comparing stories."

"Well, on *your* journey, have you developed any particular passions?" I don't let up. I'm not sure if it's because of my curiosity or because this conversation is providing a nice distraction.

Jesse grips my hand even tighter.

"Right now," he says, "I'm passionate about keeping the inn. And I'm passionate about getting you to the other side of this. And if finding a passion is important to you, then I'm passionate about helping with that in any way that I can."

I'm about to thank him when the tattoo artist tells me she's finished.

I check out my design before she bandages it.

Jesse inspects it too, and now he's the one who's wincing.

"What?"

"Nothing," he replies.

"That's not your nothing face." It's crazy I already know his nothing face, but that moment by the fire earlier showed it to me. "You were definitely thinking *something*."

He bites his bottom lip as if still debating whether or not he's going to tell me what's on his mind.

"Say it," I demand and he sighs.

"I know it's a little late to mention this. But you've only been here three days. Are you sure you want that tattooed on your wrist for the rest of your life?"

I give his arm another smack. "You're right. It *is* a little late to say that."

"You told me to tell you what I was thinking!"

Fair enough. I can't be mad. As the tattoo artist starts applying my bandage, covering up the letters *VT* that are now permanently etched on my wrist, I explain that it's just a symbol.

"This trip to Vermont is about being true to myself and reminding myself that it's never too late to start over. I think those are two good things for me to remember forever."

Jesse smiles. He looks relieved, and also convinced, that I picked an okay tattoo after all. "Yeah," he says a beat later, confirming that I also read both of *those* looks right. "I think so too."

—

"If you need help checking off an item tomorrow, can it be an easier one?" Jesse asks when we get back to our cottages.

When Jesse parked his car, we ran into a few guests getting back from dinner and visited with them for a bit, so it's late now and I'm tired, but not too tired to laugh.

"Tomorrow I was planning on starting thirty days straight of yoga," I say. "It's an easier activity *and* one I don't need help with. Seems you're off the hook on both counts."

He wipes a hand dramatically across his forehead, and I laugh again.

"Today was fun," Jesse says, leaning against the maple tree outside our cottages. "I haven't had fun in a while."

"Me either," I reply. As soon as the words leave my mouth, I think of my time with Sky and feel bad because that was fun too. It was just a different kind of fun. When I was with Sky, my heart and head were going a million miles a minute because *feelings* were involved. Tonight was no-pressure fun. With a *friend*. You really can't compare the two.

"What's on tap tomorrow?" I ask.

"Meet at the chicken coop, serve breakfast, check in guests, happy hour, then cocktails at the fire?"

"Sounds like we've got our routine down," I point out.

"Yeah, I guess we do." Jesse concurs. "Goodnight, Harper."

"Goodnight," I say as I walk up my porch steps and let myself in. It *was* a good night, I decide as I pull off my shoes. And a good day. Did I mention that I like it here? The only thing that would have made it better is a letter from Sky. I plop down on my bed and stare up at the ceiling.

How many more days do I have to wait until I can get my hands on another?

fourteen

Five. It took popping into town three times over the course of the past five days to receive another letter.

The first time I came wasn't specifically to check, though. Jesse brought me into town to get more groceries—which was a slight deviation from our routine, which I'm *loving*.

Most routines are boring. But I could do the daily routine Jesse and I have every day, and it would never grow tiresome. The guests are always changing, which keeps things interesting. The chickens keep things interesting. And trying to last at least fifteen minutes at the fire every night definitely keeps things interesting. Especially when the elements don't cooperate, as was the case last night.

Jesse and I were forced to share one umbrella while he held another over the fire during a downpour that ended with thunder and lightning. We both darted inside the second the timer Jesse had set started beeping, and Jesse had to make us a second warm drink because we were so cold and wet.

The next time I walked into town *was* to check to see if Sky had written me. That was yesterday—a full week since I'd heard from him last, so I assumed checking was a safe bet. But still, nothing.

And today I popped into Milk & Maple again because no guests were checking out or in. I had the time. And, okay, the suspense was killing me!

Fortunately, I found Letter Number Two sitting in my inbox. Sky and I are going to have to figure out a better system going forward.

111

Maybe in this week's letter I'll tell him that I check my email on Wednesdays so that I'm not holding my breath each week.

I remind myself that I can let out the one I'm currently holding. Once I do, I take a sip of my latte. I ordered a regular one this time, no flavoring, and the waitress seemed pleased. She even told me "good choice," when she set it down. I decide it *was* a good choice after taking another sip. Then I start reading.

To: Harper

From: Sky

Subject: Letter Number Two

Date: September 27

Dear Harper,

If you're wondering why this letter took me over a week to write, it's because my flight route changed and I've been adapting to a new schedule, which has been nuts. If this is the first time you've checked your email since last week and the thought of why I haven't written hasn't even crossed your mind, disregard this entire first paragraph. I shouldn't assume that I'm on your mind as much as you're on mine—which is constantly.

Now that I've got this new flight route, I'm flying to Maine all the time. I've flown there six times this week already. I'm mentioning this because each time I pass right over Vermont, and when I do, I think about you. You asked what my life in Atlanta is like. In a nutshell, this is pretty much it: fly to Maine, think about you, fly to Maine, think about you, fly to Maine, think about . . . you get the picture.

Speaking of pictures, I saw a new view on my LinkedIn from a Harper James. Were you trying to find a picture of me? I can't

112

imagine you were interested in my credentials. Although I suppose you might have wanted to verify that I am indeed a pilot. In that case, I'm sure you were pleased to see I do hold a license—at least for now. I almost lost it this week when I tried to land the plane in VT instead of ME and sneak in a special visit to an inn where this girl I'm crushing on happens to be working. (How am I doing on the flattery? Is this overkill or just right?)

It almost feels like torture that I fly over you and can't stop and say hi. In case you haven't figured this out, I didn't ask for this reroute.

Anyhow, my hope was that the real reason you were checking out my LinkedIn page was because you missed my face. If that's true, I'm happy to send you a better photo. And if you want to send any pictures my way, please feel free to do the same. I'd love to see photos of you ambling around Stowe or at work at the inn or lounging in your guest room or maybe even as you're turning in for the night just before the lights go out.

Good God, woman. Somehow you've managed to turn me on from the other side of the country without even saying a word. I'm just sitting here imagining receiving a photo of your skin against the sheets and BAM. I suppose this is a good time to say that if you're inclined to type up those fantasies you mentioned you were having, I'm clearly very willing to read them. ;)

You asked about my other dreams for my future in your last note. To be honest, I feel like they're changing. For the longest time, I thought my photo albums for the rest of my life would just have pictures of trip after trip. But now I'm not so sure about that. I'm staying open to new possibilities. And just to be clear, those new possibilities include you—at least in my imagination.

I love hearing that you're enjoying your job there. You've got eighty-eight more days to go, so make each one count. Not that

113

I have a countdown going. Okay, fine, it's pinned on my fridge. I included a photo so you know I'm not lying. (Have I flattered you enough yet? I hope I'm getting the job done.)

Until next time,

Sky

Three thoughts pop into my head when I finish reading.
Damn that Sky can write a good letter.
There are only eighty-eight more days until I see Sky!
I only have eighty-eight more days left in Vermont.
The last nearly threatens to dash my great mood, so I try to fix my attention on the first two, which put a smile on my face. Then I write Sky back.

To: Sky

From: Harper

Subject: Re: Letter Number Two

Date: September 27

Dear Sky,

I know you might not love your reroute, but I love that now each time I hear a plane and look up, I can imagine that you're right above me. Somehow the thought of this makes me miss you less.

I am thinking of you constantly too, and I did in fact check my email several times this week to see if you'd written me. And I was a little bummed (okay, a lot bummed) each time I couldn't find one in my inbox.

Let's solve this: How about you send me an email on Wednesdays? Usually this is a slow day at the inn for me, and I can get to town to read what you've written and to write you back.

Now that logistics are out of the way, I have a very important question that needs addressing: You have a *better* photo of you than the one on LinkedIn in the pilot's hat? Where? How? Because talk about giving a girl something to fantasize about . . . Please bring that hat with the condoms when you show up on Christmas Eve. I promise you'll make all my wildest fantasies come true. And now I need to change the topic . . .

Out of curiosity, is Atlanta where you'll always want to live? Or is it where you are because of work? I know you said you've moved around a lot, but do you feel settled there, or are you open to alternative home bases? Share with me in your next letter.

I have one more update to share. I got a tattoo! It's my first one and I was a bit terrified, but that was the point of it, in a way. Do you remember my list of things I wanted to try in Vermont? Well, getting a tattoo was one of the items. I'm currently in the middle of trying thirty days straight of yoga, which is also on the list, along with a handful of other things that are supposed to challenge me while I'm here. Though the biggest challenge so far is not seeing you. (There's my flattery right back at you for this letter!)

And speaking of seeing you, I love the countdown on your fridge. In your next letter, can you send me a few more pics of your apartment? I'm very visual and would like to imagine you there doing more than just looking at the countdown while standing in your kitchen. Plus, I just want to see you. :)

Fair is fair, so here's one of me in this coffee shop to hold you over for now.

Until Wednesday,

Harper

I snap a photo, AirDrop and attach it, and press send. It was the best I could do for a sexy photo in public. My shirt was pulled down a little to show some cleavage, and I was tugging slightly on my bottom lip with my teeth. I shake my head then and laugh at myself. I can't believe I even just *tried* to take a sexy photo in a coffee shop, just because he hinted at it. Who am I? Sky just pulls out this extra flirtatious side of me.

I kind of like it.

fifteen

"I like it. I really like it!" Jesse is up ahead of me on the trail, so I yell this from about fifty feet behind him as I continue to trot along on Clementine, the brown-and-white horse I'm riding.

Though there are no horses at the inn, Jesse has a friend from high school who has a stable. When he saw horseback riding on my bucket list, he must have noted it because he surprised me today by blindfolding me and driving me twenty minutes to his friend's place.

"Happy birthday," he said, when he took the blindfold off. I was shocked to find myself at the stable and that he knew it was my birthday.

I didn't tell him it was my birthday because I didn't want him to feel obligated to do something big since I'm turning thirty. And I knew he *would* feel obligated because that's the kind of guy I've learned Jesse is. But my birthdate was on my application to the inn, so he had it on his calendar already. Plus, Zoe and Grace had emailed the inn asking how they could send flowers. (Apparently, those are waiting for me in my room when I get back. Jesse went to town to pick them up on their behalf.) And my parents kept calling the inn's direct line last week until Jesse answered so they could ask him to pick me up a cake. (He did. It's in the fridge in his cottage.)

"Special occasions deserve to be celebrated," he said. "And what better way to celebrate than by crossing off another item on your bucket list."

I wrapped him in the tightest hug I think I've ever given. I know Zoe and Grace are the best friends to exist on this planet, but Jesse is quickly making his way up the ranks. "This was the perfect gift," I said. "And the perfect way to celebrate."

"I'm glad you like it!" he replied then, just as he replies now, letting me know he heard what I said. Jesse's horse, Lemon, is much faster than mine, so even though Jesse keeps trying to get him to walk, he often takes off cantering, which maintains a wide gap between us.

"Come on, Clementine," I say, tapping her sides with my heels to get her to pick up the pace. "Good girl, Clem." All the horses are named after fruit because Jesse's buddy has an apple orchard on the property. After our ride, we're going to pick as many apples as we want. I might have died and gone to fall heaven.

"So far I love being thirty," I say once Clementine and I catch up to Jesse and Lemon. The path opens up, and soon we come upon an open field glistening in sunlight that allows us to walk the horses side by side.

"That's good to hear," Jesse grins.

"How old are you?" I ask.

"Thirty-four."

"Any wisdom from the new decade?"

"Find good coworkers—they make a world of a difference."

Leave it to Jesse to find a way to make his answer complimentary. Really, *I* should be the one complimenting him—he was *definitely* employee of the week.

So many things went wrong the past few days. The refrigerator in the inn quit working. The housekeepers called in sick at the last minute one morning. A guest wanted to extend his stay an extra week, but all the rooms were full. And Jesse just handled it. All of it. In a way that was as calm and cool and collected as the way he seems to handle everything.

"If you hadn't decided to take over the inn," I say, "was your plan to continue working at your other job? Or did you have another dream you were working toward before this one?"

The question has been on my mind all week because of how well-suited Jesse seems for the life he's currently living. I really can't imagine him doing anything else.

He shrugs. "What I do has never been as important to me as the people I'm doing it with. I liked my team at my other company, so I suppose I would have stayed as long as most of them did. This inn holds Brendan's memory, so I feel like he's here, in some way. And right now, I meant what I said about having a great coworker."

I flush and fortunately he's looking ahead so he doesn't see the reaction his answer has triggered. "Does this mean you're happy at the moment?"

"Yeah," he grins. "Are you?"

"Yeah," I smile back, thinking that so many times in life you say this and don't mean it. But right now I mean it with my whole heart. That's a pretty great way to feel at the start of a new decade.

—

Jesse's friend, Will, greets us as we get back to the stable. I met him when we first arrived. He's tall and lanky and sports scruff on his face just as Jesse does.

Jesse told me when we first started riding that he hasn't seen Will since Brendan's funeral, but you wouldn't know it from the way the two of them picked up talking. You'd think they grabbed beers all the time.

When I said as much to Jesse, he said that they used to. They were buddies in high school, then lived together all through college, and have remained fairly tight since. But this year Will took over his family's farm, and for a while after Brendan's death Jesse didn't really want to socialize.

I can tell the two of them have a lot of catching up to do, so once we get off the horses and all head to the orchard, I try to give them a little space. They start collecting Granny Smith apples on

119

one side of the row we wandered down, so I start filling my bucket with the Pink Lady variety on the other side.

I can still faintly hear their conversation from where I am, though, and I perk up when Jesse shares some of the funny moments we've experienced at the inn the past few weeks—like the other night when we had to help a guest who'd had a few too many drinks get back into his room after he locked himself out. He accidently walked into the hall naked, thinking he was opening the door to his bathroom. Another guest came downstairs to inform us that he was outside his room door, trying to break it down. I rushed up with a towel and Jesse got a spare key, and we both walked away hysterically laughing.

Jesse also tells Will about the afternoon when two moms came to the front desk complaining that they couldn't find their kids. Jesse and I searched the property only to find a young teenage boy and a girl of the same age making out behind a tree. Jesse had to awkwardly clear his throat and tell them that their parents were looking for them. Later, Jesse told me he felt bad for breaking them up.

It's harder for me to decipher the conversation once Will starts getting Jesse up to speed on the farm because I'm not familiar with the stories, so I shift my focus to filling my basket to the brim. I tune back in, though, when I hear Will ask Jesse if he regrets not moving to New York.

New York? When was Jesse thinking about moving to New York?

I suddenly recall our conversation on my first day here, when I asked him if he'd ever been tempted to move anywhere else.

"*Once*," he told me.

Was New York where he was referring to? It must have been. I can't picture Jesse in New York. I've only visited once, but when I think of New York I picture people rushing from place to place. I picture late nights. I picture live shows. I don't picture all the things Jesse loves: early morning with the chickens, cocktails outside by the fire, stars to gaze at.

"Nah, man," Jesse says.

"Not at all?"

Jesse turns and catches my eye, and I avert my gaze because it seems he didn't want me to hear that. I wonder why. He's confided in me quite a bit since I've arrived, and there are times it seems we don't have any secrets between us. But then I remember I haven't told him everything about my life either. He still doesn't know about Sky, for instance. Not that I'm intentionally keeping that from him. It just hasn't come up in conversation. Maybe New York is the same and he'll tell me about it eventually.

Although, now I'm getting the sense that it's not the same because he doesn't seem to want to talk to Will about it either.

"No. No regrets," he says a second later. And that's it. He doesn't offer anything else.

He changes the subject and we all move on.

—

Jesse doesn't bring up New York on the car drive back to the inn, and neither do I, although it's on my mind. It seems as if it—or at least *something*—is on Jesse's mind, though. I notice him wrestling with it. He changes the radio station six times, even though he keeps landing on songs he seems to like. It makes me think he's frustrated that he can't change the station in his own head and is consequently taking out his frustration on the dial. Eventually, he shuts the whole thing off.

"Are you having a good birthday?" he asks, maybe thinking small talk will help.

"It's great," I say. "Thank you."

He nods and tightens his grip on the wheel. We drive in silence the rest of the way to the inn. Once he puts the car in park, he doesn't get out. He just sits there.

I don't move either.

I've noticed that sometimes Jesse takes a little time to say what he's thinking, perhaps because he's so intentional and doesn't say

121

things just to say them. He wants to say what he really means. Bucket-list item number twenty comes to mind: practice the art of patience. Perfect opportunity to work on this.

"My ex, Madison, moved to New York," he finally tells me.

His ex, Madison. I should have known the reason he'd consider a move like that was for someone else. Jesse just told me that what he does is never as important as who he does it with. I bet he also feels that where he lives doesn't matter as much as who he lives with.

"We met in town a few years after college," he goes on. "We dated up until she left. So we were close. Really close."

I nod to show I'm listening and because I don't doubt their bond. Jesse and I have become close after only a few weeks, and we're just friends. I can only imagine how close he'd get to someone—and how close she'd likely get to him—over the course of many years in the context of a romantic relationship.

"She wanted to experience something new," he says. "A big city. And she wanted me to come with her. I didn't want to go because I like it here and my family is here. But I was seriously considering it anyway because it was important to her. I looked for jobs and visited the city with her to look for an apartment and everything."

His gaze shifts from the steering wheel to his hands. "But then Brendan and Molly had their accident, and I told her there was no way I could leave then. Maybe in a while, but not right then. She left anyway. Two weeks after the funeral."

I shake my head. "What a bitch."

I meant to only think it—not say it—because I'm not sure how Jesse feels about Madison now. But the protective side of me couldn't hold it in.

To my relief, Jesse laughs slightly as he shakes his own head. "It wasn't very cool, that's for sure."

"Have you heard from her since?"

122

"She reached out once she got there and told me she still wanted me to come. But the fact that she left *then*, when she knew I wouldn't leave—and honestly couldn't—made me feel like she didn't really mean it. Like she wanted to be there alone all along." He sighs. "And I couldn't get over her leaving me only two weeks after I lost Brendan and Molly. The place I was in . . . I needed her more than ever, and she knew that. But she still went."

I hate that Madison did that.

I'm furious. How could anyone have Jesse's big heart in the palm of her hand and not be more considerate?

I knew I was starting to care about Jesse when I didn't sleep well after he told me about Brendan and Molly. And the past few days, I've felt myself caring about him even more. But the churning in my stomach from hearing his Madison story tells me I've underestimated just how much I care.

"I think I'm over it," he says, which helps my anger simmer down a bit. "I don't like talking about it, which is why I haven't mentioned it. But when I'm not talking about it, I don't really think about it. I'm not sure what that means. Maybe she did us both a favor. Maybe she wasn't right for me, after all." I can't tell if he's saying this because he believes it or because he's trying to convince himself it's the truth. Either way, it's the best way to look at it.

When I say so to him, he shrugs and replies, "It is what it is."

Then he shakes his head and tells me he's sorry.

"For what?"

"For rambling about an ex. I hope this isn't bringing up memories of your ex. That's the last thing I want you thinking about on your birthday."

"I told you already, I'm over my ex," I assure him. I briefly debate whether or not to explain how I know this for sure—but since we're on the topic and Jesse was just so honest with me, I feel I should mention it. "I actually met someone on the plane."

"Coming *here*?" Jesse asks.

I nod. "We're not formally together or anything. But we did make a promise. We have a second date scheduled for Christmas Eve, when we'll pick up where we left off. There was so much potential between us that I'm looking forward to it. And that I can believe in the possibility of it tells me I'm over my ex."

"That's great, Harper." He gives me a smile, but it looks forced.

I don't know how I was expecting Jesse to react to the news about Sky. I didn't think it through, honestly. But I realize I mildly just gave him the "more fish in the sea" talk, which is never a fun one to hear when you're bummed about an ex. It's generic. Maybe he's disappointed I didn't have something more meaningful to say, because he looks even more glum now. I'm kicking myself for choosing this moment to bring up my newfound romance.

For a brief moment, I also wonder if Jesse is jealous. Then I shake my head. Whether it's true or not, calling it out will just make things awkward. Best I don't go there.

Attempting to pivot, I circle back to his ex. "I know I don't know this Madison," I say, wrinkling my nose when I say her name, "but I'm starting to really get to know you. And all I can say is, it's definitely her loss."

I clamp my hand over his and squeeze it.

"You're a good friend," he says, squeezing mine back.

"You are too."

"I'm not being the best friend right now, though," he says.

"What do you mean?"

"We're talking too much about me. And today is about you. So tell me this: after happy hour wraps up, how do you want to continue to celebrate?"

"You've already done more than enough to make my birthday special," I say.

"Come on," he prods. "I can take you out to dinner. I know all the restaurant owners. I could get us a reservation anywhere in town. Or we can skip dinner and spend all night eating dessert. We could order a different one at every restaurant—like a dessert progression."

"Both those ideas sound fun," I say. "But can I be honest?"

"Is that a serious question?" Jesse replies. "I just bared my soul here."

"I'd rather just do what we always do. Cocktails by the fire, then dinner at your place or mine. I could let you beat me at cards, if you want to change things up a little."

Jesse laughs. I said it hoping he would. The past five nights I've won at cards, but both of us know it's because Jesse lets me. He beat me in the beginning by so much it wasn't even close, so we both know he's capable of winning every time if he wanted.

"Is that all right?" I ask.

"I'd never let you lose at cards on your birthday. But other than that, yeah. That's exactly how I'd want to spend my birthday too."

—

"When is *your* birthday?" I ask Jesse as we start our first game of cards later that night. I definitely don't want to miss it, given how much thought he's put into mine.

After cocktails at the fire, he made me steak and a salad for dinner. And then he opened a nice bottle of wine. A *really* nice bottle of wine. I'm no wine expert, but this is ten times better than any wine I've ever had. Jesse mentioned it was a bottle he was saving for a special occasion. I told him not to open it, but he insisted, and I don't know why because he's barely drinking any. *I'm* the one drinking it all. Because it's my thirtieth. And I'm happy. And this wine is *really* good.

"March 12," he tells me.

"Dang, I'll miss it!" I say this a little louder than I intended, thanks to the wine. Or maybe I'm sadder to miss his birthday than I expected to be. "I'll find a way to get you something," I say.

"You don't need to do that," Jesse replies. "I'm not a big gift guy. I'm all about quality time."

"We share the same love language," I say, happy to learn.

"The same what?"

I should have figured Jesse wouldn't have taken the love language test, given that it's straight out of a self-help book.

"There's this test that helps you identify how you like to receive love from others," I explain.

"People need a test to tell them this?"

I shrug. "Apparently. Anyway, I value quality time the most too."

"Well, then, I'm glad we're getting all kinds of that in on your birthday. Where do you think you'll be on mine?"

"I'll take next question, any category, for one hundred, Alex," I say, as I play my next hand.

"Sorry." Jesse catches himself as he studies his cards. "You're taking it one day at a time here. I get it."

I sigh. "Yeah, but I *should* probably at least start to think about it."

"You can't rush clarity," he points out.

"True. Have you talked to your parents lately? Do they have any clarity as to whether or not they're going to let you officially take over the inn?"

"They've actually stopped by twice, while you were in town," he says. "I think they could see what a good job we're doing. I'm excited for you to meet them. I know they're going to like you."

"How do you know that?"

"Who wouldn't?"

If I didn't know any better, I'd almost say Jesse was moving beyond complimenting me to flirting with me.

126

Wow, I blink. Turning thirty has really given me a big head. Or maybe it's the wine.

Jesse compliments *the guests* even. He's just a complimentary guy. That's one of the reasons he's such a great host.

"Thanks, Jesse," I say, reaching for my wine and taking another sip.

"I mean it," he says, sincerity stamped all over his features. "I'm really glad it was you they picked for this position."

I look at Jesse a moment.

I am too.

Best I don't look too closely at that thought, I think.

"What are they like?" I ask. "Your parents."

"They're really sweet. They loved this job because they both enjoy meeting people from all over the world. And because they like spending all their time together. They're best friends," he tells me.

I share that my parents are best friends too.

"That's nice," he says. "That's what I'm looking for in a partner. My best friend. Someone I like spending all my time with."

Not only do Jesse and I have the same love language, but we're looking for the same things in a significant other.

I reach for my wine glass and take another sip. "Did I mention this wine is really very good?"

—

"Whoa, birthday girl, let's get you to bed."

Jesse reaches out for my arm as I stumble while trying to close his dishwasher. I can't believe I just stumbled. Jesse's probably going to think I'm drunk. "I'm not drunk," I say. "Honestly."

Jesse smiles. "I'm sure you aren't. But I'll walk you home just to be safe."

I'm glad he does, because even though my cottage is right next door, it seems further. Maybe I am a *little* drunk.

127

When I tell this to Jesse, he laughs and says, "It's your thirtieth birthday. If you weren't a little bit drunk, I'd be worried we didn't celebrate enough."

I'm already in a cozy long-sleeve shirt and sweatpants that could double for pajama bottoms, and I wasn't wearing any makeup, so I climb right into bed once we make it inside. Jesse helps me under the covers even though I don't need him to because I'm *fine*. *Totally fine*. I don't object, however, because I like that he's here and that he's tucking me in and that he's sitting down on the edge of my mattress now. Sometimes when I say goodnight to Jesse, I find myself counting down the minutes until morning when I get to see him again. I know I'm going to do that the moment he leaves tonight.

"Did you have a good day?" he asks.

"This was the best birthday ever," I say. And I mean it. I don't know if it's because birthdays are usually overhyped and not as fun as expected and this time I didn't have any expectations, or if I just spent this one with the right person who knew exactly how to make it the best day it could be. I'm thinking it's a bit of both. "You're great," I say.

"You're great too."

"Today was so great!" I'm not sure why I just exclaimed that, but it's true.

"Goodnight, birthday girl," he says, smiling.

It's the smile that does it, I think. There's so much affection in it. Or maybe it's that I don't entirely want the day to end. All I know is one moment I'm tucked in bed and the next I'm sitting upright, pushing back my covers, and leaning in to hug Jesse. For a moment, he's still, and then his arms slide around me, and something in me just . . . settles.

A perfect day.

"Goodnight," I say, as I pull back and slide under the covers again, curling up into a ball. I can feel the contentment settling in as I shut my eyes. Jesse quietly rises from the bed and turns off the light on his way out. When I hear him shut the door, I snuggle deeper into the pillow. The sooner I fall asleep, the sooner I wake up, and when I wake up it will be Wednesday. The best day of the week.

I cannot wait to read my letter from Jesse—I mean Sky.

How much wine did I drink?

A good bit, I think, but I shrug it off and think of the minutes until morning.

sixteen

To: Harper

From: Sky

Subject: Letter Number Three

Date: October 3

Dear Harper,

It's Wednesday and here I am in your inbox. I wish I were at your doorstep instead, but I'm trying to honor your wishes (which, by the way, feels like a harder and harder task each week). On the bright side, I'm getting a lot of practice at exercising willpower over here. At this point, I could teach a class on it.

I've also attached photos of each room in my house, like you asked. I started snapping pictures of just the rooms themselves, but then I remembered you said you are very visual and wanted to be able to picture me in each room, so I switched to using my self-timer and inserted myself into the photos. (The shot of me in my bedroom is for your eyes only, babe.)

Now, on to the photo you sent me of you in the coffee shop. THAT was one of the sexiest photos I've ever seen. I look at it way too often. I had to delete it from my phone so I don't pull it up while I'm flying. Imagine that headline: *"Plane Knocked Off Course, Pilot Distracted by Beauty He's Dating."*

Sorry *not* dating. Soon to be dating. I know the arrangement. I just got ahead of myself.

I zoomed in and saw your tattoo, by the way. VT? Does this mean you've fallen in love with Vermont? Are you asking me where else I'd be up for living because you want to officially relocate to my hometown? The things I'm starting to consider for you . . .

I'll tell you this: it *is* an option for me to move elsewhere. It just takes time to put in the request and see about getting it approved. I have thought about living in places other than Atlanta, although Vermont has never been on that list. But, like I said, I'm now considering all kinds of things I never thought I'd think about before I met you.

I'm open to seeing where life takes me. That's part of the adventure, right? You can only have so much of a plan in your head for where you're going to end up. The rest is left up to fate and timing. Do you believe in fate? Do you believe in timing? (Am I using too many rom-com terms back-to-back?)

Maybe it's because a rom-com was on TV the other night: *Sleepless in Seattle.* I let it play while I was cooking dinner and definitely did not roll my eyes this time around. At least not until the end. But that was to be expected. I will never not roll my eyes at the end of that film. Don't get me wrong, it's a great movie. Out of all the rom-coms I've been roped into watching, I'd even go so far as to say I think it's the best. But I just can't get over how Tom Hanks reaches for Meg Ryan's hand on the top of the Empire State building and that's it! Neither of them explains to the other all the lengths they've just gone through to be there, including the fact that Tom Hanks' son hopped on a flight all by himself!

When I see you again, I'm going to be doing way more than reaching out for your hand. Be prepared. I will absolutely kiss you. And then I'll kiss you again. And then I'll pull out my pilot's hat and we can go from there.

131

Your admiration of the hat has been noted.

Here are things I like: your smile, your wit, and talking to you. And a part of me even likes missing you because it lets me know how much I like you.

Eighty-two days to go and counting,

Sky

You better believe the literal *second* I've finished reading Sky's letter, I'm downloading those photos he sent. They all open up in my iPhoto app, and I scroll through them one by one, laughing the entire time because Sky is not just sitting in the rooms smiling, he's enacting entire scenes and making silly faces at me. First, he's at his kitchen table, pretending to be aghast by something he read in the paper. Then he's in his living room with his hands behind his head, pretending he just saw something hilarious on TV. In his bathroom, he's hiding behind the shower curtain, sticking out his head and his tongue. In his office, he's pretending to be bored of his work. And in his bedroom, he's . . .

My God.

I forgot he mentioned this was for my eyes only.

And it really is. Because Sky is sitting on his bed wearing his pilot's hat. *Just* his pilot's hat.

And now I think I'm dead.

To: Sky

From: Harper

Subject: Re: Letter Number Three

Date: October 3

Dear Sky,

Let me start with telling you that you—mister—are single-handedly responsible for causing me to spill a full twelve-ounce latte all over the coffee shop floor. Want to know how you managed to accomplish that feat while being on the opposite side of the country? That bedroom photo. It completely did me in.

Let me explain the scene to you: I saw it. My jaw hit the floor. I froze. When I snapped into motion again, my elbow hit my cup. The cup fell to the ground. I slammed my laptop shut. Then the barista had to rush over and mop up the coffee. I stammered through an apology while all I could think of was that photo.

I don't know what else to say other than I too wish you were on my doorstep.

Now I have to change the subject because I've already created a scene in this coffee shop once today. I can't go causing another by getting even more flustered as I write down all the ways I'd show you precisely how much I like that photo if you were here in front of me.

What else is on TV these days besides *Sleepless in Seattle?* The reason I'm asking is that I don't have a TV here, and one of the things I'm most excited for when we see each other again is snuggling up with you on that couch in your living room and watching a show or a movie. It doesn't have to be a rom-com! I actually really like medical shows and scary movies. What kind of shows or movies do you like watching?

I want to know more details about you! Tell me some.

Here's a new thing I recently learned about me: maybe I am a believer in fate. I didn't think I was, but after meeting you,

I believe in it a little. I do think we have to participate in our fate by making choices that align with it. And part of me thinks that sometimes bad things just happen and there's nothing we can do about it. So I'm not sure how that factors into the equation. But yeah, I can now buy that sometimes the stars align and the right person enters our life at the right time. I mean, really, what were the odds that of all the seats on the plane, we were seated right next to each other? That's pretty crazy, if you stop and think about it.

I'm crazy for Vermont too, Sky. But not crazy enough to tattoo VT on my wrist after a couple of days because I like it. I got the tattoo because of what this trip here represents: having the courage to start over and pursue a meaningful life. I'm not sure if it's where I will want to live forever, but I was fishing to see if you'd be open to it in case Christmas Eve ends up going well *and* I want to stay a little while longer or eventually move here permanently.

Don't spare any details to my questions when you write me back.

Until Wednesday,

Harper

seventeen

I don't know why I committed to this. I mean, technically, I do know why.

I wanted to find myself.

I wanted to discover my passion.

I wanted to prove to myself that I could do hard things and stand on my own two feet after everything that happened six months ago.

But logistically speaking . . . after weeks of snacking on cheese at happy hour, drinking at the fire every night with Jesse, and refraining from any cardio training whatsoever besides walking into town every Wednesday to read Sky's letters, signing up for a 10K was probably not my best idea.

Damn you, bucket-list item number 23! Or rather, damn me for putting "run a race" on my list in the first place.

I only have half a mile to go, which isn't *too* terrible. But I think I pulled my hamstring, so I'm basically hobbling. Not great given that I walked to the start of the race and was planning on walking back.

Jesse offered to drive me. He also offered to come cheer me on, but I told him not to worry about it because I had no idea how long I would take to complete the race—or if I even could complete it— and I didn't want him to stand around waiting for me that whole time. Also, even though the race started after breakfast at the inn and I would finish it before happy hour, I figured one of us should probably hold down the fort in case a guest decided to check in or out.

Hopefully, I'll be able to call an Uber from the finish line. I say hopefully because Stowe is not like Atlanta, where there's always a driver nearby. This is a small town, and seemingly the entire population is here either running the race or lining the streets to cheer us runners on. It wouldn't surprise me if that included the Uber drivers.

To be honest, it's nice that most of the town has shown up for the event. The race is a fundraiser for the local hospital, and it's pretty neat to see people rally together around a good cause. Having so many people out here applauding is also what's gotten me this far, and it's what helps me reach the finish line in the end.

Once I cross it, a medal is placed around my neck, and the cheering coming from the roped-off area separating the runners from the crowd gets even louder. I'm surprised I'm getting this much support because I was definitely pulling up the rear. These are some seriously nice strangers.

I look over to give them a wave and say thanks when I spy Jesse right in the middle of the crowd.

I cover my mouth with my hand because not only is he standing there hooting and hollering and pumping his fist in the air as if I just came in first place, but he's also holding a sign.

It's written in bold letters, so I can easily make out what it says: *Bucket List Item Number 23.* Beside the words is a box, and in the box is a check mark.

I'm sorry, could he be any better of a friend?

I hurry (or rather hobble) over, ducking underneath the rope. When I get to him, I throw my arms around his neck. "You came!"

"Of course I came," he replies, pulling me into his chest.

"But I told you that you didn't have to."

"I wanted to. I couldn't miss it."

I pull back, still in disbelief that he's here, although I guess I shouldn't be. Jesse shows up. That's what he does. I should have known today wouldn't be any different.

"Who's keeping an eye on the inn?"

"I put a sign up that said *Be Back in an Hour.* How are you feeling?"

He lets me drape an arm around his shoulder for support as we walk to the table where they're handing out goody bags to all the participants.

"Proud, but also disappointed," I admit. "I didn't love it, and I discovered running is not my passion. I don't think yoga is either." I'm about a third of the way through my thirty-day yoga regimen, and as much as I wish I liked it enough to consider getting certified as a yoga teacher, every day I find myself counting down the minutes till my prerecorded class is done.

"At least you're ruling things out," Jesse says.

"True. I'm just starting to worry I'm going to get to the end of my time here and have only discovered a lot of things I don't like."

"One day at a time, remember?"

Before I can respond, a volunteer hands me a bag filled with candy and refreshments, plus coupons to use in town. I fish out two lollipops from the bag and hand Jesse one, then unwrap the other. "Thank you," I say. "For saying that. And for coming today."

"Are you kidding? I'd do just about anything for an orange lollipop."

I laugh as we make our way out of the crowd. In my last letter to Sky, I said that meeting him made me a believer in fate and timing. I admit meeting Jesse has made me just as convinced. And because they both came into my life when they did, I can't help but wonder if the universe knew what it was doing all along. I've been a little pissed at it for the past six months, after I lost my fiancé and my job. But now I have a great job, a love interest, *and* a new best friend. That makes me feel like the luckiest girl in the state of Vermont.

"Where'd you park?" I ask.

"About ten blocks that way." Jesse points in the general direction of the inn.

I wince. "I might've sorta pulled my hamstring."

"I could carry you, if you'd like."

"Would you?" I press my palms together. I didn't want to ask, but Jesse made it so easy by offering.

Seconds later he reaches down and sweeps me up off my feet. "Come on, my little bucket-list-crosser-offer. Let's get you home."

Forget just Vermont. Right now, I might be the luckiest girl in the world.

———

To: Harper

From: Sky

Subject: Letter Number Four

Date: October 10

Dear Harper,

My apologies for the spilled coffee, although I'm glad the photo was well received. I hope the barista made sure to give you the memo that your next two cups of coffee are on me. I called and told her you would be in on Wednesday, so hopefully you're drinking one of those free cups this morning. If not, then the barista pocketed the money or didn't recognize you from the description I gave, and I might just have to come to town and treat you to a cup in person.

I wish I could. I know from your last letter that you're most looking forward to sitting on the couch with me and watching movies when we reunite, but what I'm looking forward to the most is taking you out on the town for a real date (after we stay in for at least twenty-four hours, of course).

What are your favorite go-to dinner spots in Atlanta? And in Stowe? I want to get a jump start on planning our first couple of dates.

Let's see . . . you asked about shows and movies. I like reality TV like *Shark Tank* and *The Great British Bake Off,* and also documentaries. I'm terrified of scary movies. I would try to be all manly and act like I'm not if I were watching one with you, but I don't want to lie to you—they're not my favorite.

Here's a question for you: what are you doing for Halloween? In the spirit of honesty, I do like going out to parties. Blame the extrovert in me. But trust me, if you were around, I'd be just as happy staying in. This year, a good buddy of mine is having a costume party. I'm going as a fireman. If you were here, I'd switch it up and be a pilot. And we could ditch the party and play dress down instead of dress up. And now I've gone and changed the subject to us naked again. Admittedly, it's on my mind a lot.

While we're on that topic, I know I hinted I'd love to hear your fantasies, but after how worked up I got from that line you sent last week that wasn't even a real fantasy, just a teaser of a fantasy *(I'd show you precisely how much I like the photo if you were right here in front of me),* I'm not sure I can. At least not if I am to succeed in keeping my distance until December.

Also, in your last letter you said "in case" Christmas Eve goes well? In case? Don't tell me you are starting to doubt whether or not it will. If you are, what can I do to give you more faith?

Miss you,

Sky

139

To: Sky

From: Harper

Subject: Re: Letter Number Four

Date: October 10

Dear Sky,

I certainly didn't mean anything by saying "in case" Christmas Eve goes well. I have faith that it will go well too. I guess I meant it more as a figure of speech and because I didn't want you thinking I was jumping ahead and planning next steps when we've only taken the first few.

But go ahead and figure out our first couple of dates. I'm already so excited for them! I didn't have that many favorite spots in Atlanta since I've always been one to stay in more often than dine out. The few I did have I used to frequent with that infamous ex of mine. So, yeah . . . let's rely on your go-to Atlanta spots for our first few dates. And we will probably have to rely on your picks in Stowe too because I haven't been out to eat once since I arrived. I keep thinking I'll get around to it, but I have a routine down and haven't yet wanted to deviate from it.

The thought of you dressed as a fireman is equally as hot as you dressed as a pilot, so now you're just giving me more things to fantasize about. I'll keep those details to myself like you asked. It's too bad because here I was feeling like I might be up for typing them out . . . but you're honoring my wishes by giving me time and space, so I'll do my best to honor yours.

On Halloween, I plan on spending the night passing out candy. Reality TV and documentaries? I can't say I've spent much time watching either. I guess we're opposites in that way too. Although someone reminded me not that long ago that opposites attract.

Our night together is starting to feel like it was a while back, though. Does it feel that way for you, or is it still fresh in your mind? At least we have these letters, which help me feel connected to you.

Harper

P.S. Thank you for the coffee! What a sweet surprise.

eighteen

"**It's** going to be fine," Jesse says. "Stop stressing."

"Stop stressing?" On the center of the table I set down the bouquet of dahlias and magnolia leaves that I had Jesse drive me to town to pick up earlier this morning. "I can't stop stressing. I'm about to have dinner with my bosses."

I step back and look at the flowers. They're *not* in the center of the table. I push them to the right. There. No wait! Now they need to be a little farther to the left.

"Harper, seriously," Jesse reaches for my arm to stop me from adjusting them again and turns me toward him, resting his hands on my shoulders.

"My parents are going to love you, and they're going to think we're doing a great job running this place, and they're going to think this dinner table looks amazing. Even *if* the flowers aren't quite in the middle."

"They're not?" I take his wrists to remove his hands so I can get back to work but stop when Jesse laughs.

"If you got a ruler out, they couldn't be more centered, Harper. But please don't do that."

I can't help but laugh myself, because at this point neither of us would put it past me to retrieve one. Ever since Jesse told me yesterday that his parents were coming to dinner tonight, I've been acting like a crazy person. Last night, I stress-ate the candy we bought to hand out on Halloween. Today I haven't stood still. He keeps telling me they aren't going to be judging us, but come on. How they feel about the way things here are going will likely factor into their decision about whether or not to sell the inn or let Jesse run it for them after the holidays.

"Come on, sit down." Jesse pats the chair beside him and I groan and sink into it.

"Now turn around," Jesse says.

"What?"

"Just do it."

I'm too tired to argue, so I do. Then Jesse is rubbing my shoulders, and he's fantastic at it. He could be a masseuse, only I hope he doesn't become a masseuse, or switch to any other career, because he's a really good innkeeper and this is what he wants to do and what I want to do and I hope his parents can see that.

This is what I want to do?

"Are you calm yet?" Jesse asks.

"Yes," I say. *So calm I might not be thinking straight.* Or maybe I *am* thinking straight.

"Good," he replies. "Because my parents just walked in."

Ohymygod. I'm back on my feet in seconds, eyeing the sixty-something couple walking through the parlor toward us: a tall man nursing a limp from his fall with dark features similar to Jesse's, and a shorter woman with snow-capped gray hair and warm and inviting eyes peering out through horn-rimmed glasses.

—

Jesse was right. I had no reason to freak out over meeting his parents. Absolutely none whatsoever. In my entire life, I have never felt so welcomed and at home around people who aren't my immediate family. No wonder Mr. and Mrs. Hudson ran such a successful inn for so many years.

Sorry, Mark and Beth.

They reminded me at least three times to call them by their first names over the course of the evening, usually in between regaling Jesse and I with their most humorous stories from their years as innkeepers and complimenting the two of us on a job well done so far.

"Are you sure you don't want to stay for dessert?" I ask them now as Mark gives me a hug goodbye. I wish they'd stay longer.

I'm starting to wonder if this is a hereditary trait because it reminds me of how I feel each time I say goodnight to Jesse. The past week we've both stayed up till well after midnight playing cards and talking. Each night we tell ourselves we're going to go to sleep earlier, but when it comes around to it, we never do.

"Thank you, honey," Mark says. "But since we've stopped working at the inn, we've become early nighters."

"Plus, we don't want to interfere with your nightly fire ritual," chimes in Beth after she hugs me.

"You told them about that?" I nudge Jesse with my arm.

"He looks forward to it every night," Beth answers for him.

"Mom," Jesse gives her a look that says "please stop," and this makes me chuckle. It's cute seeing Jesse blush—he doesn't do it often. It's even cuter that he told his parents about our fire ritual. He doesn't talk much about his parents to me, but clearly he talks to them a lot about what's going on here, including how we spend our time together.

When Mark starts to mention something to Jesse about maintenance for the pool, Beth turns to me and takes my hands in hers, giving them a good squeeze. "Thank you, honey," she says. "Not just for tonight, but for everything you've done so far to help with the inn."

"It's my pleasure," I say. "I'm so grateful to you and Mark for this opportunity."

She smiles and shoots a glance at Jesse, then turns her attention back on me. "Thank you also for being such a good friend to my son. I haven't seen Jesse this happy since . . . well . . . I'm sure he's told you."

"He has," I say, squeezing her hands back. "I'm so sorry for your loss."

She thanks me. "It's been a challenging eleven months and hard for me, as his mother, to know how much Jesse has been struggling. I was worried that spending all this time at the inn would be difficult for him because it was difficult for my husband and I after what happened, but I don't see him struggling right now. In fact, I don't think I've ever seen him look so content. Something tells me you have a lot to do with that, young lady."

I shoot a glance at Jesse and catch his eye, giving him a brief smile before returning my gaze to Beth. "Your son has played a big role in my experience here being such a positive one as well," I say. "We make a good team."

"Yes, you do," Beth says.

Jesse and Mark finish their conversation, so we wrap up ours too. "All right, then," she says. "Until next time, honey."

I watch from the window as Jesse walks them to their car, still in disbelief that I was nervous tonight might not go well. Part of the reason I was so nervous might have been because the last parents I met were Sky's, and they were the opposite of Jesse's.

Not that this was the same situation at all. Sky is a guy I'm going to date, and Jesse is one of my best friends.

Still, I could see how my brain might have linked the two scenarios.

And, well, lately the thought has crossed my mind that if I hadn't met Sky, if I weren't here to find myself . . . well . . . maybe I *would* entertain different thoughts about Jesse.

But I *did* meet Sky. And I *am* here to find myself. So the what-if is sort of a dumb mental exercise.

When Jesse returns, he's beaming.

"What's up? Did they tell you they had a good time?"

His face reads like a headline announcing good news but what's the rest of the story? What's he not telling me? "My mom might have mentioned that if things keep going as well as they're going . . . they're going to let me continue to run the inn and give partial ownership to me."

"Oh my gosh, Jesse!" I launch into a hug and he hugs me back, hard. "That is such great news!"

"For both of us, really," he says. "You wouldn't have to keep working here if you didn't want to, but you would have the option to stay if you do. Obviously, I'd love you to stay, but more than that, I want whatever you decide is best for you."

"I was just thinking tonight how much I might want to stay."

"You were?"

"Yes, I really was. So thank you."

"Thank *you* for all your help."

This entire conversation takes place while we're hugging. I've felt the rumble of Jesse's voice against my cheek this whole time, we're so tightly glued together. Neither of us can seem to let the other go.

When I finally do pull away, I tell myself I held on so long because of the excitement. And any part of me that wasn't convinced *feels* convinced the following morning. Because not only did I dream about receiving another letter from Sky, but it's also Wednesday—which means I get to, and I couldn't be looking forward to that more.

—

To: Harper

From: Sky

Subject: Letter Number Five

Date: October 17

Dear Harper,

I hate hearing that you're forgetting details of our time together, but I get it. I'm forgetting some parts of our night together too.

On the one hand, I think that's a good thing, because the farther we get from that night, the closer I get to seeing you. But on the other hand, I don't like losing the vivid detail.

Which brings me to this question I'm dying to ask: have you found yourself yet? Just wondering, because if you happen to find yourself early, just say the word, and I'll be on the first flight out.

Typically, days speed up and speed past, but now that I'm waiting for something, it feels like days drag on forever. Have you noticed that too, or am I the only one experiencing this?

I thought I'd like the feeling of time slowing down because life does seem to speed up the older I get, but in this particular case I wish I could skip ahead until Christmas Eve and then press pause.

Do you sometimes wish you could play with time like that? Speed up the bad parts, slow down the good, pause the moments you wish you could live in forever?

I'm thirty-six, by the way. I don't know if I've ever told you that. How old are you?

Missing you,

Sky

P.S. Forget what I said about the fantasies. You can send them along. Hopefully those will refresh my memory of our time together ASAP.

To: Sky

From: Harper

Subject: Re: Letter Number Five

Date: October 17

Dear Sky,

I feel the same way about time. It's surprising that more people don't talk about how irritating it is that we can't seem to figure out how to manipulate it better. If I could have one superpower, it would be to do exactly what you wrote: speed up the bad parts, slow down the good, and pause the incredible.

I'd pause the moments I receive your letters, slow down how long it takes me to read them, and speed up the amount of time until I could see you again.

Well, half of me wishes I could speed it up. If I'm being honest, the other half wishes time would slow down because I don't feel like I've found myself yet. I wish I could tell you that I had so we could reunite sooner rather than later, but that's just not the case.

I'm sorry because I hate that the wait feels hard. I appreciate your patience. As a token of my gratitude, I thought I'd do you one better than reciting my fantasies. I've attached a photo that is for your eyes only, mister!

Hopefully this makes the wait a little easier.

Harper

P.S. I'm thirty. I had a birthday recently.

nineteen

"**Can't** find what you're looking for?"

Jesse approaches me in the produce section of the grocery store. I've been standing in front of the limes for a solid five minutes now. I don't even need a lime. I just stopped here to refresh my email again. And then again. And then I got in a trance because it's Sunday and I *still* haven't heard from Sky.

He never emailed me this past Wednesday. I went to Milk & Maple at the same time I always do, and there wasn't anything from him in my inbox. I waited around for as long as I could but still hadn't heard from him by the time I had to leave for happy hour. I was disappointed that night but figured he must have gotten tied up at work and I'd have an email the next morning.

When I popped into town to run an errand on Thursday, however, I checked my email on my phone and there was still no letter in my inbox. That night I did start to worry a little. Not about us. I didn't think there was a reason to. Since Sky and I started writing letters, he's always seemed as eager for Wednesdays as I am. What troubled me was that something might have happened to him. I didn't want to jump to worst-case scenarios, but what if he had been in an accident?

I used the work computer that night to look up both car crashes and plane crashes (the news would have definitely covered that), but there was no mention of Sky's name anywhere in the papers, which momentarily eased my concerns.

But then it raised others. If he was fine, what was the deal? Why hadn't he written?

149

I realized he could be *really* busy with work or something. But how hard is it to shoot a girl an email and just say that?

Not that hard.

When Friday rolled around and I still hadn't heard from him, I started to worry that the reason he hadn't emailed was because something else was going on. Something that *was* hard to say in an email.

Like that he met someone else. Or that he's tired of waiting for December. His last email did mention what a challenge waiting has been. I thought he was just venting. But what if he was dropping clues instead?

I went ahead and emailed him yesterday, just something short and sweet.

Sky,

Just checking in . . .

I know it's Saturday, but thought I'd write and see what's going on.

And even with that, still nothing has arrived in my inbox today.

Not hearing back would have bothered me any week, but given that I sent him a picture of me totally exposed in my last email, his lack of response is particularly painful. I felt vulnerable sharing that. I'm comfortable with my body, and Sky's already seen a lot of me, so I'm not embarrassed that I sent it on that front. It's more that I would have never sent it if I knew he was on the fence about us. I was hoping for a really great reaction from him, not no reaction at all.

"Harper?" Jesse prompts again, bringing me back to the now.

I sigh then, because while I don't want to get into this in the middle of a grocery store, there's no point in trying to withhold what's on my mind from Jesse. He knows me well enough by now to tell when I'm lying. Better to confide in him than make him pull it out of me.

"No, I can't find what I'm looking for," I say.

"What is it? Can I help?"

I refresh my phone one more time. No new emails.

"You remember that guy I said I met on the plane?" I ask. Since my birthday, I haven't really mentioned Sky again to Jesse, but he nods now.

"We've been emailing once a week. And I haven't heard from him the past week and a half." As soon as I say this out loud, I feel like I'm completely overreacting. It really hasn't been *that* long. Although time does seem to slow down in anticipation of something. Not only does Sky know this, but he's the one who made the observation in the first place. Which makes me think he should be sensitive to it.

"Has he ever responded late before?" Jesse asks.

"Once," I say. "But just by a couple of days. And that was before we decided we'd write on Wednesdays."

"Can you call him?" he suggests.

"I don't have his number."

"Have you tried emailing him?"

"Yeah, yesterday. I don't want to be annoying and seem needy by emailing him again."

"Wondering why you haven't heard from someone who told you he'd write to you once a week isn't needy, Harper," Jesse tells me. "It's a normal reaction to finding out someone hasn't followed through on something he told you he would do."

I appreciate Jesse for validating how I'm feeling. It makes me more accepting of my current emotional state. Although now that I know I'm not overreacting, I feel worse that Sky hasn't written.

"I'm sorry you have to sit in the uncertainty," Jesse says. "But it sounds like that's all you can do." He wraps an arm around my shoulder. "If it helps, I'll sit in it with you."

"Thanks," I say, letting him walk me out of the produce section.

—

"I'm heading into town," I tell Jesse.

"You want me to come with you?" He's in his cabin reading at the dining table, and he looks up from his book and to the doorway where I'm standing.

After Jesse and I got back from the grocery store on Sunday, he suggested I wait until Wednesday to go back to town to see if Sky had written so that I didn't drive myself crazy. I liked the idea and have stuck to it, keeping busy around the inn and checking items off my bucket list. But now that the day is here, I'm in my head again.

"That's okay," I say. "I should go alone."

"You sure?" I know Jesse would stop reading and drive me into town, even though he told me last night he's really into his current novel: *The Road* by Cormac McCarthy. He's planning on giving it to me once he's done since I just finished and enjoyed his last recommendation, *East of Eden*.

But I don't want to drag him into this anymore than I have already. I talked his ear off about it even more on Sunday once we got back from the store. I didn't let him know about the photo I sent that made me feel extra vulnerable in the face of Sky's silence. But I did continue to vent about my frustration and confusion.

And this morning, as we were getting eggs from the barn and making breakfast, I mentioned several times how nervous I was to find out whether or not I'd have a new email today.

"Yeah, I'll be fine," I say.

"You will be, no matter what," Jesse reminds me as he goes back to his book. "Here for you when you get back."

I walk fast into town because of the cold and also because of my sense of urgency to get the email ordeal over with. But as soon as I make it to Milk & Maple, I'm surprised by my self-control. I could pull up my email on my phone, but I don't. I walk to the counter first and order.

As I wait at a table near the fire for my latte, I realize it's more likely fear than self-control that's keeping me from looking at my phone or opening my computer. And caring *that* much about a relationship I'm not even *in* yet and didn't even want makes me annoyed with myself. It makes me annoyed with Sky for putting me in this position by not writing when he said he would. I'm even a little annoyed with fate for sitting me next to Sky on the plane when I was flying out here to take a trip for myself. I don't want to focus on a guy right now. And look at me. Totally focused on one!

I sigh. Maybe that's just life. You can't pick and choose when you want to work on what. We're constantly having to work on everything all at once: ourselves, our relationships to ourselves, our relationships to others, our emotions, our finances, our sanity. It's a lot. It's exhausting!

And wow, why am I on this rant in my head?

I have my latte in front of me now and my laptop out. *Rip off the Band-Aid, Harper, and just check.*

I pull up my email and . . . my heart stops.

There *is* a new email from Sky. And there's nothing suspicious about it. At least so far.

I'm just seeing the subject line and it says: *Letter Number Six.* It should say *Letter Number Seven* because this is the seventh week. But whatever. If he were writing a letter to call off the arrangement or say he'd met someone else, he probably would have titled it differently, right?

Well, I don't actually have any idea what he'd do because I don't know Sky. I'm just *getting* to know him. One night and a handful of emails isn't enough to really know a person. It takes time. It takes spending day in and day out with someone, as I've been doing with Jesse. I know Jesse.

Jesse would write something different for the email subject. Absolutely. Because he would know I'd appreciate having a heads-up before I opened a letter containing bad news.

But Sky . . . I have no clue. I guess I'm about to find out.

To: Harper

From: Sky

Subject: Letter Number Six

Date: October 31

Dear Harper,

I realized the tone of my last letter was a little depressing, so I thought I'd liven this one right up and start off with some good news. This is Letter Number Six, which means only eight more weeks until I see you!

I scan the rest of the email. It doesn't contain an apology for not emailing me last week. And nothing about another girl or wanting to call off the pact, so he hasn't met someone else. It's a completely normal letter.

Am I somehow getting this letter late?

No. I read a reference to the email I sent him on Saturday. He wrote, *I wanted to respond to the message you sent over the weekend, but you said don't email twice in one week, so I resisted.* That means this letter was written after that email, not before—it wasn't delayed in the outbox in his phone or by some other unlikely but technically possible situation. And if it had been, there would be two letters in my inbox now.

No, I can firmly cross that possibility off.

So what, then?

I sit back in my chair as the revelation fully hits me. Sky didn't . . . he didn't even *realize* he missed a week. I'm not sure whether that makes me feel better or worse. On the one hand, I'm relieved that he didn't intentionally skip sending an email. On the other, how did he forget a week?

I wouldn't forget a week. And doesn't he have a countdown going on his fridge? I guess he's no longer checking it.

Wow.

I sit back in my chair as my mind races. I don't want to overreact, but this stings. He says he can't wait to see me, but his actions don't reflect that. If he were as excited as he keeps saying, he wouldn't have forgotten to write. At least that's how I see it.

I don't want to chew him out, and I definitely don't want to write him off because of this issue alone. But I do want to call him out for it and let him know how I feel. If Sky and I are ever going to have something—really have something—honesty has to be at the foundation. I owe it to Sky, to myself, and to *us* to say that I don't like what he did, and to share all my reasons.

So that's what I do when I write him back. And then I hit send.

twenty

I've come to expect the unexpected while working at the inn. Every day poses a myriad of challenges, with different guests coming with their own particular needs. I was just telling Jesse last week that at this point, nothing would surprise me.

But I was wrong about that.

Totally wrong about that.

Because Jesse has just walked into the inn following breakfast to inform me that I have a visitor, and as soon as that visitor walks through the front door, I'm so stunned I think I might in fact faint.

"What . . ." I start, as my visitor tips his hat. His *pilot* hat.

Sky is *here*. In Vermont. At the inn. Right in front of me.

I think I'm excited. But I'm also confused. And now I'm dizzy because Sky's lips have found my mouth, and it's just as it was when I saw him last.

Only not.

Because he's not supposed to be here yet. And it's not just the two of us—Jesse is in the room.

I break the kiss off, pressing my hands to Sky's chest.

"Jesse," I say turning toward him. "This is Sky . . ."

My voice trails off when I notice that Jesse isn't where I saw him last. I cast a look around, and he's not even in the room. Over Sky's shoulder, I see the front door swinging shut.

I can't say I blame him for leaving. Who likes watching public displays of affection? Introductions will have to come later.

I turn my attention back to Sky for now.

"What are you doing here?" I'm still trying to wrap my head around the fact that he's in front of me instead of in my inbox. It's been three days since I called him out for forgetting to write me. I was expecting to hear back from him, sure, but not until next week, and definitely not in person.

"I felt so bad about not emailing you last Wednesday," he rushes to explain. "I can't believe I did that. I've had a crazy past couple of weeks at work. So crazy that the weeks sort of blurred together and I forgot. I forgot to check the countdown I had going on my fridge too."

He captures my hands and leads me to a bench beneath a window-sill. We sit, and he keeps my hands in his as he continues to explain.

"When I got your email saying how bummed out you were, I freaked. I didn't want you to question how strong my feelings were because I do still think about you constantly, Harper. It's just that I was thinking about so many other things during the past two weeks too. And I didn't think apologizing in a letter would be enough. I needed to apologize in person. I know I'm not supposed to be here until Christmas Eve. But I had to make sure you forgave me. I hope you're not mad."

I am a little mad, honestly, because this wasn't the arrangement. But it was super sweet that he flew all the way out here just to apologize. I did have doubts, and those doubts might have lingered and expanded if he hadn't shown up. He's right about that. I've also really been missing Sky, and that part of me is excited he's here.

"How much time do we have?" I ask.

"I have to catch a flight to Atlanta late tonight," he says. "I've got to work in the morning."

That's not much time. But it's more time than I thought I'd have with Sky today.

"I still have to work," I say.

"I figured as much. What can I do to help?"

157

—

Given the flirtatious tone of our emails, the kiss Sky gave me when he arrived, and all the little touches he's given me since, I'm a little surprised he doesn't immediately start kissing me when we finally make it back to my cottage after clearing breakfast. Instead, he looks around a bit, poking his head into the bathroom and checking out the kitchen before making his way to my bed and reaching for the novel sitting on my bedside table. It's the new one Jesse just finished and gave me.

"Are you a reader?" he asks, flipping through a few of the pages as he takes a seat and removes his pilot hat.

"Trying to be," I say, sitting beside him.

"I'm not," he replies in a way that seems to say "I hope that's okay." It *is* okay.

"I like our differences." *For the most part*, I think. But it's not worth adding more to the conversation because I don't want to be having a conversation.

Desire is crackling under my skin, as instant as it was the last time I saw Sky. Every casual brush—and not-so-casual brush—as he helped me pick up the breakfast plates got me heated. Seeing him on my bed only reminds me of the last time we were on a bed. It makes me want to do what we haven't been able to do for the past six weeks.

"Is this book good?" he asks, now eyeing the back-cover copy. The book reminds me of Jesse, and I don't want to think about Jesse now.

"I don't want to talk about the book," I say, taking it out of his hands and tossing it to the side.

Sky's eyes find mine, and I can tell the only reason he was leading with conversation was because he was trying to be polite.

"You're right," he says. "Conversation is overrated."

Sky's mouth covers mine before I can respond. And this time kissing him is *exactly* as it was when I saw him last. In fact, it may even be better, because I bet Sky brought condoms! Which means this kissing could lead to more.

So much more.

Chills cover my entire body as Sky presses me down onto the comforter and crawls over me, pulling at my sweater and pressing his lips to my neck.

I wish I'd worn fewer layers.

I wish I'd worn a cuter bra.

And cuter panties.

Oh, well. None of my clothes will be on very long. Sky seems determined to make sure of that. He's already pulled my shirt off over my head, and now he's sliding a hand between my legs as he reaches behind me with his other hand and unclasps my bra. When it breaks free, he pulls it off and sits back.

"Damn." His eyes are wild as they admire me. "That picture you sent was amazing, but in person . . ." His voice trails off and he shakes his head. "Damn."

More chills cover my body as I bask in his gaze.

"Okay, enough," I finally say, propping myself up with my elbows. "My turn to stare." I point to his shirt, and he pulls it off over his head in one swift motion.

Once it's on the ground, I raise a brow. "Did you get even more abs?"

He grins. "I work out whenever I'm missing you. It's a good distraction."

He must spend *a lot* of time missing me.

"Oh, before I forget!" He's on his feet, rummaging through his suitcase for something. When he returns, he has that something tucked behind his back.

"What have you got there?"

His grin grows wider as he presents me with the surprise. It's a box of condoms. A *big* box of condoms wrapped in a red bow.

"You didn't forget," I say.

159

"I didn't forget."

Only he *did* forget something. Two things, actually. To write to me. And that he's not supposed to visit me until Christmas Eve.

But why am I thinking about those things now? And why does the voice in my head still sound upset? I've already decided I've forgiven him. Haven't I?

What I need to do is refocus. Sky makes this easy when he puts on his pilot hat after setting down the box of condoms and pulling one out.

Oh, this is about to get good.

As he starts to unbutton my pants, I mess with his, and seconds later the rest of our clothes are in a pool at the foot of my bed.

Excellent.

But when Sky climbs on top of me and finds my mouth again, my attention is pulled in yet another direction.

"Do you hear that?" I ask.

"Hear what?" Sky breathes. I get the sense there could be fireworks going off and Sky wouldn't have a clue. He's that into what's happening. I thought I was that into it too, but apparently I can block out any and all noises *except* when those noises are coming from next door.

What is Jesse doing in there? Humming? Singing? Cooking? All three?

And why can I hear him? I've never before noticed that I can hear him. But I also haven't ever paid that much attention because I've never minded before—I've never cared if he could hear me. I *do* care now because Sky is capable of coaxing a lot of noises out of me. *A lot* of noises. And if I can hear Jesse, he can hear me. I don't want Jesse to hear me. That's weird. And I don't want to be thinking about Jesse when I should be thinking about Sky because that would be even weirder, and that could end up happening because he's literally right there, and I'm thinking about him now!

I press up and push Sky back. "Oh, do you want to be on top?" he asks.

I'm envious of Sky's one-track mind. I want a one-track mind too.

When I sigh, Sky seems to realize I have more on my mind than sex positions. He leans in closer. "What is it?"

I sigh again. "My coworker is right next door." I'm not sure why I just referred to Jesse as just my coworker when he's my friend, one of my best friends. But it seems beside the point to correct myself now.

"Okay, and . . .?" Sky starts kissing my neck again, trying to lure me back in.

When I sigh a third time, Sky sighs too. He must recognize I'm no longer in the mood and that I'm not going to get back into the mood. At least not right now.

"It's just too weird, having sex when he's in there and can hear us."

He sidles up beside me. "I get it," he replies. "Kinda. I mean, I wasn't thinking about it. But if I were to think about it, I could see what you mean. You're the only staff here. A person can't un-hear that."

I curl up closer to him. "I'm sorry."

"Don't worry about it."

I perk up suddenly. "Can I interest you in a consolation prize? Do you want to see the chickens?"

Sky narrows his eyes. "The chickens?"

"Yeah. They're really cute."

"You're really cute." He sits up and kisses me gently on my neck, exhaling slowly through his nose so the air hits my ear just enough to resurrect goose bumps. Seeing that my nerve endings are already primed to be tickled, he starts running his fingers up and down my sides, prompting a laugh so hard I'm sure Jesse has to hear it. But at least it's not the sound of me having sex. I can't help but blush at the thought of Jesse hearing me having sex.

twenty-one

I thought showing Sky the chickens would be a fun activity. But after being in the coop with him for ten minutes, I'm rethinking that. Sky's hands are still in his pockets. He looks uncomfortable, grossed out, and as if he's counting down the minutes until we can do something else. Anything else.

"You sure you don't want to hold one?" I try one more time. I've got Xylo in my hands and—not to offend the other chickens or anything—I think Xylo is the cutest. How could anyone not want to hold her?

"I'm fine," he says.

I try not to act bummed out even though I am. I want Sky to be into this. But that's not fair of me. That's wanting him to be someone he's not. That's wanting him to be like Jesse. He's not Jesse, and that's a good thing because I don't have a thing for Jesse, I have a thing for Sky. And if Sky doesn't want to be here, I should come up with another idea for how to spend our time. We don't have much of it.

Xylo looks confused when I set her down because I usually like to hold her longer. She also looks confused that Sky is here and Jesse is not. I feel the same way, so it's probably a good thing that Sky and I are headed elsewhere.

Reaching for Sky's hand, I lead him out of the barn . . . and right into Jesse.

I clear my throat. I've been wanting to make introductions, but now that I have the chance, I'm nervous. I think it's because Jesse is my good friend, and I want him to approve of the guy I like, and

162

on the flip side I want Sky to like my friend, Jesse. "Jesse," I say, "meet Sky. Sky, this is my coworker, Jesse."

Jesse's jaw hardens and I instantly know why. I just referred to him as my coworker, not my friend. But it's too late to fix it without drawing too much attention to it.

What is wrong with me?

Sky nods and says, "I know."

Oh, right, technically they met earlier when Sky first arrived. They probably introduced themselves.

"Jesse and I went to high school together," Sky informs me.

Okay, way earlier.

"You did?" I don't know why I'm so surprised. It's a small town. I should have figured they knew each other. Or knew *of* each other.

"Yep," Sky says.

"Were you two friends?" I ask.

"He was older," Jesse says, at the same time as Sky says, "He was younger."

That didn't answer my question. Or did it? I guess in high school, your grade often determines who you hang out with. To be honest, even if they were in the same grade, I can't really picture them being friends. Sky is so . . . adventurous and athletic and charismatic. And Jesse is so . . . calm and outdoorsy and intentional with every single word he says. I imagine Sky was popular and Jesse was probably too busy doing his own thing to care about popularity.

"I was in Jesse's brother's grade," Sky says. "How is Brendan, by the way?"

It's normally pretty quiet on the property, but even so, you can always count on hearing something—the chatter of guests, the cluck of the chickens or, at the very least, birds chirping. In this moment, however, the entire property is silent.

Clearly Sky has no idea about the accident. You'd think his family might have found out and told him since it's such a small town.

Then again, Sky isn't close with his family. Maybe they did find out but never shared the news.

Jesse looks at me, and I can tell he doesn't want to talk about it. I don't blame him. I feel bad that this topic came up, and so soon into the conversation. I wasn't expecting Jesse and Sky to become best friends, but I was hoping all of us could bond. They're both important people to me. That's clearly not going to happen in this moment.

"I'm going to finish giving Sky the full tour," I say. Jesse nods and heads into the barn. I take Sky to the parlor. It's in the opposite direction and there are cocktails in the parlor. I know it's only noon, but today has been full of surprises. That calls for shaking things up a bit.

—

"What was that about?" Sky asks once it's just the two of us and I'm pulling out the alcohol from behind the bar.

"Brendan passed away," I share.

"Seriously?" Sky is behind the bar with me, putting ice in two glasses. He stops and shakes his head in disbelief. "How?"

"Car accident," I say. I don't share more because I don't know if Jesse would want me to share more. Jesse shared his feelings about the accident with me in confidence, and I've always tried to be the kind of friend who keeps what's shared with me between me and the person who shared it. It's not my place to tell another person's story.

"That's awful," Sky says. And that's all he says. He doesn't ask me any follow-up questions, and I'm kind of relieved because I don't have to worry about which details I should share and which I shouldn't.

Instead, I shift my focus entirely to the task at hand and open a bottle of tonic. I didn't even ask Sky what he wanted to drink. I just decided I'd make us gin and tonics because ever since we drank them together in the air, I've thought of it as our drink.

"You remembered," Sky says when he sees me start to pour the gin.

"Of course I remembered."

Sky comes up behind me and wraps his arms around my waist. I lean back into him, reveling in the fact that it's so easy to touch him.

"I've had a few gin and tonics since I landed," I say. "And every time, I can't help but think how they aren't as good on the ground as they are in the air."

"Well, I've had one gin and tonic in the air without you since we met, and I'm thinking drinking this one on the ground with you is going to give that a serious run for its money."

I smile as I reach for a lime to slice. "I forgot how much I love when you say things like that."

He kisses my earlobe and tugs on it gently with his teeth. Goose bumps break out on my skin.

"What else did you miss?" Sky whispers in my ear before lowering his mouth to the side of my neck.

I grin as I drop the lime slices into the drink, an idea forming. I also forgot how playful Sky can make me. I spin around in his arms and say, "Lots of things."

"Like?"

"Like your lips," I say, leaning in and kissing those.

"And your neck," I say, kissing him there next.

"I also missed your ears and your . . ." I've just kissed Sky's second ear and am about to name his nose when I see his eyes widen at something behind me.

"There's someone at the bar, isn't there?" I ask.

He nods.

I assumed an empty room when I shouldn't have. I turn around, mortified to address the guest. Only it's not a guest. It's Jesse.

And now my cheeks must be at least five shades darker.

"Can I steal you for a second?" Jesse rubs the back of his neck, embarrassed, as if he didn't want to see what was just happening any more than I wanted him to see it.

"What is it?" I ask.

"Xylo's missing."

The gate to the chicken coop. I must have left it open when Sky and I walked out. "Shoot, Jesse, I'm sorry. I'm so sorry," I repeat, moving from behind the bar and following him outside.

"Just start looking," he says.

I nod and begin to scan the property. While I search, I can't help but steal glances Jesse's way. He's normally calm in a crisis, but he looks totally stressed out about this one. I know that Xylo is his favorite chicken too, but that alone doesn't seem like the cause. Especially since we'll obviously find her.

"There she is!" I spot her a second later, hiding in the brush by the small pond behind the barn. After reaching down to pick her up, I cuddle her into my chest. She clucks happily when she sees me and even more exuberantly when Jesse comes up from behind. Then again, she's just a chicken. Her anthropomorphic reactions are likely all in my head. Jesse strokes her feathers, and we escort her back to the coop together, setting her in with the others.

"That's a relief," I say.

"Yeah," Jesse says, although he doesn't look relieved. He still looks stressed.

I reach out and rest a hand on his shoulder. "What's up? Is this about Brendan?" I'm sure he wasn't expecting to have to talk about him today, and I still feel terrible that Sky brought up the topic. Though, in Sky's defense, he honestly didn't know not to broach the subject.

Jesse shakes his head.

"Is this about Sky?" I probably should clarify that he won't interfere with my duties while he's here, which isn't for very long. I'm still planning on dealing with my responsibilities, including checking in the two guests arriving at three-thirty and hosting happy hour.

But Jesse shakes his head, so I don't bother mentioning any of that.

"What's it about, then?"

He doesn't say anything. Jesse has *always* told me what's on his mind when I've pressed him, ever since I first got here. So why not now? The only subject I can imagine he might not want to discuss with me is me.

"Did *I* do something?" I try. Is this because I called him my co-worker earlier?

I open my mouth to ask or apologize, but he shakes his head.

"No," he says adamantly. "No. I'm not mad at you, Harper. It's just . . ." He looks as if he wants to say something but isn't sure if he should, which must mean he hasn't fully thought it through yet. Jesse is too purposeful to share a thought he hasn't completely processed. "I should get back to work," he concludes.

He walks away before I can press him further.

twenty-two

Sky and I are at dinner. A really romantic dinner at a restaurant in town called Plate. We're seated at the best table in the joint because Sky called last night before he flew out here and made us a reservation, requesting the table right in front of the fire.

We came straight from happy hour at the inn. Sky said I had to try it, and he was so excited he could take me himself. Ever since we arrived, we've been talking. The conversation is fluid and flirty, and I think it's going to lead to sex—really *good* sex.

But as we sip red wine and wait for our food to arrive, the thought keeps crossing my mind that this is the time of night when *Jesse and I* usually sit at *our* fire.

I keep trying to shake it, but I can't. Part of me wonders if it would be easier if we were sitting at a different table—one that wasn't next to the fire. I ponder claiming I'm too warm, but a scan of the room tells me the rest of the tables for two are taken. So I'm forced to keep staring into the flames. And each time I do, I think of Jesse.

I wonder if this is why Jesse was upset earlier. Did he know I would miss our ritual tonight? Was he upset about it and didn't know how to tell me?

I'm upset too, I realize, as our food arrives and we start eating. I miss our ritual. I'm surprised how much I miss it.

And I feel terrible about missing it because, first of all, Sky is right here in front of me. He's such a great date. And I've missed him and dreamed about seeing him again and spending time together since the day he left. (Sure, in all these imagined scenarios, I pictured us together after Christmas Eve, but still.) Second of all, what if this is the night Jesse's and my streak ends? I wonder if he's sitting by the fire alone or if he bagged it. And if he is sitting by the fire but I'm not with him, does that count, or do we both have to be there for it to count? We never discussed this. I never imagined there'd be a night where either of us would have other plans. We're always at the inn.

Half of my heart feels as if it's there now, and at one point Sky picks up on this. "Is something wrong?" he asks.

I'm not sure what to say. I need to tell him something. I believe in honesty in relationships. I especially believe in honesty before a relationship officially starts.

I set down my fork and reach across the table for his hand. "The meal is lovely. And you being here makes me so happy. It's just that Jesse and I have this ritual where we sit outside at the fire every night at this time. It's something he used to do with Brendan, so it means a lot to him. And I feel bad missing it."

Sky squeezes my hand, then releases it and reaches for his glass of wine to take another sip. "I'm sure he will understand," he says. "It's just one night."

Just one night. Put that way, it doesn't sound like a big deal.

But it feels like a big deal.

"True," I say. "It's just that we're trying to see how far into the season we can last sitting out there in the cold, so missing one night sort of blows the whole thing."

Sky nods and begins to trace his thumb around the stem of his wine glass. "Do you want to head back?"

I can see in his eyes that *he* doesn't want to head back. Honestly, why would he? We're in the middle of a date on the only night we have to spend together until Christmas Eve. Still, it was sweet of him to offer. Really sweet. It shows he was willing to sacrifice our date, and that should make me feel more at peace with my decision to be here with him.

So . . . why isn't that happening?

"I've probably missed it already, anyway," I say, because it's the truth. I should have thought about this before we left. But Sky had the reservation, and I was wrapped up in him, so I wasn't thinking about Jesse and the fire. And I didn't anticipate how much Jesse and the fire would consume my thoughts, or that I'd feel as if I'd somehow made a mess of things.

"I'm sure he will understand," Sky says again as he goes back to eating.

I hope he's right.

—

Sky and I finish eating soon after that. I started to pick up my pace when it occurred to me that if we wrapped this up sooner rather than later, I could make it back in time for the fire (or have Jesse make another fire), sit with him for fifteen minutes, *then* have sex with Sky in my cottage before Sky has to head to the airport. Sky matched my pace and didn't seem to mind. But now that we're in his rental car, I'm realizing he probably thought we were in an unspoken agreement to get out of there fast so we'd have enough time to have sex at least once before he left, maybe even twice.

He started kissing me as soon as we got in the car, and he's *still* kissing me in a way that makes me think he's down to do it for the first time right at the end of this dead-end street.

It's not the worst idea in the world. All the lights are off in the houses surrounding us. Plus, we're doing a good job at the moment of fogging up all of the windows. And Sky rented an SUV, so there's plenty of room if we move from the front to the back. Yet another bonus is that we wouldn't have to worry about Jesse overhearing us.

But *I'm* still worrying about Jesse. That's the annoying thing.

Sky cups my face with both hands and drives his tongue into my mouth as if he's trying to push everything out of my mind. And it works. It is quite the kiss, after all.

For a moment, I can't think of anything but the feel of his shoulders under my hands, his tongue against mine, and how we're going to come together in a window-fogging tangle in that back seat. I'm flushed and panting, and I want . . .

To be by the fire.

Dammit. Dammit!

I'm still worried about Jesse. I can't stop seeing him all alone at the fire. And I can't stop feeling guilty about this. And sad. Like I'm not where I'm supposed to be.

I am not supposed to be here right now.

And that kicks off the anger I thought I'd let go of already: Sky isn't supposed to be here yet.

I want to shake myself. Why can't I just love that he's here?

I hate all these emotions. I don't want to feel any of these things when I'm kissing Sky. I definitely don't want to be feeling them when I'm about to have sex with Sky for the first time. I've fantasized about this moment so many times, and this isn't how it's supposed to be.

I break off the kiss just as Sky starts to shift us into the back seat.

"I'm sorry," Sky says, panting. "Is the back of a car tacky? It is tacky. I promised you our first time would be amazing, and I just . . . I got carried away."

He's giving me an out here, and I could take it. But I'd feel too guilty blaming this on him. Plus, if I tell him that's it, he's going to want to rush right back to the inn and have sex there. And if we go back to the inn . . . I know myself. The first thing I'm going to have to do is check on Jesse.

I know myself.

Did I just say that? I almost laugh. Of all the times to feel as if I'm figuring out who I am, this is *not* an ideal moment.

171

"It's not you. It's me." As soon as I say this, Sky's eyes grow wide. Oops. I've probably freaked him out. Those are often the words a person uses to end things. I'm not trying to end things. I just want them to start right.

"I wasn't expecting you to be here tonight," I try to explain. "And because it was so unexpected, it's been hard for me to recalibrate—to get work off my mind or all that I'm missing back at the inn. I want to be fully in this moment with you, but I'm not."

Sky always seems to have the right words up his sleeve. But he's quiet now for a solid minute.

"I thought flying out here was the right thing," he says finally.

"It wasn't the wrong thing," I say, trying to make him feel better. "It just wasn't . . . good timing."

He hangs his head, and I rest my hand on his back, wondering if I made the wrong decision. We could be having sex right now. We could be moving forward. Instead, I'm choosing to put us on pause—again. And this time pausing us doesn't feel as exciting as it did last time because Sky's feelings are hurt.

"Do you want me to take you back?" Sky's hands are on his steering wheel as if he already knows the answer to his question.

When I nod, he starts the engine.

I don't like the direction this night is taking. But I don't know what I can do to correct its course.

—

Sky doesn't get out of the car when we get back to the inn, so I don't move either. I'm not sure if it's because he doesn't want to come in or he's waiting for an invite.

I contemplate extending one, but there doesn't seem to be a point. Neither of us spoke once on the car ride here, so I can't imagine the two of us talking in my cottage for the final hour before he has to leave for the airport. We're both in a pretty negative mood.

Thanks to me. But also thanks to Sky.

I am more than willing to admit I'm at fault here. I feel terrible for my role in the turn this night took. But I'm also frustrated with Sky for flying out here in the first place. We came up with the arrangement we did for a reason, so we'd both be fully available and ready to dive in. He might be ready, but he knows I still have things to unwind.

I share some of these thoughts out loud with him now, even though I'm mostly just repeating what I told him earlier. But the silence between us was becoming too weird. I have an urge to fill it, and all these thoughts feel worth reiterating.

Once I finish, Sky looks up from his hands.

"So where does this leave us?" he asks.

I stare into Sky's eyes and am reminded of everything I like about this man: the way I feel when I'm around him, how playful he makes me, how fun everything is when we're together, his willingness to put his heart on the line for me, despite his past.

Since the moment I met him, he's brought so much good into my life. He's also brought the promise of something good to come. I have loved looking forward to his letters every week, and a big part of me still loves the idea of reuniting with him on Christmas Eve. I know we have real potential to be good together. So even though tonight didn't go as either of us hoped, I don't want to say anything that I will regret upon waking up tomorrow.

"I want to stick to the pact. I'm still looking forward to reuniting on Christmas Eve," I respond.

"*Will* you be looking forward to it?" Sky asks.

"Yeah. Will you be?"

Sky doesn't immediately answer me, which hurts. It hurts so much that it makes me wish I could go back in time and make different choices tonight. If I had handled all of this better, we could have been having an entirely different conversation right now, one about how much *more* we're anticipating Christmas Eve after this second incredible day together.

I force myself to remember that Sky could have made different choices too. He could have never forgotten to write me in the first place. He could have chosen to apologize in several letters instead of flying out here. I can't take all the blame for the situation we're in.

But I have to release any and all blame and just accept what is. This night didn't play out as we both would have liked. But it doesn't have to mean it's over.

Does it?

Sky still hasn't answered me.

"Will you be looking forward to it?" I repeat.

"Yeah," he says finally. His voice doesn't sound convincing, though.

"You're scaring me," I say.

"You're scaring me," he shoots back, then braces his hands on the steering wheel and stares straight ahead. "I think I might go see Andrea."

"Now?"

"Now."

Clearly he's also telling me it's time for me to get out of the car. And to say goodbye. But is this goodbye for now or goodbye altogether? I don't know, and not knowing sends a fizzle of panic through me.

We had a pact, didn't we? I want to hold fast to the plan. I want to keep my promise. But I'm not sure Sky does.

"Will you still write to me next Wednesday?" I ask.

He nods.

"I'll write back. I promise," I say.

I know Sky needs reassurance right now, but so do I, and I don't feel I'm getting any. I'm relieved when this dawns on Sky and he finally shifts toward me and gives me a hug. I want him to kiss me too, and he does that next, but I regret I wished for it because it's not a reassuring kiss. It's a desperate kiss. A sad kiss. A confused kiss. *Confused.*

That's how I feel when I get out of the car and wave goodbye.

Very, very confused. And I wonder where we stand and if I still have someone waiting for December with me.

—

As soon as Sky pulls away, I want to sulk and possibly even cry. But I can't do either of those things because I haven't forgotten why I pushed Sky away in the first place.

Jesse.

I shake my head as if to get rid of the sadness, and square my shoulders. It's very possible I'm heading toward another person who is upset with me, but it doesn't matter. I need him to know I'm sorry. I need to repair the damage.

It's just past seven o'clock now, which means Jesse is probably in his room. I say *probably* because he normally is, but Sky's appearance threw both of us off our routine, so there's a chance he's elsewhere instead.

When I knock, he doesn't answer right away. I wait a minute and try again. When he still doesn't answer, I turn to leave, but then I hear the doorknob twist, and a second later Jesse pokes his head out. I wish he would come all the way out or invite me in. His hesitant greeting makes me think he's definitely mad at me.

"Can we talk?" I say.

"It's not really a good time."

Yep, clearly mad at me. I don't blame him. I should have mentioned Sky's and my dinner plans ahead of time so he and I could have nailed down a plan B for our fire routine.

"Look, Jesse—" I start to explain. "I won't be able to sleep if we don't talk about this tonight. I'm assuming I missed the fire. And

I feel so bad about that. Really bad. At dinner, all I could think about was what a terrible friend I was, and I was wondering if you've already sat by the fire, and if so, how you'd feel about making another so I could join you because it's still before midnight so technically we can keep our streak—."

The sound of Jesse's bathroom door opening distracts me. When I hear footsteps on the hardwood floor, I fall silent.

"Do you have company?" If I sound surprised, it's because I am. He nods.

Talk about changing up our routine. Jesse hasn't had anyone over since we started working together. He's spent every night with me. Then again, I wasn't here tonight, so I guess it makes sense that he might have invited someone over to hang out.

"Who?" As soon as I say it, I recognize I'm being nosy. But I'm curious why he's being so secretive and not just introducing me. Also, it would have been really nice if he could have told me he had plans tonight so I wouldn't have felt so bad about the plans *I* had. There's no cell service here, so he couldn't have made last-minute plans on a whim. He must have known before Sky and I drove to dinner that this person would be coming over.

Rather than answer my question, he turns and looks over his shoulder. "Give me a minute, will you?" he says to the person behind him.

"Okay," I hear a voice reply. A female voice.

He steps outside and closes the door behind him.

What the hell?

"Who's in there?" I say. At this point, I don't care about being nosy. His behavior is weird.

Jesse leans against the porch railing and folds his arms over his chest. "Madison," he replies.

"Madison, Madison?" I don't know his ex's last name, so this is the only way I can think to clarify her.

176

When he nods, I swallow. I don't know why finding out she's here made my throat dry suddenly.

"Did you know she was coming?" I ask.

"No."

"When did she get here?"

"About an hour ago."

"What's she doing here?"

This question takes him a little while longer to answer. He drops his gaze down to the deck, studying it as if there's something much more interesting down there than floorboards.

"She misses me," he says.

She misses him. Is she here to get him back? Is he going to take her back? Does he miss her? So many questions fill my head, but I want the answer to one the most: Why are these possibilities making my stomach twist and turn?

Am I annoyed because I cut off my time with Sky to get to the fire with Jesse only to find Jesse hosting Madison and not thinking about me or the fire at all? Am I feeling protective of Jesse because I want to make sure he's not going to get his heart broken again? Or am I . . . I don't think I can finish the last thought.

But it pops into my head nonetheless.

Am I jealous?

My stomach sinks. Is this the real reason I kept pushing Sky away all night? Is this why I couldn't get Jesse out of my mind? Do I have feelings for him?

"Is she staying with you?" I ask.

Jesse nods, and this bothers me way more than it should. So much so that it lets me know without a shadow of a doubt that I am jealous.

Shit!

"I'm sorry. I should probably get back inside," Jesse says.

I just nod. I'm sort of relieved because I can't talk right now. I need to think. Or cry. Or sleep. Probably a little bit of all three.

Jesse walks slowly to the door. I'm waiting to hear the twist of the doorknob, but instead I hear him say, "Harper?"

"Yeah?" Now I'm the one studying the deck. For the record, it's not interesting.

"I did sit by the fire," he says. Then he opens the door and steps inside.

—

I don't know why Jesse told me that, but I can think of two possible reasons. One, he was trying to let me know he was hurt I wasn't here and that our streak is over and it's my fault. Or two, he was trying to let me know he did his part and that if I make another fire and do mine, we can still sustain our streak.

I do not want to make a fire right now. I want to head back to my room and crawl under my covers and not come out until I feel more sorted. But for a reason I don't want to analyze too closely, I don't let myself do what I want to do. I push myself to gather the wood and make an outdoor fire.

I set my timer once the flames get going and stand as close as I can to the heat because it's late and freezing. I'm there exactly fifteen minutes. No more. No less. Then I grab a bucket from inside, fill it with water, and put the fire out.

twenty-three

I didn't sleep well last night, which I guess was to be expected. While my heart was exhausted, my mind was wide awake, trying to decipher if I was tossing and turning because of what happened with Sky or with Jesse.

I woke up wishing I could call Sky, which I took as a good sign. It made me realize I am excited about our potential. I *want* to still want Sky. I want that new beginning on Christmas Eve. I hope that in his letter to me this week he tells me he still loves the idea too, and we really do go back to the way things were before he showed up yesterday and ambushed me.

But I also woke up wondering what was going on inside Jesse's cottage, and praying that Jesse and Madison were doing nothing more than talking. Which is a bad sign because it means I do have feelings for Jesse. And I don't want them. I don't want to see him as anything more than a friend. The friendship the two of us have is good. Strike that, it's great! It's one of the best friendships I've ever had. I don't want things with us to change, and they would change if I leaned into my feelings or ever admitted them out loud.

Besides, Jesse is possibly reconciling with Madison, and I've got Sky—and that only makes my feelings more complicated.

With all this commotion going on in my head, I tried to ignore my emotions all morning. As I was dressing, I did my best to focus on the present moment as I've been practicing in yoga. And when that didn't work, I tried to focus on Sky. But no matter where I tried to direct my thoughts, I still found myself listening to the low murmur of conversation in Jesse's cottage, and my stomach took a nosedive every time I wondered if (and when) I'd start hearing other noises.

Eventually, I decided I had to leave. I needed fresh air. I needed to get busy.

What I didn't need was for Jesse to decide that today was "bring your ex-girlfriend to work" day. He invited Madison to join us in all of our usual duties.

She was there with us in the barn as we fed the goats and chickens. She was there when we made breakfast. And now she's accompanying Jesse on his wood-chopping duty and other daily tasks while I check in guests and attempt to mentally check out from this hellish day that's only half over.

I wish I knew how long Madison was staying and what was going on between the two of them, but I haven't had a chance to talk to Jesse in private. I also wish Madison wasn't so nice. I was hoping I wouldn't like her so that if Jesse asked me what I thought of her, I could tell him it wasn't worth giving her a second chance. But if he were to ask me at this point, I couldn't say that in good conscience. I don't know her well enough to know whether or not she is a good match for Jesse, and I still don't like what Jesse told me about her leaving for New York without him, but I'm not seeing any major red flags in terms of her personality.

Which isn't to say I want to become best friends with her. But I would like to go back to being best friends with Jesse, and if there's any hope of that, I need to get away from the inn for a minute before these feelings I'm having grow even more complex.

As soon as I'm done hosting happy hour, I walk straight into town to get dinner. Alone. I finish my entire meal even though I'm not hungry, just to eat up time. Then I order dessert. I don't attempt a single bite, but I stare at it for a while until the waitress comes over with a box and asks if I want to take it to go. I'd tell her I'd like to stay and stare at it for a while longer if the place weren't about to close, but it is, and I'm the last one here.

Since it's late, I call an Uber and have the driver drop me off at the inn. Once he does, I see the fire outside is made. No one is sitting at it. I don't know if Jesse sat out there already or not. In case he did, I clock in for exactly fifteen minutes, again by myself. And then I hurry to my cottage and turn off the lights.

—

When I wake the next morning, I'm expecting to feel better, but I feel even worse than I did last night. I'm in such a bad headspace, in fact, that I do something I haven't done since I arrived at the inn: I tell Jesse I need the day off. He's in the barn with Madison when I walk in and say so. As soon as I do, he stops collecting the eggs and rises to his feet.

"Are you feeling okay?" he asks, approaching me.

"I don't know," I say, because it's not a lie. I don't know what I feel, but I know it's not great.

"Do you need anything?"

Before I can answer, I spy Madison, out of the corner of my eye, picking up Xylo.

Not fucking Xylo!

This makes me way more upset than it should. But come on!

There are twenty-five other chickens, you know. Get your own favorite chicken, Madison!

I just had an argument with Jesse's ex. Over a chicken. In my head. That very well could be my low point over the past forty-eight hours.

I decide then I need to go into town again.

"No, thanks, Jesse," I say. "I'll be fine."

Not long after, I walk into Milk & Maple and get a latte, which reminds me of Sky. I check to see if he's written me even though it's

181

not Wednesday. He hasn't. I contemplate writing to him but decide that could be disastrous. My feelings are too all over the place. Until I nail them down, I should steer clear of expressing myself.

After that, I wander into the bookstore and select a novel, which reminds me of Jesse. I leave the bookstore at a near run, then wander into every other store in town. I text Zoe and Grace and tell them I can't wait to see them next week. I don't fill them in yet. I can't even wrap my own head around it. I spend a lot of time wishing next week were this week. I wonder if Madison will still be here next week. I spend a lot of time hoping she's not.

It's a small town, and after a couple of hours I've done everything one could possibly do in it, so I decide to face the inn. I'm not sure what I'll do there the rest of the day. Sleep, maybe, if my brain will let me.

As I'm walking, a car pulls up beside me and I hear its window roll down. I should look over. What if I'm about to be kidnapped? Well, at least then I wouldn't have to run into Madison and Jesse again.

My sense of humor sucks right now.

"Harper?" I hear a voice from the car say. I know that voice, which means I know that there's a green Jeep Cherokee beside me and that Jesse is driving it. The only reason I still don't look over is because I'm worried Madison is in the car too, and right now, I don't think my heart can take seeing the two of them together.

"It's just me," Jesse says a beat later, so I do stop and look. I don't know if Madison left or she just didn't accompany him on his car ride. I'm too afraid to ask because it will show that I care, and I'm afraid to show Jesse that I care because for starters, I'm not sure I *should* care. I still have feelings for Sky. Those didn't just disappear, and these feelings for Jesse might. They came out of nowhere. What if they just as easily vanish? Sure, that seems unlikely, given that I haven't just met Jesse. I know him—better than I know Sky. And I'm pretty sure my feelings are based on all that I know. Still, there's a chance they could tone back down to a friend level. And I'm hoping that's what happens. Because then everything can stay the same. Besides . . . what if Jesse doesn't have any feelings for me? Then I'll have embarrassed myself and ruined our friendship for no reason.

"Want a ride?" he asks.

"I'm okay walking," I say, even though I'm tired of walking and tired of not talking to Jesse too.

"You sure?"

"Yeah, I'm fine." These are the first lies I've ever blatantly told Jesse, and they feel terrible.

"Get in the car, Harper."

"Okay." I like that he knew I was lying. I also like that he called me out for it. I've never wanted to be called out for a lie before, but I did just then.

As soon as I climb into his car, he pulls a U-turn so he's heading away from the inn. I don't know where he's taking us. I don't ask. I don't speak a word. And neither does Jesse. I'm not saying anything because I'm not sure where to start. So much has happened since Jesse and I have had a *real* conversation. Sky visited. Madison visited or is still visiting (I still don't know). We went two nights without sitting by the fire together. I realized I have feelings for Jesse. The list goes on.

I have no idea why Jesse isn't saying anything. I also still have no idea where he's headed. I let him continue a few more miles before I finally ask.

"Where are we going?"

He doesn't turn his head even though I'm looking at him. "Item number nineteen."

"What?"

He takes one hand off the steering wheel and runs it through his hair. "A road trip with no destination in mind."

My bucket list.

Jesse is helping me check an item off my bucket list. Right now. Even after everything over the past few days.

I want to hug him because this is exactly what I didn't know I needed. But then it hits me that I also want to kiss him. The way he shows up for me, the way he knows me, the way he always seems to want what's best for me—all of these things put together make it impossible not to have feelings for him. Even when I don't want to have feelings for him. Even when I shouldn't have feelings for him.

"Why do you look upset?" Now Jesse's looking at me and I'm the one with eyes fixed on the road.

"I'm not upset," I say. It's my third lie. Jesse sees right through this one too.

"Fine, I'll admit it first," he says. "*I'm* upset."

"You are?" I've never seen Jesse upset. Maybe this is why I didn't recognize this emotion on him.

"You completely blew off the fire," he says.

So he *was* disappointed. I knew it.

"I tried to apologize," I say. "And I lit a fire and sat out there alone after you went inside."

"I know," he says. "I saw."

"You saw?" *He saw?*

He nods. "I even set my own timer to make sure you didn't cheat."

That he did this and admitted it makes me smile. "I didn't cheat last night either," I say. "I sat out there then too."

"I know," he says, gripping the steering wheel tighter. "I sat out there last night before you, and I left the fire burning in case you showed up. I saw you sit down for fifteen minutes when that Uber dropped you off."

Now I'm not smiling. I'm blushing. *Both* nights he was in his room with Madison, he was watching me, suggesting he was more concerned with maintaining our ritual than with what was happening between the two of them. Which makes me think nothing was going on with Madison.

"Did you get back together with Madison?" I can't help blurting this out.

"Are you and Sky together?"

"I asked you first."

Wait, why did he ask about Sky? Does he care if I'm with Sky? The tone of his voice implied he does care. Why would he care unless he was jealous of Sky the same way I was jealous of Madison? Was that why he was acting strange the whole time Sky was here? Does Jesse have feelings for me too?

Jesse pulls over to the side of the road. I look around. I have no idea why he's choosing to stop right here. We're in the middle of nowhere. I guess it is a road trip with no destination in mind. I conclude right then and there that road trips with no destinations are overrated. I'll be sure to write that down when I cross it off my list.

"I told Madison I don't have feelings for her anymore," Jesse says. He doesn't need to be concentrating on the road anymore, but he is. I don't know if this is because the decision was difficult and talking about it is tough, or if it's because he's nervous to see my reaction to his confession.

I can't say I care. I'm just glad he's not looking at me because I'm so relieved, I can only imagine it's written all over my face. If he were to look over and see that, he'd know how I feel, and I still don't know if I want him to know.

"She kept trying to apologize," he goes on. "And I told her I forgave her. I just . . . I wasn't into her like that anymore."

"Then why did she stay so long?"

Jesse takes his hands off the steering wheel and sets them in his lap, studying them as he answers me. "Madison's always been confident. She saw the whole thing going differently in her head. She assumed I would want another shot. So she didn't have a return flight. When I told her the first night she was here that it wasn't going to happen between us, she tried to find a flight out the next morning but couldn't get one until this afternoon."

"So she's gone?" I clarify.

"Yeah, she's gone."

After he's answered me, he finally looks at me. "Why did you call me your coworker in front of Sky?"

I nearly shut my eyes just to hide from Jesse. "I . . . I don't know."

"Harper."

"It just came out. I didn't understand why I said it." Except now I know things about myself that I didn't then. "You know what you mean to me, but I think I . . . I—"

"—wanted to distance yourself from me in front of Sky," Jesse finishes.

"Maybe." I swallow. Then, in a rush, I add, "In case he was the jealous type."

At this, Jesse says nothing.

Does he think I was just worried Sky would be jealous of *any* guy, or is he thinking it's more specific than that?

Because now I know the reason I told Sky that Jesse was my coworker was because I didn't want Sky to question my relationship with Jesse.

"What happened with Sky?"

I should have predicted this question. I reach up and rub my temples, feeling like a terrible person for sitting here so grateful that Jesse told Madison there was no chance of tomorrow when I didn't say the same to Sky. I told him the opposite.

To cut myself some slack, my feelings for Jesse didn't occur to me until after I told Sky I still want the promise of a someday. But in my next email to Sky, I intended to tell him that I'm still looking forward to Christmas Eve. I've been pressing forward, determined to keep our pact and hopeful about what could develop between us. Would this change if Jesse were to admit he has feelings for me? I wish I knew the answer, but I don't.

"The trip didn't go like either of us expected," I answer honestly. "But I think we're still considering sticking to our pact."

Jesse doesn't react. I wish he would so I could get a better read on him. Better yet, I wish he'd just confess his feelings for me if they exist. But how can I expect him to do something I'm not willing to do myself?

"I told you I was upset with you about the fire when Sky was here," Jesse says. "But why were *you* upset when Madison was here?"

I swallow. I can't answer that. Not without admitting my true feelings. But I also can't deny I was upset. Jesse would see straight through that lie. I didn't exactly hide it well.

I shift in my seat.

"Why, Harper?" he presses.

When I fix my eyes on Jesse, he seems to be sitting closer. Or maybe he's always been this close and it just feels as if he's closer because our eyes are locked and I'm sensing he wants me to admit I was jealous. I'm also sensing that if I were to tell him how I feel, he would kiss the hell out of me right here, right now. The way my heart pounds at the thought tells me I'd like that. *A lot.*

But would that be for the best? Or would it ruin everything?

So many answers are on the tip of my tongue. Why was I upset?

"Because Madison being here made me insanely jealous and realize that I like you as way more than a friend."

"Because from the moment I've met you I've been trying not to have feelings for you, and I thought I was doing a damn good job, but now look at me!"

"Because I'm supposed to reunite with Sky on Christmas Eve, and part of my heart feels like it still wants that, but another part of my heart can't imagine not spending Christmas Eve with you."

But I don't say any of these things.

187

Instead I say, "Because I didn't want to see you get hurt."

Jesse blinks. "Are you sure that's the only reason?"

I wasn't expecting him to press me. But I think him doing so means he does have feelings. Feelings that he'd like to explore. I'd like to explore them too. I nearly open my mouth to admit it.

But in the back of my head there's this pilot whom I've been emailing every week. One who flew all the way out here a few days ago to apologize in person because he likes me *that* much. One who I made a promise to before I met the man in front of me.

Because of him, I can't do it.

"I'm sure." This time when I lie, I hope Jesse believes me.

twenty-four

I decide to spend as little time with Jesse as possible until I can sort out my feelings. It isn't easy, but it's the right thing to do for everyone's sake. Except for cooking breakfast together and sitting by the fire for fifteen minutes every night (Jesse and I decided our streak could continue even though we each sat out there two nights alone), I do my own thing.

I try not to analyze how Jesse feels. I try just to home in on how I feel about Sky. That's what I need to do first. Unfortunately, without Sky here, it's hard to get clarity on my feelings. When I'm with Sky, there's this dynamic current between us. Sky makes me adventurous and flirty and fun. And I like that. But then I remember how off we were at times on his surprise visit, and I don't know if that was the shock of it or something else. So, for a few days, nothing progresses.

But come Wednesday, I do get clarity on *his* feelings when I get another letter. In it he sounds so normal, so like the Sky I first met—it's almost as if his trip out here didn't even happen. He stresses that he's still just as excited about Christmas Eve as he was before his visit. He even says he's sorry he didn't give me the same reassurance I gave him before we parted ways that night.

I flinch slightly when I read that apology. Then I push my doubt aside and write him back, keeping it light and normal too. I don't say anything about how confused I am because I don't want to plant seeds of doubt in his mind if I don't have to. And I don't know that I need to. I think. Well, I just really don't know.

One thing I do know is that there has never been a time in my life where I've been looking forward to seeing my best friends more. The timing couldn't be better for their arrival.

They were originally thinking to come for Thanksgiving since they both have more days off work for the holiday, but prices for plane tickets were crazy, and even though we're as close as family, we decided it was silly for them to miss celebrating with their parents and siblings, who are all in Atlanta. Grace is also married with a baby on the way, and I told her she shouldn't miss this holiday with her husband, Noah. They opted to fly out two weekends before instead. Though they're only staying for two nights, at this point, I'll take whatever amount of friend time I can get.

"You're here!" I squeal, wrapping them in a group hug as soon as they step out of their rental car.

"We're here!" echoes Grace. "Look at this place!" It's a cold day, but with clear skies, so the property is shining. "Look at you!" she says, giving me a once-over.

"Look at *you*!" I reply. Though it's still too early in her pregnancy for her to be showing, her face is glowing.

"Look at *him* . . ." says Zoe.

When I shoot a glance over my shoulder, I see Jesse walking toward us. *In his damn cutoff shirt.*

I've filled Zoe and Grace in a little via text about Sky's visit, Madison's visit, and how I'm now conflicted about my feelings for Sky and for Jesse. They know I'm pining for their advice on who I should choose while they're here, and I'm pretty sure Zoe just chose her side.

"You must be Zoe and Grace," Jesse says. "I've heard so much about you both." I had no idea how Jesse would act around my friends since we've only spoken about their arrival in terms of logistics: how many nights they're staying, what room we're putting them in. But he's acting normal, like the Jesse I first befriended, and a tenderness I'm not sure I want blooms once again in my stomach.

"Congrats on your exciting news," he tells Grace. I mentioned she was pregnant over a month ago. He remembered. Of course, he remembered.

"Thank you." Grace smiles as she places a hand on her stomach, and I can tell he's having an effect on her too. But Sky is at a slight disadvantage because he's not here. At least now my friends will understand the reality of my dilemma when I lay everything out on the table for them later this afternoon.

We make small talk in a circle about Zoe and Grace's flight here and how things have been going in Atlanta since I left. Then Jesse and I tell them about life at the inn. All our stories take place prior to this past week, and recalling our good memories causes even more tenderness to sweep over me. The feeling is followed by a burst of nostalgia for the way things were before I started to develop feelings I didn't know what to do with.

I'm relieved when Jesse tells us he should get back to work because seeing him be *my* Jesse again is too much. I can't handle it.

"I'll take up your luggage," Jesse tells Zoe and Grace when they open the car to get their things. "I'm sure Harper is anxious to show you around the property."

We all thank him as we turn to leave, but before we get very far I hear Jesse say, "Hey, Harper?"

"Yeah?" When I turn back around, his eyes find mine—really find mine—for the first time since we were on that car ride without a destination, and my entire body fills with a longing I can't describe.

"I can cover for you for happy hour tonight," he says, "if you want to take your friends into town."

I swallow and nod. "Thank you, Jesse," I say. Or maybe that's not what I say. The truth is, I'm too distracted by what's going on in my heart to pay attention to anything going on in my head.

191

—

"Okay, I'm just going to say it," Zoe says once we're seated in a booth at Harrison's, an upscale American restaurant known for its comfort food, where we settled on for lunch. "I like the innkeeper. And *you* like the innkeeper."

I'm honestly surprised it took her until we got into town to speak up. I was sure she would blurt out something to this effect on our tour of the property or during the car ride here. Likely the only reason she held out was because she knew it was going to prompt a long discussion and so waited till we had the time for it.

My eyes well up, and Zoe must notice because she rushes to apologize. "Oh, I'm sorry. I thought you wanted us to weigh in!"

"I do," I say, as she hands me a napkin. "It's just that I don't *want* to like the innkeeper."

"Because of the pilot?" clarifies Zoe, as she twists her long, dark hair up into a bun.

"Exactly. I *want* to like the pilot. I met the pilot first. The pilot is great."

"I like the pilot too," offers Grace. I forwarded parts of my emails between Sky and me to Zoe and Grace in preparation for this discussion.

"It's not that I don't also like the pilot," adds Zoe. "I'm just saying we shouldn't rule out the innkeeper."

"I know," I sigh, my frustration growing. "I have no idea what to do."

Grace reaches over and rests a hand on top of mine as our food arrives: soup and salad for us all. Once the waitress leaves, Grace says, "Do you have to focus so much on figuring that out? I thought you came here for you."

I'm almost embarrassed when she calls me out for this. But she's right. Here I am stressing about two guys when I didn't come here for a guy. I came here for me.

"You're right," I say. "You're totally right."

We spend the next half hour talking about the progress I've made. I tell them about the items I've crossed off my bucket list. I tell them that while I haven't found my passion, I do like it here. I tell them I value my work at the inn and the slow pace of life that comes with living in a small town.

And then I get caught up to speed on everything going on with them. Grace tells me she has some challenging new therapy clients. She can't go into detail, which suits her fine because she doesn't want to. On the home front, she and Noah have painted their nursery yellow and have picked out baby names: Leslie if it's a girl, Lucas if it's a boy.

Zoe then fills me in about a recent yoga retreat she hosted at her studio and about the dentist she just started dating. "I cracked a tooth. And it was the best worst thing to ever happen to me," she says.

I smile and reiterate how happy I am they're both here. There's something about sitting with good friends—you feel as if all is right in the world. Or will be all right.

We continue catching up in the comfort of our booth long after the check has been paid, and then we walk around downtown for the remainder of the afternoon, popping in and out of all the shops. Both Zoe and Grace pick up sweatshirts and other Stowe souvenirs from The Country Store on Main. They plan to give them as Christmas presents for loved ones back home. Then we opt for a late-afternoon coffee at Milk & Maple.

Once dinnertime comes around, we decide to try another new restaurant, Whip Bar and Grill, and although it's lovely and the food is delicious, we eat quickly because the girls are tired from the long day and tell me they want to retire early.

When we pull back into the inn, it's just past nine o'clock. I glance at the fire pit and notice Jesse sitting out there by himself. It's later in the evening than it usually is when we sit out there, but he had to cover my evening duties and his, so it makes sense that he's just now getting around to it.

"I need to join him," I say, nodding to the fire once we climb out of the car. "Just for fifteen minutes. Do you two want to join before you call it a night?"

"Isn't that *your* special ritual?" Zoe says. I've told them both about it over text.

"Yeah, but you're our guests. You're more than welcome to join."

Zoe pulls her jacket tighter around her chest. "I flew here to catch up with my best friend, not catch hypothermia, so I think I'll pass."

"That claw foot bathtub in our room is calling my name," says Grace.

"Okay. I'll meet you up there," I say. We already decided at dinner I'd sleep on their fold-out couch at the foot of their two queen-sized beds. Their trip isn't long enough for us to spend any of the hours apart.

"How many minutes did I miss?" I ask Jesse when I approach the fire.

"Three," he tells me. "I'll restart my timer."

"You don't have to. I can just wait out here for three minutes after you finish up."

"Already reset," he says.

I nod and take the seat beside him, reaching for a blanket to drape around my legs.

"How was town?" he asks.

"Nice," I say. "How did happy hour go?"

"Fine."

"Thanks again for covering for me."

"No worries."

This conversation is so not like us, it makes me cringe. I can tell it's making Jesse cringe too. He's not even attempting to hide it. He was just shaking his head, and now he's rubbing a hand down his face and getting to his feet. "Look, Harper," he says. "We need to talk."

194

"I know," I whisper. He's right. We can't keep tiptoeing around each other.

"I was jealous." He blows out a breath as if he's struggled with keeping this in as much as I have. "When Sky showed up, I was jealous. When you gave him a tour, I was jealous. When you went to dinner instead of being at the fire, I was jealous. Every time I saw him touch you, I was so *goddamn* jealous."

He's pacing back and forth, his movements quick and jerky. Suddenly, he stops and whirls around, his eyes slamming into mine. I think I stop breathing, but I'm not sure because he looks as if he's about to say something every part of me wants to hear.

"I like you, Harper," he says, and there's such certainty behind the statement that it punches me in the chest. "I like you as way more than a friend. I like you like I could fall for you."

I'm feeling his confession everywhere. It's thirty-two degrees out, and I might need to strip off a layer. Or several layers.

I didn't realize how badly I wanted these words until they came out of his mouth.

I don't know what he sees in my face, but he shuts his eyes for a moment, and when he opens them he says, "I know you have an arrangement with Sky, and I respect that and don't want to get in the way of it if being with Sky is what you want. The last thing I want to do is to get in the way of what you want, Harper. I will bury my feelings, if that's what you want me to do."

I know he would. That's just who Jesse is. He puts other people first.

"But I needed to share this because I want you to know that if there's any part of you that has feelings for me too, then my hat's also in the ring. I will wait for you too."

A beat goes by, then another, and he breaks eye contact with me and half turns away.

"You don't need to respond if there's nothing to say," he says. "It's okay. It'll be okay. I just had to say it once."

But I do need to respond. I've been so worried about not being fair to Sky, but not saying anything in this moment wouldn't be fair to Jesse.

"I wasn't completely honest with you in the car," I confess. He faces me again, and I push the rest of the words out. "I was jealous of Madison. And my feelings didn't just appear when she got here. They've been developing for awhile, but that's when I realized how strong they were, because for the first time I couldn't ignore or excuse or fight them."

I watch as Jesse lets out a quiet exhale.

"I don't know what to do with this, Jesse," I continue. "I'm not with Sky, but I feel I've made a commitment to him, and I do have a connection with him. I'm really confused, but I need you to know that your feelings aren't one-sided. I just need you to know that."

When I finish my confession, I drop my head into my hands because I don't know how to handle any of this. I feel frustrated and exhausted.

I hear Jesse walk back to his chair beside mine and sit down. Then I feel the weight of a steady, comforting hand on my back, and I know Jesse will stay here like this as long as I need.

It makes me want to cry.

It makes me want to kiss him.

Dammit.

When I lift my head from my hands, I see he's closer than I anticipated. Close enough that it wouldn't take much for my lips to find his.

"Did you almost kiss me in the car?" I ask. I know the last thing I should be doing right now is asking for more confirmation of Jesse's feelings, but I haven't been able to get that question off my mind.

"It took everything in me not to kiss you, Harper." Jesse brings his forehead close to mine. "It's taking everything in me not to kiss you now."

My heart is pounding so hard I can hear it thrumming in my ears. I half want to say, "Just kiss me, then," and I half want to leave.

I should leave. I battle with myself as the timer goes off. Maybe it's a sign, but neither one of us shifts an inch.

I don't know how long we stay like that, letting the timer blare.

"I need to think," I finally whisper against his lips.

"Okay," he breathes against mine.

I do not know how he finds the strength to do what I can't, but a beat later he gets to his feet. He shuts off the timer. And then he walks away from me. By the time he's halfway back to his cottage, it occurs to me that he was able to find that strength because he cares for me. And because he meant what he said: he will bury his feelings if that's what I want. He will give me whatever I want.

I'm as relieved as I am disappointed. And I have no idea where that leaves me.

—

Zoe and Grace don't ask about the fire when I get upstairs, even though I was out there much longer than fifteen minutes. I don't offer any details because I'm still processing everything that just happened. Instead, we talk about our plans for tomorrow as we get ready for bed. I propose that we hang around the inn all day so they can accompany me on my normal routine and we can make dinner after happy hour in the parlor.

They both tell me they love that idea, although they sound so tired I think they'd agree to just about anything. They've already buried themselves under the covers.

Zoe made up my bed on the sofa, so I get under the covers after brushing my teeth even though I feel wide awake. We all mutter goodnight, and a few minutes later I hear Zoe's signature heavy breathing and nothing from Grace, which means she's probably passed out too. Grace has always slept in complete silence with both hands crossed over her chest like a mummy.

I roll over onto my side, which is how I usually like to fall asleep, but that doesn't seem to help. My mind is still racing.

It strikes me that this is the first time in more than eight weeks that I won't be sleeping next to Jesse. Not *next to him, next to him*, obviously. I just mean in the cottage beside him. There's always been something comforting about knowing he's just a few feet away. I didn't realize just how comforting until now, when I'm here and he's on the other side of the property. What does that mean? What does that tell me?

I roll onto my back again and start my staring contest with the ceiling, thinking of Sky's cute snore as well as our night together in his room and all the letters he's written me. Those still make me smile with a giddy sense of joy. What does *that* mean? What does *that* tell me?

My mind jumps to an unpleasant memory: when Jake left me right before our wedding. I remember him telling me that the choice was incredibly difficult, that his heart was being pulled in two directions. I thought he was just saying that to soften the blow of his decision and maybe justify his broken promise to me. I thought it wasn't possible to have a heart as conflicted as he described. But I believe him now. I understand in a way I didn't before. And maybe that's all I'm going to get tonight: better understanding of how my last chapter ended, not clarity on how this one will play out.

twenty-five

Having Zoe and Grace help Jesse and me the following day is amazing—not because we need the extra hands but because having them around makes it easier for Jesse and me to act normal around each other. Without them, we'd probably have to talk more about what happened last night. Or I'd avoid him again until I had more time to process my feelings. But their presence allows us to focus on showing them a good time, and consequently we get back into a comfortable rhythm. In fact, today I feel I have my third best friend back, and I couldn't be more grateful.

This makes me really wish Jesse and I could go back to just being friends. Wouldn't that be the best of both worlds? I could be with Sky, hang out with Jesse, and not have to lose either of them.

But as the day goes on, I come to understand that even if I could shake my romantic feelings for Jesse and kept working at the inn beyond December, the dynamic between us wouldn't stay the same. Because if Sky were to become a more prominent part of the picture, I would devote most of my free time to him, not Jesse. And, in time, Jesse would meet someone else, and that woman would consume a lot of his time. I know I wouldn't like that. The extent to which I know I wouldn't makes me think my feelings for Jesse are here to stay. And I hate that realization because it means there is no best of both worlds.

"Do you want to join us for dinner?" Zoe asks Jesse after happy hour ends. "We're making salad and pasta."

Jesse poked his head into the inn's kitchen to check on us just as we started cooking. I should have been the one to extend the

199

invitation, but since I wasn't, I reiterate Zoe's invite so he knows he's welcome.

"Sure." He shrugs now that he knows I'm comfortable with it. "Why not?"

He offers to help cook, which is nice because it makes the process go by quickly and gives us all more time to stand around and talk while we wait for the lasagna to bake. Jesse seems to enjoy Zoe and Grace's company as much as I do, and the feeling on their part appears mutual. Several times, my mind jumps ahead and pictures all of us hanging out years from now—here in this kitchen and in Atlanta at Grace's house or Zoe's. I don't know if this will happen, but I can see it so clearly.

I feel bad then that Sky hasn't had the opportunity to meet my friends. I know they'd like him too. He's such a natural charmer that I can see them laughing alongside him.

But Sky isn't here.

And he hasn't been here.

Just the *idea* of him has been here. But that was my decision, not his. And even with his absence, even with our pause, he's a damn good idea. So good that even though I'm feeling the way I am about Jesse, I'm still hanging on to the promise of a someday with Sky.

Ugh! I'm so tired of not knowing what to do.

Once the food is ready, we carry it into the parlor and take a seat at one of the tables. Jesse and I sit opposite each other, and Zoe and Grace do the same. Jesse reaches for the bottle of wine at the center of the table and takes the liberty of filling all our glasses. Once he's finished, he surprises me by getting to his feet and raising his glass.

"I'd like to make a toast," he says. Jesse isn't one for speeches, although he did give quite the speech at the fire last night. I push that out of my mind and refocus.

"To Zoe and Grace," he begins, smiling at them both. "I'm so glad you're here and that I've had the opportunity to meet Harper's closest friends. I hope you two know you always have a free place to stay whenever you want to make the trip."

I feel a flutter in my chest. Being nice and inclusive to a girl's friends isn't a love language, but if it were, it'd rank high on my list.

"And to Harper," Jesse says, turning his attention across the table to me. My heart begins pounding in earnest as I wait for him to say more.

But he doesn't.

I'm not sure if he was planning to and lost his train of thought or if saying my name was all he could say. It doesn't matter. Because somehow the way he said my name seems to affect me as much as—if not more than—it would have had he used all the words in the English dictionary.

—

"That man is in love with you," Grace says once we're in bed with the lights out following dinner, dessert, and a fifteen-minute stint at the fire. (Zoe and Grace joined Jesse and I this go-round, although begrudgingly. They did not see what the hype was about and voiced several times that our plan was crazy.)

"I think you might be right," I say. I haven't had a chance today to tell them what happened at the fire last night, but I share the details now.

Once I finish, Zoe reaches for one of her pillows and throws it at me. "I can't believe you didn't tell us this sooner!"

"I'm sorry," I say, dodging it. "I was processing."

"That was very selfish of you." Grace throws her pillow my way too. "Next time process your thoughts out loud. Because we are *here* for these Jesse details."

"But what about Sky?" I groan.

"I'm here for those details too," Grace says.

"Yeah, I definitely haven't minded those either," pipes in Zoe.

"So what should I do?"

When neither of them responds, I throw their pillows back at them. "If you want me to process my thoughts out loud, you need to weigh in on my dilemma."

"I wish we could," Grace says with a sigh. "But we can't answer that question for you."

I moan and roll away from them, feeling even more lost. I was really hoping for some guidance.

"What I *can* say," she continues, "is that I've known you most of my life, and I've never seen you more lit up than you were today. I don't think it's because of either one of these men, Harper. I think it's because you followed your heart here, and that was a good decision for you. Just trust you'll make the next right decision by the time Christmas Eve rolls around."

I've heard a lot of good speeches since I got here, both from Sky and from Jesse. But this speech from Grace takes the cake. It was exactly what I needed to hear. It was the perfect reminder for this moment.

I sit up and turn back toward Zoe and Grace.

"I have the best friends in the world, don't I?" I say. While I may not be clear on my feelings when it comes to my romantic life at the moment, my feelings about the two people in front of me couldn't be clearer.

"Hell yeah, you do!" Zoe replies.

This time I take my own pillow and chuck it at her bed.

"I was waiting for that," Grace laughs.

twenty-six

Zoe and Grace are gone, and Jesse and I (and the guests) are alone again. At least until Thanksgiving, which is in a week and a half. Then Jesse's parents will join us, which I'm looking forward to, and the guests will clear out for the holiday and the day after, giving us a break.

Closing down for Thanksgiving and the following day is a tradition Jesse's parents established when they were running the inn, and they recommended Jesse and I continue it. They said at our dinner together that the tradition was always the break they needed before shifting into high gear to prepare for the Christmas season. Plus, the few years they did stay open for Thanksgiving, the inn was less than half full, so they reasoned it wasn't a big deal to shut their doors and fully enjoy Turkey Day with family.

I'm a little uneasy about how things will go between Jesse and me during the period when it's just the two of us. Now that his feelings for me are out there, my feelings for him have expanded so much, and it's getting harder for me not to act on those feelings, even if I don't want to. And I don't—not unless I come to the conclusion that I'm more curious about a possible future with him than I am with Sky. Because I would hate to lead Jesse on. I won't.

I mention this to Jesse two nights after Zoe and Grace have left, and he tells me that he'll take his cues from me, which makes me feel a little better. But the following night, I begin to question my own resolve when Jesse and I end up in the hot tub following our coldest night ever at the fire.

Jesse in a cutoff shirt gets to me.

203

Jesse with his *entire shirt* off gives me a whole other set of feelings, and I'm pretty sure he can see these feelings all over my face as I sink into the bubbles beside him.

"I still don't have my mind made up," I say, just so he's clear that our intense eye contact is not an invitation. It's not going to lead to anything more.

"I figured," he says. "It's only been one day since you last told me you needed more time to think."

"It feels longer," I say. Maybe because resisting my feelings just became ten times harder. The jets have kicked on, Jesse is leaning his head back, and he just let out an "ahh" sound that makes me think I'm a complete goner. Two seconds later he half-moans an "oh yeah," and I sink down lower until my lips and ears are underneath the water.

When I finally come up for air, Jesse's staring at me again. When I notice his eyes briefly dip to my lips, it takes everything in me not to close the gap between us, because *holy hell* I want to know what it's like to kiss Jesse.

I bet he kisses as intentionally as he speaks. I bet he'd mutter something incredibly sweet into my mouth before he slipped in his tongue. I bet once we started kissing we wouldn't be able to stop, and it would lead to more things with hands and lips and moans.

"We're going to need a code word," I mutter, blinking. I set a boundary with Sky during our night together, and it's time to set a boundary with Jesse.

"For what?" He lifts an arm out of the water to run a hand through his hair. My eyes land on his bicep and linger.

"So that you and I don't kiss each other."

"I already told you I won't kiss you until you tell me that's what you want, Harper." He splashes some water my way as if to let me know I can lighten up.

"I'm not worried about *you* kissing *me*," I say. "I'm worried about *me* kissing *you*."

He doesn't respond right away. When he finally does, his voice is lower, less playful. "Doesn't the fact that you want to go there tell you something?"

It does. Of course, it does.

"If Sky weren't in the picture, there would be no part of me questioning my feelings for you, Jesse. But Sky is in the picture. I need to sit with all of this a little longer. It's been too much, too fast."

He nods as if he heard me. "What about *Xylo?*"

"What *about* Xylo?"

"For our code word," he clarifies. "Thinking about a chicken is a turnoff, isn't it?"

"Sort of, but she reminds me of you."

He grows pensive. "How about *bumfuzzle?*"

"What?" The corners of my mouth curl into a grin. I wasn't expecting him to say that given how serious he just sounded.

"I read it in a novel once and thought it was the funniest word I'd ever heard."

"What does it mean?"

"Confused."

"Very apropos," I admit.

He nods as if he hadn't thought of that.

"Try saying it without laughing," he encourages me.

"Bumfuzzle," I repeat and snort out a laugh less than one second later.

"You see." He brings his arms out of the water and drapes them around the ledge. "Now we've got nothing to worry about."

Only that's not entirely true because the way Jesse delivered that line gave me chills.

In a hot tub.

And when Jesse gets out and I get a last glimpse of his bare chest before he wraps himself in a towel, I mutter *bumfuzzle* to myself six times, and my feelings don't go anywhere.

So I'd say we have a lot to worry about. Or I do, at least.

I have a lot of thinking to do too.

—

Fortunately, come Thanksgiving Day, even though Jesse and I are spending the morning beside each other in the kitchen, we have so many dishes to prepare that I'm convinced there won't be time for any intimate moments.

At least I don't think so.

Jesse's parents are arriving at two, and knowing they're coming has been keeping both of our heads in the right place. This is also the second Thanksgiving Jesse and his parents have experienced without Brendan, and Brendan was big on the holidays, so Jesse's tone today is a little subdued.

"How are you feeling?" I check in with him as he dices the onions for the stuffing and I mash the potatoes. I already asked him this earlier this morning.

He gives me the same shoulder shrug as before. "Brendan would be in here right now making us Irish coffees."

"That was his contribution to the meal?"

"Yeah. He would make them every Thanksgiving, Christmas, and New Year's Eve. And Molly always made the stuffing on Thanksgiving. I'm using her recipe, but last year it tasted different than when she would make it. I have no idea why. It needs her touch, I guess."

He looks at me shyly. "Having you here makes it better than last year, though. I know my parents will feel the same way. My mom has mentioned several times how much she and my dad are looking forward to seeing you again."

206

I smile, glad I'm able to make things a little bit easier on everyone just by being around.

"Being with you guys is going to make the holiday easier on me as well," I say. "This is the first one I've spent away from my family."

My parents considered coming out, but they're hosting both sets of grandparents, who stopped traveling a couple years back due to various health conditions. I already explained this to Jesse.

"Do you want to call your parents?" he asks.

"Yeah, I might do that now, if that's okay?"

"Sure. I can handle things in the kitchen."

I wipe my hands off on a dish towel and head to the front desk, using the landline to dial. It's good to hear their voices once I get them on the phone. My grandparents are there already and it sounds as if everybody is having a good time, which warms my heart and makes me miss them. It doesn't make me wish I were there, though. I wish my parents and grandparents were *here*. I'd love to celebrate together, but I'm glad I'm celebrating in Vermont, at the inn. It really cements my feelings about this place. It feels like home, which is crazy because it's not home, or at least not a home I've known for very long. It's *become* home, though.

The thought momentarily crosses my mind that I might be leaving this home at the end of December, depending on whether or not Jesse's parents officially let him take over running the inn and who I realize I have stronger feelings for—Sky or Jesse. But I push the thought away because today is not a day to dwell on future decisions or anything stressful. Today is a day to celebrate and to be grateful for my many blessings.

—

Beth and Mark show up with several side dishes and a pie for dessert, even though Jesse and I told them we'd take care of everything.

"You can never have too much food on Thanksgiving," Beth tells me as she gives Jesse a hug and then comes over and embraces me.

Once Mark's given out his round of hugs, he decides to make Irish coffees in honor of Brendan, and we take the warm drinks from the kitchen into the parlor and sit on the sofas as we wait for the turkey to finish cooking.

When Jesse gets up to stoke the flames from the fire he started earlier today, Mark and Beth ask me about Zoe and Grace's visit. Jesse must still be talking to them daily if they know they were just here. I wonder if he told them about Sky's visit or Madison's, or if he mentioned that we seem to have feelings for each other that we're not sure what to do with. They don't inquire about those visits or that topic, so maybe not. Although if Jesse did tell them anything, they'd know better than to bring it up and potentially ruin our lovely afternoon.

It honestly couldn't be more enjoyable. We play board games and tell stories. Beth shares that she's picked up some hobbies lately, including knitting and archery, and Mark fills Jesse and me in about a trip the two of them are planning to take to Ireland in the new year.

"It was hard to travel while we were here," he says. "Probably the only downside of running this place. So we're excited to take more trips in the years to come."

Brendan comes up a couple of times once the turkey is carved and we are at the table eating. Beth wanted to hear some of my favorite Thanksgiving memories from years past, and after I shared a few, I felt weird not asking all of them to share theirs. Of course, all of their memories included Brendan. For the most part, everyone holds it together during those stories, and by the end of the meal we're commenting that years from now, when questioned about our favorite Thanksgiving memories, this year will be one we share unequivocally.

"Thank you," Jesse says as he and I wash the dishes while his parents bundle up to join us at the fire. They insisted on being part of our tradition tonight, even though the last time I looked out the window I saw a couple of snow flurries—the first of the season.

"For what?" I say as I hand him a soapy dish. I'm rinsing, he's loading into the dishwasher.

"For just being you. And for being here today. And for helping me run this place. I'm incredibly grateful you came into my life this year."

"I should be the one thanking you," I say. "For helping me with my bucket list. For welcoming me into your family. For being patient with me."

I dry my hands on a dish towel and reach for one of his hands to squeeze it. I only meant for the touch to be friendly, but my palm lingers in his a little longer than I intend, and then Jesse traces his thumb over mine, and neither of us can seem to let go. My stomach stirs and warmth spreads up my neck into my cheeks. If this is how much I feel for Jesse when I'm *resisting* my feelings, how much would I feel for him if I *leaned into* them?

I rest my forehead against his, wanting to find out the answer to that. But instead I mutter, "Bumfuzzle."

It works.

Thank God it works.

Jesse releases my hand and we both smile as we pull apart. I know nothing between us technically happened, but still, when we rejoin his parents, I feel as if I'm trying to hide a certain look on my face so they don't think something did. Because of how absorbed I am in that task, I almost don't hear it.

But Jesse hears it, and his parents hear it, and because they all start walking toward the front door, I turn my attention that direction, and then *I* hear it.

Someone is knocking.

I don't know why I feel as if I should be the one to get it. Maybe because they all look confused, as if they have no clue who it could be, and I've been surprised once before. I hurry in front of them and get to the handle first.

"Special delivery."

twenty-seven

"**Are** they from your parents?" Beth is standing beside me, admiring the bouquet arrangement as I set it down on the check-in desk.

I don't have to open the tiny note card sticking out of the flowers to know these are not from my parents. My parents would never send something this extravagant. They also wouldn't send roses because they know my favorite flower is a lily. But you know who doesn't know that and *would* send a bouquet as big as this? Only one name comes to mind.

I peek at the note card and read it fast: *A rose for every day since I've seen you last. Only one more holiday to go. Sky*

Oh, that's so . . . so . . . My heart can't find the right word. It doesn't know how to react.

"Yeah, they're from Mom and Dad," I lie. "They miss me and wanted to mark the holiday somehow."

"That is incredibly sweet."

Beth buys it. Mark buys it. But Jesse doesn't buy it, and I didn't expect him to. I see him swallow and tug on his shirt collar as if he could use some air.

"How about we get out to that fire, huh?" I suggest. I could use some air too.

Jesse and I end up across the fire from each other because of where his parents sit down, which sucks because I was hoping to whisper an apology in his ear. So I send my message across with my eyes, body language, and facial expressions instead, and Jesse picks up that I'm saying some version of "I'm sorry. I didn't know those were coming."

211

I read him as he silently communicates something back along the lines of "It's fine. I get it. I already told you I get it."

Me again: "It's *not* fine. That couldn't have been fun for you to see."

Now him: "It wasn't. But I can handle it."

Me one more time: "I don't want this to ruin tonight. Today has been so perfect."

Him: "It won't. Don't worry."

Now, somehow, Jesse and I are smiling and talking to his parents again, and we seem okay. And I think the rest of the night will be okay.

Beth and I discuss Christmas decorations for the inn as we sip on the cocktails Jesse made, and shiver as snow flurries land on our heads. On the other side of me, Mark playfully curses Brendan and Jesse for developing this tradition.

Once the timer sounds, we all hurry inside and warm up by the indoor fire. Mark stokes it as Jesse retreats to the kitchen to cut slices of apple pie. He carries them out in bowls with scoops of vanilla ice cream, and we savor each bite.

After we finish, Jesse and I clear the dishes, and then we walk Mark and Beth to the door so they can get home before the snow really starts coming down. While Mark gives Jesse a hug, Beth turns toward me.

"I know I said this before, honey, but I feel it's worth mentioning again: I've never seen Jesse so happy, and I know a big reason for that is because you're here."

Tears instantly spring to my eyes and I try to blink them away, but I don't do it fast enough.

"Is something wrong?" Beth asks.

No, I think. *Everything's right.* And that's why I'm crying. Because I still don't know what to do about that.

twenty-eight

When I wake up the day after Thanksgiving, I look out my window and see that the entire property is blanketed in white. I step into boots and walk out onto my patio in my robe and a jacket, only to find Jesse already outside in a jacket and jeans.

"What do you think?" he asks, looking over.

"I've never seen anything like it," I admit.

It's gorgeous. In contrast with the snow the red barn looks bright, as if it had a new paint job, the fields are glistening with thick powder, and it's so quiet I can hear my own heartbeat.

"The first day it snows is always my favorite day of the year," Jesse says. He leans against his railing and gathers some of the snow on the ledge with his hands, packing it into a ball. "Do you ever get snow in Atlanta?"

"Rarely," I share. "It's always a big deal when we do."

It's also always a day off, I think. A day off from school, from work, and from any other responsibilities. The thought crosses my mind that maybe that's how I should treat today—as a day off.

Maybe today I don't think about my dilemma. I can pick that back up tomorrow.

I walk a little farther out onto my porch in my boots so I can hear the snow crunch beneath my feet. Then I turn back toward Jesse. "I know decorating for Christmas is high up on the agenda today. But what do you think about checking off a bucket-list item and teaching me to ski or snowshoe first?"

The faint smile that appears on his lips lets me know that, as always, he's up for the challenge.

"I'll do you one better," he tells me. "I'll teach you how to snowshoe and ski, and we can check *two* items off your list."

———

There's a large shed near the barn filled with snowshoes, skis, boots, and poles that Jesse opens once we're both dressed. Everything's organized according to shoe size and pole height, so it's easy for him to find our gear.

"Will one of us be out here helping the guests on snow days?" I ask as we take a seat on the bench outside the shed to put on our boots and fasten our snowshoes. Since snowshoeing is easier, we decided to start there.

"That's how my parents used to do it, yeah."

"Are they the ones who taught you how to do these winter activities?"

"They used to take Brendan and me up to Spruce Peak or Mount Mansfield every weekend in the winter. Those are the two mountains around here. Once they bought the inn, though, cross-country skiing through these trails became our weekend winter entertainment." He gestures to the acreage in front of us.

"Sounds like an idyllic childhood."

He nods and leans down to help me tighten my toe and heel straps. "What was winter like back home for you?"

"It took place mostly indoors. Picture Christmas movies with popcorn by the fire."

"Sounds pretty idyllic too."

"No complaints here."

After fastening his own straps, he hands me my poles and shows me how to step into the binding, then instructs me to lead with the poles and keep my feet wider than I would when walking. After we get going, I'm surprised when he circles back to the topic and asks what kind of childhood I'd like to give my kids, if I want kids. "*Do* you want kids?" he clarifies.

Jesse and I have covered most topics since I've been here, but we haven't covered this one; I think because it's more normal to discuss it with a guy you're dating than with a friend. Given that neither of us is exactly sure what category our current dynamic falls into, it makes sense we're delving into uncharted conversation territory.

"I do want kids," I share. "I can't say I've given much thought as to what our weekends, summers, or winters would look like. That would require me to know where I plan on settling, and I'm not sure that's Atlanta anymore, but I don't really know. As for how I'd like to raise them, I'd love to give them unconditional love and the tools to help them be the best versions of themselves. That's partly why it feels so important to me to figure out how to be the best version of myself first, so I have a way to help them on their journeys."

I briefly take my eyes off the trail and look at Jesse as I ask him the same question.

"I want kids, yeah," he says. "Several, if possible, since family is so important to me. I suppose I'm open to where I raise them, although I do love the idea of that place being here. As for how I'd like to raise them, I've only gotten as far as knowing I'd like to give them an example of a loving relationship to look up to. I think having that foundation is everything."

I try not to have an emotional response to his answer, but I lose that battle fast. Jesse's not even talking about loving me specifically, but his words make me wonder how good it would feel if he and I were to ever fully open up our hearts to each other. The idea causes my heartbeat to kick up and my breath to catch. If Jesse notices this, he doesn't let on. He doesn't say anything, in fact, for the rest of the loop. It's not until we're stepping out of our snowshoes and into our skis that it strikes me that maybe he wasn't saying anything because the same exact thought was on his mind too.

—

"How are you feeling about the bucket list and your progress?" Jesse finally asks me another question once we reach the bottom of our first hill on skis. I watch as he climbs it, then follow his lead, angling my heels out just as he's doing.

"I'm learning a lot about myself. But I still don't know that I'm any closer to discovering my passion." I pause. "What if I don't?"

"Then you don't," he says with a shrug, as if it wouldn't be that big of a deal.

I wish it weren't such a big deal to me, but it is. I'm breathing hard, so I wait until we reach the top of the hill before I share this with Jesse.

He looks out at the snow-covered trees and then down at the slope before responding.

"I think the important thing to remember is that if you're truly searching for answers, you need to be open to all the possibilities, not just looking for confirmation of what you think you're supposed to find."

Jesse's comment hits me on so many levels. Is that what I'm doing? Am I so set on expecting my newfound passion to reveal itself in some dramatic fashion that I've overlooked how I've fallen into a career that fits me? And have I been so determined to wait for Sky that I've ignored all the signs that it's Jesse who's captured my heart?

"Are you saying I should let go of my original intentions?"

"I'm saying I don't think it's a bad idea to just trust the ride and see where it takes you."

And with that he kicks off down the hill.

So much for trusting the ride. Halfway down the hill, I tumble. I wish I could say it was a casual fall, but I roll several times before coming to a stop at the bottom.

Jesse is at my side in seconds, crouching down and asking if I'm okay.

I spit out snow to answer him. "I think so," I say, doing a quick mental scan of my body. "I just have snow in my hair, and now I'm wet and cold."

"Here." Jesse tugs off his gloves and brushes the snow out of my hair, then pulls off my gloves and rubs his hands over mine.

Funny thing: I'm not cold anymore. I also decide maybe falling isn't so bad, after all. In fact, for this kind of treatment, I'd consider falling on purpose on the next hill we climb.

Okay, maybe not. The fall hurt.

Jesse brings his lips to our hands and blows on them a couple of times as if he's trying to make everything better. And he does. Jesse always makes everything better. And he has since I got here.

He blows one final time and then looks at me.

"Better?" he asks.

I feel a burst of yearning and then a rush of something more. Something deeper.

"Better," I grin.

Then he pulls me up and helps me get back on my feet.

twenty-nine

By the time Jesse and I make it back to the shed after our last run, the temperature has seemingly dropped five to ten degrees. My guess is the wind chill is just making it feel a lot colder than when we set out, but my teeth won't stop chattering, and my fingers and toes are numb. At this point, I don't think even Jesse's magic touch could warm me up. It's going to take more than that. It's going to take a warm bubble bath, a cup of hot chocolate, and a crackling fire. I suggest the hot cocoa and fire idea to Jesse as we hurry to pull off our gear.

"I'm in," he says. "Meet me in the inn in half an hour?"

"Deal."

I beat Jesse there even though I take longer to bathe than usual. Maybe he decided to take an extra-long shower. I heard his water turn on and wasn't paying attention to whether or not it was still running when I walked out. I was too busy trying to figure out how to get over here without undoing all the progress I made warming up in the tub. The snow started coming down again, and the wind is currently whipping through the trees, causing them to bend and blow in all directions. I decide to start the hot cocoa.

It's ready by the time I hear Jesse walk in. Or, rather, stumble in. I'm in the kitchen, so I can't see him, but when I hear him grunt as if he's in pain, I hurry out into the parlor.

He's not in pain. He's hauling in a Christmas tree. A big Christmas tree.

"Where did you get that?" I rush over to help him carry it to the corner near the mantle.

"Last week I ordered it to be delivered. Since we have so much decorating to do today before we reopen tomorrow, I thought it would save us some time. I'm glad I did, because with today's weather, cutting one down would be a challenge."

He grunts again as we set it down, and the sound reverberates through me, catching me off guard.

"What do you think?" Jesse steps back to assess the tree while I assess my feelings, something I said I was *not* going to do today. Although maybe that was an unrealistic expectation. On an average day, it's hard to turn off that little voice in my head. Add the extra challenge of trying to turn it off when everything Jesse is doing and saying is stirring up so much emotion and I suppose I should have known I was setting myself up for failure.

"I think it's a keeper." I train my eyes on the tree and not on Jesse.

"I agree."

"Where can I find lights and ornaments?" I ask, deciding staying busy might help.

"In the hall closet."

I head in that direction. "Hot chocolate's in the kitchen," I call out.

"Want soup and a grilled cheese too?" Jesse offers.

"Sure."

When he returns with our food and drinks twenty minutes later, I have one strand of white lights untangled and all the ornaments out. I found an old record player with Christmas music in the closet too, so Nat King Cole is currently serenading us in the background.

"Where are all the ornaments from?" I ask, turning one over in my hand. They're all different shapes and sizes, an eclectic collection that looks as if it's been gathered over a lifetime.

"Each year we all gift each other a new one," he tells me.

"That's a sweet tradition." I set the ornament down and join him at the table, stealing a glance out the window as the wind continues to whistle and howl, kicking up snow. We certainly picked the right time to ski. It would be miserable out there now.

"My parents started it in their early marriage and have kept it going since," he tells me.

"Where did they meet?"

He swallows a bite of his sandwich, then shakes his head as he picks up his mug.

"What? You're not going to tell me?"

"It might weird you out to hear it."

"You can't start a story that way! Now I only want to hear it more."

He hesitates, then says, "They spent one holiday season working together at an inn."

I shouldn't have doubted Jesse. He's right. I *didn't* want to hear that. It is too weird given everything going on in my head right now.

He must read the expression on my face because he grins and says, "Told ya."

"You know me well."

"I do."

I pick up my sandwich, pulling off the crust just so I have something to do besides look at Jesse. "Well, now that it's out there," I say softly, "tell me the rest."

Jesse takes another sip of his hot chocolate and says, "They both got hired at an inn in Burlington during their sophomore year in college. On their first day of work, they met and hit it off right away. They fell in love with the place and with each other, and that experience taught them that one day they wanted to open up an inn together."

My voice is even quieter than before. "That's sweet."

"Yeah," Jesse echoes.

Neither of us says anything the rest of the meal.

We do go back to talking again once we get the lights strung on the tree and start hanging ornaments. But for the most part we just listen to Christmas songs, occasionally humming along to the ones we like.

Every so often Sky's roses catch my eye. They're still on the check-in table. I left them in here last night because I felt weird bringing them back to my room since Jesse and I walked to our cottages together after his parents left. I want to move them, but I don't want to draw attention to them either. I haven't figured out how to do that—I only remembered them after Jesse emerged from the kitchen—so I'm forced to live with them sitting there for now. But each time I see them, I can't help but ruminate on the clear difference between what I have with Sky and what I have with Jesse.

Everything about the way Sky shows he cares is so big, so loud, so dramatic, and what Jesse and I have is a lot quieter. But that doesn't mean I feel it any less.

In fact, when Jesse hands me the angel to put on top of the tree and his fingers gently brush against mine, I understand that what I feel for Jesse is unequivocally stronger.

thirty

I want to blurt out my realization the second I have it.

"Jesse—" I begin. But I pause as the lights on the tree and overhead start to flicker. The next second, the power goes out completely.

Jesse curses beneath his breath. It's the first time I've heard him swear. "Luckily, we don't have guests," he says, as if trying to see the bright side. He walks to the window, searching for a downed power line.

"See anything?" I ask.

It's only three-thirty, so it's not completely pitch black out there yet—or in here—but this time of year the sun sets around four, so it will be soon.

"Not out this window." He walks to another window and tells me he doesn't see anything there either. "I'm going to have to call this in on the landline," he says. "And see if I can find out when the power's coming back."

I nod and ask if I can help by finding candles or lanterns somewhere.

"There are pillar candles underneath those." He motions to the benches along the windowsill as he makes his way to the front desk.

I lift the seats up after removing the cushions and find an assortment of candles with glass coaster plates for them to sit on. After pulling out a couple boxes, I set a few candles in the windowsills, then cluster a couple on each of the tables. There's a lighter on the mantle, so I retrieve that and light them all.

By the time Jesse returns, it's darker outside, but it's glowing in here. And it looks . . . romantic. My confession dances on my tongue, but Jesse still looks as if he's in crisis mode.

222

He runs a hand through his hair. "The estimated wait time for power to be restored in our zip code is five hours and thirty minutes."

"So it will be on by the time guests arrive tomorrow morning," I point out.

He nods and stuffs his hands in his pockets. "That just leaves tonight."

"Right."

"I'm going to start a fire, for heat," he says. "You . . ." He seems to register the room as he looks from all the candles to me. He visibly swallows. "You definitely took care of the light."

When our eyes lock, my heart thuds at the prospect of spitting the words out. But I hesitate. And in that gap, Jesse asks, "Want to start hanging the garlands while I get going on the fire?"

I want it to be special when I tell Jesse how I feel. I want it to be the *right* moment. This isn't it. We still have so much more decorating to do.

"Sure," I say, and we get to work.

It's not the right moment when we finish decorating a couple hours later either. Next, we prepare dinner and while we wait for the food to cook on the gas stove, we play a game of cards. Jesse keeps talking about what we'll make the guests tomorrow if—for some reason—the power isn't back on when they arrive.

Not the right moment.

I don't even consider it while we're outside by the fire. It's way too cold tonight. And the wind! The wind is blowing so forcefully that once we open the door to come back inside, it blows wide open. We both reach out to push it closed, and Jesse's hand covers mine.

It clicks closed, cutting off the howling wind, but Jesse doesn't move.

I don't ask him to.

We stay like this for several breaths, and then I pull my hand out from under his and turn around to face him. My back is against the door and he's half leaning over me. Heat pools low in my stomach.

It's dark in the entryway, but I can see the flicker of candlelight dancing across his face.

He must see more on my face than candlelight because the next second he asks, "What's going through your head, Harper?"

His voice is low, a rumble, and I shiver.

This *is* the right moment. No question.

My pulse quickens.

"I'm going to have to mutter the code word here, Harper, unless that look you're giving me means you are okay with me doing what I'm thinking about doing." His eyes are on my lips, so I *know* what he's thinking about doing.

I want him to do it.

I've never wanted to be kissed by someone so badly in my entire life.

I swallow so my words don't stick in my throat. "It's you, Jesse," I breathe. "I want *you.*"

He blows out a quiet breath of relief and shifts closer. So close I can feel his scruff on my face and his heartbeat against mine. If either of us moves an inch, our lips will touch. I can't stop thinking about what it will be like when they *do* touch. Although I should—

Oh no.

No, no, no.

Don't think it, Harper!

But it's too late.

"I need to . . ." I begin.

This is going to kill me.

"What?" Jesse says thickly, just as his lips are about to meet mine.

". . . tell him first." I finish the sentence. I don't know how I manage to, but I do.

I also don't know why the thought popped into my head in the first place. All I know is that it did.

"Sky?" Jesse clarifies.

His name spoken aloud destroys the moment. But maybe that's why I stopped the moment from going further. I didn't want the kiss to be destroyed. Things with Sky need to be completely over before I indulge my feelings for Jesse, or I could end up feeling guilty. I don't want guilt to be any part of my first kiss with Jesse.

"Yes."

Jesse closes his eyes a moment, then backs away from me and leans against the windowsill, rubbing his forehead.

"I'm sorry," I say, and I am, I really am.

Jesse looks at me then. "No, I'm not mad at you. You make a good point. I don't want anything else in your head when I kiss you, Harper. *Anything.*"

The last word has such force and such promise behind it that I nearly take a step toward him. I lean back harder against the door to ground my feet.

Jesse huffs out a breath and continues. "I backed up because now that your feelings are out there . . . not kissing you is going to be a serious challenge for me the rest of the evening."

His face is filled with desire, and after a brief glance at his jeans, I can see the desire there too, and the heat burning in my stomach travels lower. I close my eyes thinking about all the things he'd be doing to me if I hadn't just stopped him.

I am on fire.

"I see your point," I say, but the words come out on a shaky breath. "We should call it a night."

When I blink open my eyes, I see that Jesse has already left the entryway and is heading into the parlor, blowing out candles along the way. I stay put, knowing that if I follow, we'll blow out the candles faster but then will be alone in a room together. In the dark. With this white-hot desire.

For both of our sakes, I stay put until he's put out all the candles and extinguished the fire, and once I hear him treading my way,

I open the door and step outside, walking a few paces ahead of him back to our cottages.

Neither of us even bothers saying goodnight. I hurry up my porch steps and hear him hurry up his, and we both shut our doors at the same time. I lean against mine just as the power pops back on. I know it does by my digital alarm clock's blinking red numbers across the expanse of dark. I can't help but think it knows I'm counting down the moments until Jesse and I can pick up where we left off.

thirty-one

This should be a phone call.

It's Tuesday, and I'm dragging my feet as I walk into town. Now that my heart is leading me in another direction, there's no point in delaying the inevitable till Wednesday. I need to tell Sky about my decision now, no matter how much I'm dreading writing the email.

I *would* call if I had his number. I suppose I could email him and ask for it. But I've never asked for his number these past couple of months. Not even after his surprise visit, when a talk would have probably made sense. What if asking for it causes him to feel the same dread I now am? I have to deliver bad news, but I can at least save him from anticipating it.

Although *I'd* want a warning about bad news.

But if giving him a warning possibly also gives him a full day of dreadful anticipation, it's not worth it. I know nothing of Sky's schedule. If I ask for his number, I don't know when he'd get back to me. If I don't receive his email with his phone number until tomorrow, that's an entire day. And that's if he's not flying when I finally call. If not, it's even longer.

No, that could be worse. And I want to be as sensitive in my treatment of Sky's feelings as I possibly can.

In some ways, ending things doesn't seem like that big of a deal. I mean, it's not as if Sky and I are together. We've technically only spent two or three days together, and we've gotten to know each other mostly through letters. But in other ways, this feels immensely difficult because the connection Sky and I have is stronger than any other connection I've had in my life—until Jesse.

I can't say I'm mad when I walk into the coffee shop and find that the line is longer than usual. I should have expected traffic given the influx of tourists. The inn is booked solid from now through Christmas, and after briefly taking in the downtown area on my walk here, I can see why. Jesse and I weren't the only ones putting up the holiday decorations yesterday. Stowe transformed overnight into a winter wonderland.

The light poles have all been wrapped with white lights, garlands, and red ribbons. Oversized ornaments and bows are hanging in most store windows, including Milk & Maple's. And there's a tall, bushy Christmas tree covered in colorful lights at the end of Main Street near the church steeple. Most of the storefronts have Christmas trees up as well, either out front or in their windows.

I give my attention to the one inside Milk & Maple, which is draped in white lights and coffee cup ornaments. Then I sweep my eyes over the rest of the room, checking out the other decorative touches. I spy twinkle lights along the counter, green stockings hanging from the fireplace mantle, and—

Sky.

I swing back around toward the register in a blind panic. Was that really Sky? Or is my mind playing tricks on me?

I take a deep breath before shooting another glance over my shoulder. I peer at the same spot, but this time he's not there.

My nerves settle a little, but I scan the room again, feeling crazy. I could have sworn I saw him.

I spy him then, hiding behind the Christmas tree.

When my eyes meet his, he shrugs, admitting he's been caught, and then he makes a silly face that reminds me of those photos he sent me all those weeks ago of him in his apartment, and before

I know it, I'm laughing. I can't believe I'm laughing, but I am. I forgot how easily he makes me laugh.

He waves me over to him, and I bite my bottom lip as I step out of line. When he makes another silly face, my lip breaks free, and I grin again as I walk toward him.

He's out from his hiding place by the time I reach him, and before I can ask what he's doing here, he takes me into his arms and holds me as if he's trying to make up for all our time apart. He presses his lips into my hair a beat later, and a shiver works its way down my spine and all the way to my toes. I don't have time to process my reaction—to process anything—before he starts apologizing.

"I'm only in town because my mom had a health scare," he explains. "I didn't let you know because I didn't want to screw up again. I wanted to keep my promise and give you the space and time you told me you needed."

He wanted to keep his promise.

My stomach drops.

"I didn't think you'd be here today," he goes on. "That's the only reason I came in. I thought you only came to Milk & Maple on Wednesdays. What are you doing here?"

My stomach sinks even more because *oh my god*—if he knew I was here to break our pact after he's done everything he can to honor it . . .

I swallow and blink as the room begins to spin.

"Harper? Are you okay? You've gone pale," Sky says. At least I think he says that. There's a chance I misheard him because I do feel funny.

I reach a hand out to Sky. I feel so unsteady. He reaches down and swoops me up into his arms in response. I'm so caught off guard by the sudden gesture that my eyes dart to his, and when his eyes meet mine, I have a flashback to when he picked me up just like this the first night we met, right before bed.

The memory warms me all over and I blink, trying to snap out of it, because recalling heated and happy memories of our time together is not what I need right now.

What I need is to pull it together and remember why I came here in the first place.

To end things.

I thought I should call him, didn't I? Fate did me one better.

I look away from him after he sets me down on a seat at a table before claiming the seat across from me.

"Are you okay?" he asks, reaching over and resting his palm on top of my hand. My skin tingles beneath his, and I draw in a deep breath, knowing I should pull my hand back, but I'm unable to move.

How do I answer that? I don't feel okay.

"Is your mom okay?" I ask, dodging the question. I can't imagine Sky would have come to town if his mom's health scare wasn't serious, given how much he actively avoids his family.

"She had a stroke," he says.

"Sky—" I flip my hand over so I'm holding his and squeeze.

"She's fine now," he continues. "At least that's what the doctors are saying. Although maybe they're just telling us that to get her out of the hospital. Luckily her speech wasn't affected so she's managed to keep bossing everyone around as if she owns the place." Sky chuckles and so do I.

"I'm glad she's okay."

"I am too." There's a beat, and then Sky says, "And another bright side? I get to see you, even if it wasn't my intention. And just before I head back to Atlanta tonight too."

He squeezes my hand happily, and I swallow the sudden lump in my throat.

"You leave tonight?"

He nods. "Mom will be back home by then, and I need to return to work."

I have to tell him. I have to tell him the pact is off now. That's what I came here to do, and I've already made up my mind.

Right?

I nearly growl at the question. *Right.*

I gently let go of his hand and place mine in my lap. Then I open my mouth, but before I can say a word, I hear my name, followed by Sky's.

When I turn around, I spy Sky's sister, Andrea, standing behind me. "I should have told you my sister was meeting me here," Sky says, getting to his feet to grab her a chair.

I rise to give her a hug, not sure if I'm grateful she showed up or if this just made things worse.

Once we embrace, Andrea and I sit. Sky, who couldn't find an empty chair, stays standing.

"Please tell me you two just bumped into each other and my brother didn't break down and invite you here."

"I didn't!" Sky says, holding up his palms. "I swear. This is just a coincidence."

"Good," she says.

"I told Andrea the truth about everything—including our pact—last time I was in town," Sky clarifies. He never mentioned how his conversation with Andrea went when he left the inn after our argument, and I never asked. We both just put that night behind us and have been pretending it didn't happen—probably not the best approach, but one we've stuck with. "I made her promise to keep me honest on not reaching out to you this go-round."

"He's been dying to contact you," she tells me. "But I've been proud of him for keeping his word and abstaining."

For keeping his word.

My stomach knots.

"Let me order us all coffee," Sky says. "Harper, you want a latte? Andrea, a cappuccino?"

We each nod, and Sky plants a brief kiss on my forehead before heading to the register. There's no line now.

I try to brush off the tingles from that brief contact with his lips as Andrea starts talking.

"I want to vouch for my brother and tell you that any mistake he's made so far is just an honest mistake. He *really* likes you. I could tell when you two were at my parents, and I could see it in his eyes when he stopped by my house during his most recent trip. I can see it now too. He hasn't been like this since Julie."

"Yeah, he told me about her and how much he regretted ending things," I say, just to participate in the conversation.

"He didn't end things with Julie." She pauses. "Oh, you must mean Lucy."

I'm not sure how Andrea interprets my blank look, but she continues after a second.

"Makes sense you mixed them up. I'm sure you two haven't spent all your time emailing about his two big exes. But I was talking about Julie—you know, the one who left him the night he proposed."

Huh?

Sky had an ex who left him the night he proposed to her?

"You didn't know about Julie?" Andrea must have read my expression.

"No," I admit.

She pinches the bridge of her nose. "Christ. I mentioned her at my parents' house, and you nodded along like you recognized the name . . . but now I'm remembering that's because you were acting." She shakes her head a couple of times and stares across the table at me. "I'm sorry. It wasn't my place to share that part of Sky's past."

"What part of my past?" Of all moments for Sky to rejoin the table.

Andrea winces as she meets Sky's eyes. "I mentioned Julie. I'm sorry. I thought she knew."

232

Nervousness flashes across Sky's face as his eyes briefly connect with mine before they drop to the tabletop.

"It's a difficult topic for me," he says. "I felt weird writing about it in a letter, and we've had so little time together in person."

"That's understandable." I can imagine Sky wanting to wait for the right moment to share this story, and we haven't had that yet. That isn't Sky's fault. I'm the one who asked for three months to find myself. Sky would be happily dating me right now and likely sharing all kinds of stories otherwise.

Andrea gets to her feet. "Listen, I'll wait for my coffee at the counter and take it to go. That way you two can continue talking. I'll see you back at the house, Sky. And Harper," she smiles, "see you on Christmas Eve."

Christmas Eve. Not a day I want to be reminded of right now.

Sky takes Andrea's seat, scooching closer to me, and when our eyes meet, his expression is pained.

"I really would have told you," he reinforces.

"Sky, stop, it's okay. I know you would have."

Sky looks down at the table, and when he looks back up, he sighs and says, "It was my junior year of college. We were high school sweethearts and both went to college in Boston to be near one another. We were young, I know, but I was really in love with her. Hours after she'd accepted my proposal, she told me she had a change of heart, that she couldn't keep her promise to me because she was in love with someone else. It crushed me."

Just as it crushed me when Jake told me he had feelings for Anna. I'm going to cause Sky that kind of pain again.

I'm going to be sick.

"For years after that, I told everyone the story I told you on the plane: that I was never going to get married," Sky goes on. "And I think I really believed that. But eventually I realized I was just afraid of getting my heart broken again. I put myself out there with Lucy a few years

233

ago, but then I ended that because I was afraid of one day getting hurt, which I know I already shared with you." His head snaps up. "I'll never make that same mistake again, Harper. I'd never make it with *you*."

I just about prevent myself from flinching at his words.

"Sky, I—"

I what?

I . . . want to break things off with you? How can I possibly get those words out now? After he just told me his story with Julie?

Sky pulls my chair toward him as our lattes arrive, then pulls me onto his lap. "Look, I didn't mean to kill the mood."

His arms encircle me loosely, and goose bumps break out along my skin.

"You didn't kill the mood," I say, trying to refocus.

"Well, just in case . . ." He suddenly squeezes my sides, tickling me. I'm not expecting it and I burst out into giggles.

"Sky!" I protest, reaching out to push his hands back, but he easily captures both my hands in one of his. Then he looks at my lips with that look of his, and my breath quickens.

What am I doing?

What *the hell* am I doing?

I don't know.

Suddenly I want to cry, because it hits me that my decision, although difficult, seemed certain when I had distance from Sky. A whole other Harper 2.0 appears around Sky, and I fall into her—and into this—so easily, so quickly, so naturally. Sky is so *fun*. Life is an entire ride with him.

My experience with Sky is what opened my heart back up. We were both willing to be brave again because our connection seemed worth that risk. I've been trying to resist the power of that connection, but that's lying to myself.

Sky and I share something in another realm than what I share with Jesse. While Jesse supports me, understands me, and makes me feel seen, Sky thrills me, lightens me, and makes me feel alive. They draw out different sides of me.

Maybe if I knew myself, the choice about who to be with would be easier because I'd know what kind of love I couldn't live without.

It's so clear to me in this moment what I need to do.

"I should go," Sky says, filling me with relief. I need be alone. "I told you I wouldn't see you again until Christmas Eve, and no matter how hard it is to keep that promise with you in front of me, I will keep it."

He lifts me up off his lap and gets to his feet in one swift motion.

He touches one hand to my face, tilting up my jaw so I meet his eyes.

Please don't try to kiss me.

That would be such a betrayal to Jesse. And to my conflicted heart.

Sky slowly brushes his thumb across my bottom lip, eliciting a chill down my spine, before dropping his hand.

"I'm not going to kiss you, Harper, because each time I do, it's harder to walk away." He grabs my hand, raises it to his lips, and places a kiss on my knuckles with all the charm he's always possessed. "But I'll be thinking of you."

At his words, my heart goes haywire. Then he releases my hand and turns toward the exit.

Just before he walks out of the shop, he stops in the doorway and looks back. He winks at me, and I can see all the promise, all the adventure in that one little wink.

And then he walks out into the snow.

thirty-two

There's a knock on my cabin door, and I'm not ready for it, even though Jesse has given me plenty of time since I returned from Milk & Maple. He's been so considerate, likely assuming I've been in here decompressing from writing the difficult email I told him I was heading into town to send Sky. It's going to destroy him when I share what really happened.

It's going to destroy me too.

Oh God, did I make the biggest mistake here?

"How did it go?" he asks, taking a seat on my bed beside me and wrapping an arm around my waist for support.

His innocent touch nearly breaks my resolve.

"Not well?" he guesses.

I shake my head, even though I know I need to do more than that. I need to speak up and explain. But how do I explain this to Jesse? Despite mulling for hours over how to do so, all the words leave me.

"Harper," Jesse says softly, "talk to me."

"I . . ." *Out with it.* "I ran into Sky," I confess.

Jesse's arm tightens around me. "He's in town?"

"I had no idea," I say. "He didn't tell me because he was trying to keep his promise to me and give me the space I asked for until Christmas Eve."

"Did you tell him in person, then? That you want to end the pact?" When I hesitate, I hear him suck in a sharp breath, as if he knows the answer, and then he pulls his arm back, a choked sound escaping the back of his throat as he gets to his feet. He begins pacing.

236

"I had every intention of telling him," I rush to explain, but even to my own ears the excuse sounds hollow. "I went in decided. My feelings are so strong for you, Jesse. But then . . . I ended up finding out some details about his past that made it too difficult to tell him what I planned on saying. It made me realize exactly how much I was going to hurt him, and I have to be sure before I cause that kind of pain."

He stops pacing and looks at me. "Sure? Sure of how to say it or sure of your feelings?"

I close my eyes because I can't stand to see Jesse's reaction to what I am about to say next.

"Both," I admit, that one word cutting like a knife through the air.

I know this contradicts my certainty last night. I know he probably doesn't understand. I don't yet fully understand why I made the choice I did. That's the problem.

"I thought you *were* sure of your feelings."

I swallow, then blink, pushing through it. I'm so frustrated with myself, I want to scream, but I owe it to Jesse to at least try to put my feelings into words.

"I thought I was too, but seeing Sky confused me." I take a deep breath and spit out the rest of my defense. "I wish it was just the regret of not keeping my promise to him, but it's more than that. What I have with Sky compared to what I have with you, Jesse, it's not similar. It's not even close. I feel like two entirely different people with each of you. But . . . but both connections are powerful."

I hate that I need to say this. I hate that it's true.

"When Sky was in front of me, I could see who I'd be with him, how'd we be together. And here, I can see who I'd be with you, how'd we be together. And it hit me then that I don't know who I am or who I want to be. And if I don't know that, how do I know what future I want? How can I be sure?" My words have been coming faster and faster, as if I think that by filling the silence, everything will be okay. I force myself to slow down. "Seeing Sky again got me so in my head, Jesse. I thought . . . I realized I need to take this time until Christmas Eve to really double down on figuring out who I am. It's what I came here to do. It's also the only way I'll know exactly what my heart is telling me."

When I finish, the silence is thick.

"Harper."

The amount of hurt packed into my name nearly rips my heart right open.

Dammit, dammit, dammit.

"It's so unfair to you, me changing my mind again," I say, fighting back tears. "I'm being unfair to you."

Jesse groans, the sound coming from deep in his chest, and he goes back to pacing. "That's—yeah—but it's not that," he says with a slight shake of his head. "I get that you're conflicted. I'm not mad at you for that. I never have been. I know you met him first and made a promise. I know that *this*, between you and me, wasn't part of the plan. But it happened, Harper. And I can't turn this off. I can't turn this thing between us off."

He stops pacing then and stares at me with so much heat in his eyes that I stop breathing. Stop thinking. Stop wanting anything but Jesse.

I'm on my feet in an impulse, stretching my hand out for his. He resists my touch at first, but when I try again, he gives in and pulls me toward him, drawing me close and pressing his forehead against mine. The outside world fades away and my heart drums faster and faster. We stay like this, with his arms wrapped around me and our foreheads pressed together, for a solid few breaths until he reaches for my hand and tugs me down on the bed so we're sitting as we were before.

Only closer.

"I don't know how to control this anymore." His words come out in a warm sigh on my skin, and when he caresses my cheek,

I close my eyes and fight back the whimper that wants to escape from the back of my throat.

I was expecting this conversation to hurt. I was expecting it to be hard. I don't know why I didn't anticipate that it might end up with me back *here,* feeling like this for Jesse, wanting him to do all the things I made him put off doing to me last night.

His free hand finds my other cheek, so he's cupping my face now. A wave of heat ignites under my skin.

When I blink open my eyes, they lock with his.

"Since last night, all I've been thinking about is this moment, Harper," he says, his thumbs rubbing a slow path on my cheek. "All I could picture when I fell asleep was what we'd do right now, right here, you and me."

I grip the sheets with my fingers, wanting to tell him to do it, wanting to tell him how much I want it.

"Jesse," I breathe.

His name brings him closer. "I don't care if you haven't told him yet. If you're planning to, that's enough. I won't stop this time. I'll drive everything else out of your mind, I promise. You just say the word."

His promise vibrates everywhere inside me.

Everywhere.

I want to say yes. God, do I want to.

The struggle inside my chest right now is unbearable. I can feel the battle of the dueling sides. *Pick Jesse, are you out of your mind?! Give in to this. Hang on, remember how you felt around Sky, though. And remember that promise you made. Don't you dare make a mistake.*

"Jesse—" I repeat, and he comes even closer so that his lips are almost touching mine. I didn't think my heart could pound any faster, but it just proved me wrong. It's going so fast it almost hurts.

Or, wait—maybe the pain is coming from knowing that *this* is going to hurt.

This phrase I know I have to say.

I do have to say it.

But I don't want to.

Harper, you must!

It's not fair to Jesse to come to my conclusion in the heat of the moment. And it's not fair to Sky either.

"I can't Jesse. I need to think."

There.

It's out and . . . I don't feel relief. Not an ounce.

All I feel is Jesse as he releases a deep exhalation of disappointment onto my skin. And then I feel my own disappointment and an ever-mounting frustration with myself. For not being more decided. For putting this man I care for so deeply through this ringer.

I close my eyes, fighting back a fresh wave of tears, when I feel Jesse's hands drop from my face and the warmth disappear. By the time I open my eyes, he's on his feet again, standing above me.

"I know I said I'd wait, but given how I feel, given how high my hopes got yesterday, I . . ."

"I'm so sorry," I say, my pain and regret filling his pause. "Please know how sorry I am, Jesse."

I want to get up and reach out for his hands again, but I don't because I'm not sure I could let go. He puts his hands in his pockets before I can second-guess myself. "I need some distance today, okay? With everything you just said, it's too hard for me to be around you right now. I hope you can understand that."

"I do," I say. "Of course I do."

Jesse nods and walks to the door. But then his earlier words come back to me.

"I said I'd wait, but—"

"Jesse!" I half-shout, shooting up to my feet in a blind panic as he reaches the door. He stops but doesn't turn around. "Will you give me the time? Will you still wait?"

I know I have no right to ask that of him. None whatsoever. I just hurt him, and I'm *still* hurting him. I hate myself for asking. I want to take it back.

I've made such a mess.

I turn away from the door, unable to bear the answer I think is coming, unable to face it if he gives me no answer at all.

I hear movement right behind me, but I don't turn around. I can't look at him.

He's so close I can feel his body heat radiating toward my back. I hear his inhale and brace myself for whatever he's about to say, but instead he closes the distance between us until there isn't any. Not an inch.

My breath catches and I lean into him almost without thought. His hands firmly grip my hips, burning imprints on my skin. He inhales, deep and slow, and I feel the rise of his chest behind mine, and the fall as he blows out a long breath into my hair.

Everything in me stills, settles.

Then he slowly leans down to place a scorching kiss on my neck.

"I'll wait," he says, sliding his lips along my skin to my ear, "because I'm sure."

Then he's gone, and my cabin door swings shut.

And I don't move from that spot for a long time.

thirty-three

Even though I know I've hurt Jesse, he tries not to show it the next day. Or the day after. Or the day after that. Often while we're working side by side in the barn or the kitchen, I'll see a flicker of sadness on his face, and I can tell how much effort it takes for him to disguise it.

But he does disguise it. Every single time.

He's not doing this out of pride. That would require Jesse to have an ego. He's doing it for *my* sake because he doesn't want anything to take away from the last few weeks of this journey I'm on. He knows how important it is to me to figure this—myself and my heart—out.

One day, no matter what happens, I will thank Jesse for handling this situation with such maturity and for giving me the gift of time. For now, I just accept this gift, since time is what I need right now.

The day after I met Sky in the coffee shop and confessed my conflicted emotions to Jesse, I went back into town and emailed Sky. He had gone back to Atlanta the night before. I found myself grateful for the space and nature of a letter—the format let me choose my words more carefully than I ever could in person. And I had needed to choose them well because Sky was in the dark about so much.

In the email, I was as honest with him as I had been with Jesse. I told him about Jesse and how conflicted I felt and apologized for not having more certainty. I apologized for any hurt the letter would cause. And I also warned him that this would be the very last letter I'd write to him before Christmas Eve because I needed to spend the rest of my days here remembering why I came to Vermont in the first place. I was honest that doing so was not only important to me, but the only way I could figure out how I felt.

Then, I wrote to him about Christmas Eve. I explained I'd understand if he didn't want to show up for the big party at the inn anymore, given that it wasn't certain we'd be picking up where we left off as planned. I'd understand if he didn't want to wait for me to decide—he'd already been waiting for so long. And I assured him that no matter what he decided or what happened, he'd always hold a special place in my heart.

The moment I pressed send, I knew it was the right thing to do.

Even if my chest still tightens at the memory of it a week later. Even if I hold my breath as I open my email today and expel it in a rush when I find a response from him.

Sky surprises me by thanking me for my honesty. He admits that what I told him hurt and that finding out I have feelings for Jesse triggered some old insecurities from his experience with Julie. But he also says he appreciates that I recognize this rather than ignoring or being dishonest about it. He likes knowing that he and I will be starting out on an honest foot if we ever get the chance to give our romantic relationship a real shot. And then he tells me he still wants the chance of a real shot. He will still be waiting for me on Christmas Eve.

I journal about his response as soon as I get back to the inn. I started journaling the very first night after Jesse left my cabin. I had to—I didn't know how else to process what I was feeling. I wrote down everything I'd felt about Sky and Jesse since I arrived in Vermont. Then I decided to make journaling a daily practice for the remaining time I had here.

Every day, I write down everything I'm feeling about not only Sky and Jesse but also myself—who I feel I am and who I feel I want to become. And I make myself look inside my heart repeatedly. Because that's what I came here to do. That's what I must do now.

I know I'm getting clearer and clearer on my feelings. As challenging as it is to listen to what my heart has to say, by being quiet and not requesting advice or feedback from anyone else, answers slowly start to surface—and not just about my choice between these two men, but about what I want to do after December ends.

thirty-four

"I have some news," Jesse tells me, five days before Christmas Eve. We're at the outdoor fire. I can't believe we're still doing these fires, but we are. It's no longer a question of if we'll make it until Christmas Eve. We've already made it this far; it's just what we're doing.

It's not about the challenge of beating Jesse and Brendan's old record anymore. I think we both continue showing up because, for some reason, during these fifteen minutes, Jesse and I are still able to be "us." Perhaps that's because we're out here for such a short amount of time that we don't overthink anything we're saying. Or because it's so cold that both of us like to talk to distract ourselves. Or maybe it's because Jesse keeps making the drinks stronger to help us stay warm, and the alcohol loosens us up. Whatever the reason, it's nice to have this time, especially now that so much of our days are spent doing our own things.

"What is it?" I ask.

Jesse blows on his hands before answering. We're both on our feet, standing near the flames. "My parents have made their decision."

The temperature is in the low teens tonight, and it's snowing. I'm so cold I assume I'm completely frozen—inside and out—but apparently my heart is still capable of movement. A lot of movement.

Holy hell. What is happening inside my chest?

I've known this was coming, but I thought it wouldn't happen until after Christmas—no idea why. I also have no idea what Jesse is about to tell me because his face is giving nothing away. I didn't realize just how much I want this for Jesse until now. I want this for him more than I've ever wanted anything for myself.

"What is it?" I press.

I'm getting a taste of what it's like to wait for an answer I really care about. Now I feel even worse for what I've put Jesse and Sky through these past few weeks.

Waiting isn't fun. It's torturous.

Jesse reaches for the drink he had set down earlier on an armrest on one of the chairs. I hope he's picking it up again to toast to the future and not because he's going to need a drink to dull the disappointment. But either way, I just need to know—*now*.

Jesse turns toward me. "They're going to let me keep the inn."

"Oh, Jesse!" I scream. We *do* toast then, and I jump up and down, spilling my drink everywhere, but I don't care. I fling my arms around Jesse in the biggest hug, my heart dancing.

I've never been so happy for someone in my life. Since I've gotten here, Jesse has been such a champion of me figuring out my dream. It's so fitting that this holiday season is culminating with him getting his.

When we break apart, my vision is blurred with tears. "These are happy tears," I clarify. "I'm *so* happy for you, Jesse."

"Thanks," he says, grinning, all that joy spilling over. But then he turns serious. "I also want you to know that no matter what happens between us, you have a job here after December."

"Thank you, Jesse."

"No matter what, Harper," he stresses.

I hug him again. I can't not hug him again. Jesse has always wanted what's best for me, and although the dynamic between us has changed over the past three months, in both good and bad ways, *he* hasn't changed.

I know who Jesse is, and because of his help, I've learned who I am.

"Merry Christmas, Jesse," I say, grateful to know that no matter what, he and I will be okay.

thirty-five

The annual Christmas Eve event at the inn is a way bigger deal than I thought. When I first arrived, Sky told me the whole town attends, but I just didn't think he meant literally the whole town. I should've known, though; the 10K race for the hospital showed me that Stowe turns out for events. That, and Jesse has been talking about what a big production this party is for the past month.

But it's not until two days before Christmas, when volunteers start materializing by the carload to donate their supplies and their time, that I fully grasp the scope of this tradition.

I have never seen so many people working together to build something so magical. The local music store brought a stage that their employees are helping to set up now for a concert performance by the high school show choir. At least twenty-five families showed up early this morning with thousands of strands of lights, which they're now wrapping around the trees lining one of the trails behind the inn for a mile-long horse-drawn carriage ride through the woods. (Jesse's friend, Will, and a few other residents with horses will bring them over in trailers on the big day.)

The owners of Milk & Maple are here too, setting up a drink cart that will serve hot chocolate. Beside it, a local bar, Hannigan's, set up another drink cart that will provide hot adult beverages. Jesse has a whole list of food trucks offering dinner and dessert that will arrive the night of. Two men are wheeling in a gazebo on a truck past me to set up for Santa and his elves, and several others are bringing in insulated tents and space heaters to keep guests comfortable.

I feel as if I've been transported to a Hallmark movie Christmas set, which is good and bad. It's good because I've never been a part of something like this, and it makes me love Stowe even more. It's bad because at some point, I'm planning on talking to both Sky and Jesse, and this party will be a very public place for such private conversations.

I consider the possibility of waiting to talk to each of them until after the party, but it goes till midnight, and then it will be Christmas Day, and how would that even work? We'd all be dancing uncertainly around one another for hours.

Plus, at this point, I'm completely clear on my feelings and don't think I can wait any longer to get them off my chest.

—

On Christmas Eve morning, I find Jesse putting big red bows on the chicken coop for guests who wander into the barn.

"Hey," I say, walking toward him. "I was looking for you."

"Hey," he grins, handing me a box to help. We've been tag-teaming so many tasks the past few days. I keep thinking we must be done, but then more decorations seem to come out of nowhere. "What's up?"

"Am I in charge of a particular booth or station tonight?"

"You've done the upfront work. Tonight you don't have to worry about anything." *Except I do,* I think. *I'll have to worry about your feelings and Sky's.*

"Oh, okay. Does the same go for you?"

"Yeah, pretty much. I'll just walk around to see if anyone needs help with anything."

I nod and tuck a strand of hair back behind my ear. This gesture alone causes Jesse to stop what he's doing and face me.

"Will you . . . need me for something?"

"I just want to make sure we have time to talk."

248

"Talk, talk?" he clarifies.

I nod. Jesse has been so patient the past few weeks, but now there's a look of desperation on his face, as if he wants me to just say what's on my heart right now. Part of me wants to. I want to be as careful with Jesse's emotions as I can. Maybe I should just tell him now.

I clear my throat. "Jesse—" But then the chickens all start to cluck at once, and a familiar voice calls out my name, followed by Jesse's name. I look over my shoulder.

It's Will.

"I've got the horses in the trailer. Where do you want them this year?"

Jesse stares at me and I stare back at him, and for a moment I think he's going to tell Will to *get out right now*.

But he only shakes his head and sighs. "Follow me, Will. I'll show you."

thirty-six

Jesse and I are busy with tasks until six o'clock, when the party begins, so I'm not able to head back to my room to get ready until then. As I pull off my work clothes, I hear the commotion outside: indistinct chatter from guests who have already arrived, car doors opening and closing as more people show up and park, the show choir singing "Jingle Bell Rock."

My heart goes into overdrive just thinking about the conversations I need to have tonight and wondering when Sky will arrive. He and his family could show up in a few hours, but they could also be out there right now.

I'm nervous to see him. I'm nervous for tonight in general. But at least I'm not undecided. Tonight will be hard and sad, exciting and new. I focus on the positive part of that statement as I pull out a festive look from my closet. Inspired by all the snow on the ground, I decide to go with a winter white outfit: white pants, a cream snow jacket over a white cashmere sweater, and a snowflake necklace and earrings.

As I clip my earrings in, I spy my bucket list on my dresser. Every single item on it is checked off. All of them. I can't help but feel proud of all the progress I've made since I've been here.

It's amazing what changes a person can make in her life in three months if she really dedicates herself to doing the work. I like that I've learned this. I like knowing it's possible to start over. No matter how bad things get, there is always a new life waiting. A better life waiting. We just need to have the courage to take the necessary steps to go after it.

This newfound wisdom has given me the quiet surety that no matter what happens next—good or bad—I'll be okay. I'll be able to figure it out. I might not have found my passion while I've been here, but gaining this confidence is an even better gift. At least that's what I wrote in my journal last night.

I tuck my bucket list inside my dresser now and walk to my bed, pulling my journal off my bedside table and jotting down a few thoughts I haven't had a chance to note yet today.

I'll hold on to this practice even after tonight. In fact, I think I'll keep a lot of the habits I've developed in my time here.

I won't go back to using my phone as I did before, for instance. I've really benefitted from the separation from technology. It's made me more present. I don't think I'll go back to watching TV either. I've missed a few of my favorite shows, but I've discovered novels, and reading is the nicest replacement.

I'll never go back to the hectic, unfulfilling lifestyle I had before. I like rising early and working hard in a setting that brings me joy. I like ending the day with gratitude and good company. And I know the inn isn't the only place where I can live like this. I can live like this anywhere. I just have to make the conscious choice to do so.

And I won't regress to the person I was before. I don't think I can, honestly, given all I've learned about myself and the changes I've made since I've arrived.

I really like the person I am now.

And I really like one other person . . .

I close my journal, setting it aside.

It's time to tell that person how I feel.

thirty-seven

I spy Sky seconds after stepping outside my cottage, and my breath catches in my throat. He's near the cocktail cart with his entire family. He spots me almost immediately, as if he sensed where I was and knew right where to look. That wouldn't surprise me given the strength of the connection we've had since we first met.

When our eyes lock, my pulse kicks into high gear, and I give him a little wave. He waves back, and I see a faint smile on his lips, as if he's not quite sure whether he should be happy to see me or dreading it.

I think he's waiting to see how I react. Out of the corner of my eye, I notice Jesse helping out at the hot cocoa cart, passing out cups to little kids. In case Sky's following my gaze, I don't react. Both of them deserve a private conservation.

I just nod my head in the direction of the gazebo, indicating that Sky should meet me there. I don't head toward him because I don't want to talk to his entire family right now. And knowing Sky, he wouldn't want that either. I bet he's happy for an excuse to extract himself, honestly.

A couple of benches behind the gazebo where Santa and his elves are seated are empty. Families are lined up in front, waiting for their turn to meet him and have their pictures taken. Assuming parking ourselves behind the star attraction is probably our best bet at not being disturbed, I take a seat beside a space heater there and wait. When Sky doesn't join me right away, I look around, wondering if he didn't understand my nod or where I was nodding to. Just as

I'm about to rise to my feet to go check, he appears, and my heart starts to hammer.

He looks the exact same as the last time I saw him . . . only better. He told me once that he works out whenever he's missing me. Well, either he's been missing me a ton or he found new motivation; his jeans are fitting him just right, and once he spots me, he pulls off his black jacket—maybe because he's the overheated kind of nervous—and I see that his fitted forest-green sweater is clinging to his biceps and abs.

He's taking me in as he approaches, and gives me another faint smile when he's finally standing before me.

"Hi," he says.

"Hi," I reply.

He reaches a hand behind his neck as if he's unsure whether to hug me or just sit down. I get to my feet and hug him, making the decision for him. Only once we're wrapped in each other's arms, I'm reminded how difficult this entire decision has been, and tears instantly come.

Sky must feel them spilling onto his neck because he starts to withdraw. And then he's looking at me and sees my tears, and I know he knows what's coming next.

"I'm so sorry," I say, a quiet sob escaping with the words. He lets out an exhale that's so deep, he must have been holding his breath since we wrote each other last. Then he wipes away my tears and brings his forehead to mine.

"Are you sure?" he asks.

I'm so sure.

But that doesn't make this any easier. In fact, I'm reminded why this decision was so hard to make. There are real, strong feelings here, on Sky's end and on mine.

What I have with Sky . . . it could be great if we ever gave it a real shot. But this thing I have with Jesse—it's already here. And it's not going anywhere. It's become an immovable, essential part of me.

A million times I tried to run through scenarios in which I chose Sky, and I *could* see us being happy. The promise was there. But what I couldn't imagine in any scenario was saying goodbye to Jesse.

I asked myself which love I couldn't live without. This was my answer.

Still, that doesn't make it hurt less.

I step away from him and reach for his hand, pulling him down onto the bench beside me. I keep his hand in mine as I tell him how much I struggled with this decision and how sorry I am for both the pain I'm causing and the additional layer of hurt I know he must feel given that he's experienced this kind of rejection before.

"I've been in your shoes," I remind him. "I hate that I'm causing you to feel something that was so difficult for me to feel. But do you remember our letter to each other about fate and timing?"

Sky nods, letting me know he's listening. Good. I wasn't sure if he was. He looks as if he's in his head right now. Not that I can blame him.

"I don't know why I met you on my flight here and not in Atlanta before that," I say. "I don't know why life works out the way it does. I don't want you—or I—to go there. But I really believe we met each other for a reason. I believe we went through all this together for a reason. And I'm trusting the timing of my life, Sky. I think trusting it, in addition to trusting myself, is the best way to live. And my hope is that you can go forward trusting the timing of your life and yourself too."

Sky looks away and I give him a minute. I'll give him all the minutes he needs. I wish I could give him a cure for the broken heart I've caused too. But the only cure I've found for that is time. And the willingness and courage to get on your feet again and start over.

Sky finally turns back and meets my gaze. "If you ever change your mind—"

"I won't," I reply. I don't want him to cling to any false hope. I've already made him wait too long. I want to set him free, the same way Jake set me free when he was finally honest about how he felt. I understand Jake now, better than I ever have.

"Okay," he nods, bringing my hands to his lips and kissing them softly, kissing me goodbye.

I know how difficult it must be for him to accept my decision. Fresh tears fall down my face. Sky is a such good man.

But I also learn something about him: Sky will be okay. Maybe not tonight. Maybe not for a few days or even a month or two. But he will get back on his feet. And when he does, I hope he can learn to trust his heart again when the timing with someone *is* right.

Sky looks up and around, dazed, as if he's realizing it's time to leave and search for his family—or rather one member of his family, Andrea. I'm glad she's here so he can talk to her after this.

"Wait," I say, fishing in my pocket. I pull out a folded piece of paper and hand it over.

"What's this?" he asks, opening it.

"One last letter," I say. "I wrote everything down in case I didn't find the right words tonight. I wanted to make sure you always knew how grateful I am to have met you. And how much I'm wishing nothing but the best for you."

"I feel the same," Sky says. "I do."

He folds the letter back up and stuffs it into his pocket. Then he draws in a deep breath and gets to his feet.

thirty-eight

When I was trying to imagine how this night would play out, I wasn't sure how I would feel once I broke things off with Sky. My plan was to talk to him early enough in the evening that I'd have time to shift gears and get excited about owning up to my feelings for Jesse. I assumed it would take at least a couple of hours for me to get to this point—maybe longer. But I think it's a testament to the immensity of what I feel for Jesse that as soon as my conversation with Sky ends, all I can think about is finding him.

Out of respect for Sky, though, I wait. I watch from a distance as he connects with Andrea. I spy her giving him a hug, then draping her arm around his back and walking with him toward their car. The rest of his family follows shortly after. I say a silent prayer then that Sky finds what he's looking for—and soon—because he deserves a happily ever after as much as I do. Once their cars pull out of the parking lot, I jolt into action, searching for the man who makes my heart happier than it's ever been.

My first stop is the hot chocolate booth where I saw Jesse earlier, but he's no longer there. I scan the other booths, and when I don't see him at any of those, I walk inside the inn. Everywhere I look, large groups of people are chatting and drinking cocktails. I weave in and out of them, searching their faces but not seeing his. I spy Mark and Beth in a group by the tree in the parlor, but I duck behind the cocktail bar so they don't see me. I'll talk to them later. Right now, all I want to do is find Jesse.

I check for him in the kitchen next but don't see him there either, so I head back outside and over to the line for horse-drawn carriage rides. Will is returning from leading a ride just as I approach. He stops the horses and looks at me.

"Have you seen Jesse?" I ask.

"Not in a while. He came on a ride with me about thirty minutes ago."

I nod and thank him, heading toward the barn since I haven't checked there yet. I peek in, but it's pretty empty—just a couple of kids and their parents standing outside the chicken coop, petting the chickens' heads.

Where is he?

My heart is thrashing as I exit the barn, frantically looking in every direction. Now that I'm certain of my decision, I want to shout it at the top of my lungs. I want Jesse to know it's him I choose without a doubt in my mind, without an ounce of confusion. The truth of it beats through me like a drum.

It's him. It's him. It's him.

"Looking for something?"

"Jesse," I breathe, pivoting toward his voice. He's walking toward me from the direction of our cottages. I'm so relieved I'm not even sure if I smile. I just know I'm moving, and then I'm meeting him in the middle.

His hair is windblown and he's wearing my favorite jacket of his: it's blue-and-green plaid, and because it's so cozy, some nights he brings it to the fire for me and lets me bundle up in it. I've never told him that all those nights he let me borrow it, I mostly loved wearing it because it smells like him.

I can tell him that kind of thing now. Later. After I get what I need to say off of my chest.

Tears are welling in my eyes, and I don't want Jesse to see me crying and think I'm about to deliver bad news, but I can't control

257

the few that break free. I open my mouth, to tell him they're happy tears—that I'm not here to break his heart—but he speaks first.

"This is for you," he says, handing me a gift I hadn't even noticed he was holding.

"Jesse—" I start to say, but he stops me, pressing a finger to my lips.

"Just open it first, okay?"

I can't. I can't wait a minute longer to tell him how I feel. But that focused look is on Jesse's face, the one that tells me he really cares that I open it.

"Please?" he says, cementing my impression.

"You didn't have to get me something," I say, taking it.

"I told you I would."

He did tell me he would. When I first got here, he said he'd be sure to get me something good for Christmas. And I got him something special too, but it's in my cottage.

I remove the ribbon and wrapping paper slowly. Underneath, there's a green box, and inside the box is an ornament. I pull it out.

Not just any ornament.

A beautiful handmade one.

Santa is hanging from the string and he's holding a scroll of paper. On top of the scroll, Jesse inscribed *Harper's Vermont Bucket List*, and beneath it is a giant check mark along with the word *complete*.

"I don't know what choice you've made tonight," he says. There's a flash of anguish in his eyes, but then it's gone. "But in case that choice was to leave, I wanted to make sure you left with a reminder of what you came for."

Selfless Jesse.

My hearts swells against the walls of my chest, and tears are falling down my cheeks in earnest now. Jesse reaches out to wipe them away, his fingers leaving a tingling trail on my skin.

"I love you, Jesse," I say, unable to contain the words anymore. "I'm so in love with you, I don't know how I was ever unsure of it."

I see a smile sweep across Jesse's face as if I've just given him the greatest gift in the world, and my heart expands, thrumming fast behind my rib cage.

"I might have come here for my bucket list, but I found so much more: I found you. I'm so grateful to you for being patient with me as I listened to my heart. I love you, Jesse. I love you so much."

He pulls me into his chest then, and I feel him exhale what seem like a thousand pent-up breaths all at once, and then a laugh, as if his joy can't be contained, and my stomach somersaults at the sound.

"I love you too, Harper," he tells me. He kisses the top of my head and holds me even closer. "More than you can know."

I already knew I made the right choice. But as soon as these words leave his mouth, I'm convinced of it ten times over.

This is where I belong. This is where I'm meant to be.

Here. Here with Jesse.

When he finally releases me, I gently place my gift down on the snow beside us and reach for his hands. I want to tell him everything. But he lifts a hand to my cheek instead, sliding it along until it cups my jaw, the tips of his fingers anchored in my hair.

"I've been waiting so long for this," he says, his eyes on my lips.

"How long, exactly?" I want to know the precise moment Jesse realized he had feelings for me. I want to hear everything he wasn't able to tell me while he was waiting for me to come to terms with what I think I've known deep down inside me all along.

"That's a story for another day," he says.

"Jesse, tell—"

He steps closer, his eyes heating with an intensity I've only seen twice before: the night the power went out and the day he almost kissed me in my cabin. And suddenly, I can't speak. I can barely breathe.

I feel the shift within me, the flash of desire so intense that I lean toward him without thinking. I feel his stubble on my temple, and memories, one on top of the other, flash through me: every near kiss, every denied touch, every too-long look, every single casual brush. All of them leading to this moment.

The world narrows to Jesse and me, to here and now.

As if he can hear my thoughts, he says, "Right now, Harper, I just need you."

Then his hands are on my hips, my hands are on his chest, his lips find mine, and I'm . . . I'm on fire. Everything within me is ignited. I'm consumed with the power of it, of the want, of the need, of the love, and when Jesse tilts his head and deepens the kiss, I moan, and it vibrates from me through to Jesse, and I feel the answering vibration in his own chest, beneath my hands. A pulse takes flight somewhere within me, a pounding wave of heat spreading across my limbs, demanding more, more of—

This. I never imagined passion like this. I've never loved like this.

I don't know how long the kiss goes on for. We can't seem to stop, as if we're trying to make up for weeks and months all at once. But I know that when Jesse finally lifts his head, my chest is heaving and his breath is coming in short bursts, little rapid puffs I can see in the air. I whimper at the sudden loss of heat, missing his lips and tongue and hands, and Jesse slams a quick, hard kiss onto my lips in response to the sound.

"Jesse." I cut a glance at the cabins behind him, then at his lips, then at the party in full gallop around us.

We look at each other a moment, and then Jesse swoops down to grab my present off the ground and seizes my hand, tugging me toward our cabins, and I'm laughing. He looks back at me as we stumble through his door, and a new smile illuminates his face, one I haven't seen before but have a feeling I'll be seeing often now. It sets my stomach fluttering, sends little sparks into my chest.

"Harper," he says in the quiet of the cabin. "Harper."

And then my back is against the door and Jesse's lips are on mine and it's—

The.
Best.
Christmas.
Ever.

epilogue

One year (and one day) later
Jesse

Harper's still asleep next to me.

I know this with certainty before I even open my eyes because I can hear her light snoring. I grin at the sound.

I've had that same reaction every morning since she first slept over a year ago. I love that the sound confirms that she's here in my bed, where for months I only imagined her being, before I reach for her warmth and find out how she slept and what she dreamt and whatever else might be on her mind first thing.

Grinning like an idiot and not caring in the least, I open my eyes and turn my head to look at her.

I've got it so bad.

Her eyes flutter open at that exact moment, and she smiles when she catches me staring, then turns on her side toward me, tucking one hand beneath her head under the pillow. When she starts to laugh, I seek out her other hand and thread my fingers through hers.

"What's funny?" I ask.

"You—looking at me all adoringly when I can't imagine what I must look like after last night."

I make a show of examining her. Her eyes are a little puffy with sleep, but still bright. Her blonde hair is mussed and messy, and she's wearing only one Christmas tree earring, the other lost in the sheets. Her lips are pink and still a little swollen, and then there's just skin for days.

I send her a heated look, speaking in that silent way we sometimes do. *My adoration stands.*

You're crazy, she says with her widened eyes.

I grin again and bring her hand to my lips, pressing a kiss to her knuckles, then pull her closer to me beneath the sheets. Out loud, I say, "Remind me what happened last night."

"You don't remember?" Her tone is flirtatious. She knows I could never forget.

We celebrated our official one-year anniversary last night at the annual Christmas Eve party, but halfway through the night, we escaped from the crowd and ended up back here—in my cabin that we now share. What followed somehow rivaled what happened behind closed doors last year when we came in here to finally give in to all we'd been resisting. A part of me hopes this becomes a tradition.

"Joggle my memory," I say, pulling her even closer.

"Well, it started a little like this." She closes the remaining gap between us and releases a groan into my mouth. I swallow it, feeling the fire building in my chest, the one that burns only for her.

One kiss turns into two until our kisses flow into one another, languid and teasing, and become something else, something that begins to heat my blood and test my restraint.

I've got it so, so bad.

Her lips slide over to my earlobe, and she tugs on it gently with her teeth. "Do you remember now?"

"I'm starting to," I breathe, bringing my hand behind her head. I pull her mouth back to mine.

Kissing leads to touching. Touching leads to Harper muttering my name. And the way she mutters my name damn near makes me unravel. When her arms encircle me and I feel her nails dig into my back, any last ounce of control I have is gone, and I shift us, rolling on top of her.

"Looks like your memory is back," she grins.

I settle my hips against hers, hovering above her and holding her gaze for a brief second before dipping my head down and smiling against her lips. "Not completely. Help me remember what's next."

And she does.

And it's even better than last night.

Every time is better than the last.

Every day is better than the last.

How in the world did I get this lucky?

———

"I *really* need to get going this time." Harper is sitting on the edge of our bed buttoning up her shirt.

It's her second attempt at getting dressed. The first time, she gave in to the kisses I pressed into her neck as I knelt on the bed behind her, falling back in my arms. I'm trying the same tactic now.

"It's Christmas morning," I say in between kisses. "Where do you have to rush off to?"

"Just an errand."

She's not usually one to keep things vague or to keep secrets from me, but I don't push it. She must have a reason.

Once she finishes the last button, she spins toward me and smiles, linking her arms around my neck.

"You should get up too, mister," she grins. "We're hosting breakfast for our families, remember? And we have guests."

"You make me forgetful," I say, leaning in and kissing her again.

At first I thought my constant need for Harper—for *this*—was out of a desire to make up for the months I was unable to act on my feelings and could only fantasize about being together. But it's been a full year now, and my desire for her—this nearly impatient need—hasn't waned, it's only grown. So I've concluded it's something else entirely.

It's what happens when you fall for your best friend.

The connection is deeper, more intense, more . . . everything.

I break off the kiss before it goes on too long because I know she's right. We both need to get moving.

She smiles against my mouth before I pull back. "To be continued . . .?"

I kiss both corners of her mouth, then her forehead. "Absolutely."

She waits for me to get dressed and we walk out of the cabin together, hand in hand. Snow must've fallen last night, because fresh powder is covering everything in a new and pristine blanket. The sun is just beginning to rise, and it's painting the sky and the snow a variety of colors. The air has that crisp smell, and the birds are starting to chirp.

Our boots leave fresh tracks in the snow as I escort Harper to my car, which we now share, and open the door for her.

Once she's off, I head to the inn. A couple of guests are staying with us for the holiday, but because they have family in the area and plan to celebrate all day with them, they only requested coffee this morning rather than a full breakfast.

I prepare that coffee now, deciding to hold off on starting preparations for the breakfast Harper and I are making for her parents and mine until her parents surface from their room upstairs and mine arrive.

After I carry the coffee into the parlor and say hello to the few guests who stop in, I wait till the room empties out. Then I take a minute to sit in an armchair by the Christmas tree and enjoy the glow of lights. I haven't been able to relax here the past couple of days, as we've been busy preparing for and hosting the Christmas Eve celebration. But the work we put in panned out.

It was the most well-attended Christmas Eve celebration we've ever had at the inn, which made Harper and I feel good, given that it came on the heels of our first official year running it together. It was also fun to have Harper's parents here for the party. We haven't yet been able to visit them in Atlanta, given that it's hard for us to get away, but they don't seem to mind coming out here; they've visited a couple times since Harper called them last Christmas morning to tell them about us—and her plans to remain in Stowe and run the inn with me.

What a year running this place together has been. It's not yet more successful than it was under the management of my parents, but it's as successful, which was our goal. Both of us are incredibly grateful for the success and for having a job that allows us to spend so much time together. For some couples, this much alone time might drive them crazy, but for Harper and me, it's perfect. We can't seem to get enough of each other.

I feel a smile creep onto my lips as happens anytime I think of that woman. Sometimes I reflect on what I had with Madison and how torn up I was after she initially walked out of my life, and I realize what a blessing in disguise that was. Harper has mentioned feeling the same way about her breakup with her ex-fiancé, Jake. I wish we could tell everyone struggling to get over somebody that there is someone better out there. Your person will show up, and life will make sense again. It just might require waiting. But the wait is worth it.

So worth it.

I hear the front door open and a voice call out my name.

Harper's voice.

I can't believe there was a period of my life where I didn't get to hear it every day. Now I can't imagine not hearing it every morning, afternoon, and night.

"In here," I say.

When she walks into the parlor, I notice she's holding a bag. I rise up out of my chair, and when she hands it to me, I look inside. It's cream.

"I noticed last night we didn't have any," she says. "We need cream to make Irish coffees."

Brendan's signature holiday drink.

Whenever I think I've reached my threshold for how much I'm capable of feeling, somehow Harper pulls a new emotion out of me. Sometimes it's an affection. Sometimes it's a sharp burst of desire. And sometimes it's a deep connection to a part of my soul, *like the one I feel now.*

Since we took over the inn, Harper has made a point of preserving both Brendan's memory and Molly's, in small ways like this and in bigger ways, like helping me to create a foundation in their honor. The foundation helps support local businesses to keep Stowe a thriving downtown, something we felt was fitting given Brendan and Molly's love for the city. Harper's support in this endeavor means so much to me. She means so much to me.

If I were told I had to go back in time and endure all the angst and the uncertainty that accompanied the last holiday season to guarantee my arrival at this moment, I'd suffer through it ten more times—without question.

God, I love this woman.

"Come here," I say, drawing her into my arms and kissing her softly, then smoothing down her hair with my hand.

"Don't move," I say. She eyes me curiously as I leave her side and walk to the tree. Crouching down, I retrieve a box beneath it.

All weekend I've been trying to find the perfect moment to give her something I've worked on for weeks. I thought I'd give it to her in front of everybody, but something about this moment spurred me to want to give it to her now, when it's just the two of us.

We've talked a lot about everything we went through last year, and in one of those conversations, we broke down the two times Harper told me she'd chosen me. The first time, once it clicked that I was the one, she waited for the perfect moment for hours. She held off as the feeling built up, until she was overwhelmed by that press of *yes, now* to say it. And the second time, she said she was frantic with the need to tell me, that it exploded out of her when she couldn't contain it anymore. Right now, I feel a blend of the two.

She frowns when I hand it to her. "I thought we said we weren't getting each other anything."

We *did* say that. We bought gifts for our families but decided our gift to each other would be buying Harper's parents their plane tickets so we could enjoy their company and they wouldn't have to stress about pricey holiday travel fares.

"It's not exactly a gift," I say. "Open it."

She continues to eye me as she peels back the wrapping paper, but once she finds the sheet of paper inside, her focus shifts, and I hear her breath catch. I watch her scan the page and I see tears fill her eyes as she reads the bucket list I wrote, one filled with twenty-five items for us to check off together . . . before becoming husband and wife.

Because the last item on the list she's holding reads *Marry Me*.

I reach into my pocket for the ring, knowing I won't have much time.

The ring I chose is simple and elegant. Harper won't have to worry about it snagging on anything during our daily duties, and she won't have to take it off when gardening, one of the many hobbies she's picked up over the past year.

She decided that hobbies were a lot less pressure than passions and told me that's what she'll be sticking to from here on out. I've done my best to encourage every single one, helping her to be the most her that she can be. And she encourages me to be the most me I can be too.

I think that's the true definition of a soul mate: someone who loves you for exactly who you are but also supports you in being the best you.

When her eyes seem to reach the bottom of the list, I drop to one knee. As soon as she looks down, I ask, "Will you marry me?"

"Yes. Absolutely, yes."

No hesitation. No wait.

I jump to my feet and slide the ring on her finger, relieved that it fits perfectly. She kisses me right after in a mix of laughter, tears, and love.

I hold her close and tight as if she might slip through my fingers. After loss, that's just what you do with the people you love who are still here. You appreciate them more. You love them harder than you knew was possible.

And as for the people who are gone . . . you continue to look for signs that they are still around. Right now, I can sense from a gut feeling that Brendan and Molly are watching. The same gut feeling that told me Harper might one day be my wife.

I felt it when I first spotted her dancing by herself in the parlor before we'd even had introductions. Then again, the morning after I told her about Brendan, when she'd had that look of complete determination on her face and demanded that we name the chickens. And then again, when my parents told me I could keep the inn and my only thought was that I couldn't imagine running it without Harper.

I fell in love with Harper over a holiday season, and I would've waited for her as long as she asked me to wait.

When Harper and I finally break apart, I hear applause, and we both look over to the doorway, only to realize we've had an audience this whole time. Both sets of parents are watching.

They rush over and give us hugs, congratulating us and sharing in our excitement.

Christmas Day has arrived, our families are here, and Harper just agreed to be my wife. There's nothing more to wait for.

Except happily ever after.

Yeah . . .

I like to think that's what's waiting for us next.

acknowledgements

This book would not be in your hands if it weren't for Jordyn McCoy, my newest team member, who read this story week-by-week as I wrote it and gave instant feedback so that I stayed on course. Jordyn, getting to work with you has been a dream! I can't thank you enough for your constant encouragement, never-ending ideas, and enthusiasm for my books.

I wrote *Waiting for December* mostly in coffee shops last holiday season alongside my good friend, Aliza Wilson. Aliza, I will always have the fondest memories of our #TeamJesse versus #TeamSky chats. Thank you for helping me with this plot, for letting me interrupt your work to brainstorm ideas when I was stuck, and for sharing in my excitement for the story.

Yet another champion of this book was my editor, Katrina Diaz Arnold, founder of Refine Editing. Katrina, each time I received an installment of your edits I couldn't wait to open my email because I knew how much stronger you were making the story and was dying to see the improvements. Hearing the excitement in your voice over the phone as we talked through the edits also kept me going when the process got tough. Thank you for your feedback on how to improve this story! Thank you, Jaime Brockway, my copy editor, as well for your attention to detail and suggestions for improvement.

My mom and brother combed through this manuscript several times to help me nail down the timeline and catch any last errors. I know this was not a fun job. Thank you both for making the time!

Thank you also, Mom and Dad, for continuing to support my

dream of writing stories and encouraging me to stick with this work on the hard days.

A few other people are always just a phone call away to remind me to keep going. Thank you: Chelsea Kovacevich, Ketara Alani, Christy Bittner, Olivia O'Connor, Aunt Leslie, Aunt Georgette, Aunt Betsy, Francine Kovacevich, and Casey Costello.

To all the book bloggers who read my first novel, *Waiting at Hayden's*, your support helped me write this one. Thank you for encouraging me, for connecting with me, and for getting behind that story.

Meghan Krueger (@megreadsnovels), thank you for your thoughtful feedback on the novel I wrote before this one! It was invaluable and helped guide my decisions when writing *Waiting for December*. It's been wonderful getting to know you too!

I almost lost the last draft of this manuscript when my computer crashed, but Clint and Monet helped resurrect the file. Thank you both for keeping me calm and working a miracle.

Rafael and everyone else at Formatting Experts, thanks for the beautiful interior of this book and being the best team in the industry. Thanks Ryan Selewicz for my author photo and for your never-ending support, Lindsey Kath for my cover illustration, Danielle Christopher for my cover design, and the entire team at Sullivan & Shea publishing!

During the pandemic I stumbled upon Instagram photos of Edson Hill in Stowe, Vermont and this became the inspired setting for the novel. Though I used my artistic license to make many changes to it, I always imagined my characters here. Thank you, Edson Hill, for providing the inspiration I needed. To all my readers, I hope you get to visit one day!

Many of the stores mentioned in the novel I've visited in person and if you plan a trip to Stowe yourself, I highly recommend wandering into The County Store on Main or Bear Pond Books, or any of the other charming shops and restaurants on Main Street. Please note, some of the stores mentioned including Milk & Maple do not exist and were created purely for the storyline.

To all the book clubs who read *Waiting at Hayden's* and to each and every reader who picked up a copy of that story, or shared it, or talked about it with friends, or reached out to talk with me about it—thank you! Not only has this helped allow me to continue writing, it's also made my job much more fun. Writing is a solitary pursuit and it's been a joy getting to meet so many of you.

When I set out to write this story, all I knew was that I wanted it to be about someone starting over. I hope this book serves as a reminder that change can be good, and that having the courage to course-correct when life doesn't go according to plan can be surprisingly wonderful and just what we never knew we needed. Hopefully this story warmed your heart and maybe gives you the courage to try something new or to take time this holiday season to listen to your heart and see what direction it's trying to lead you next.

If you enjoyed this book, I would be so grateful if you'd consider leaving a review on Amazon, or Goodreads. Reviews help allow authors to continue writing stories and I look forward to the opportunity to share many more. Thank you for your support!

If you are part of a book club and would like me to join in on the discussion, please email me at rileybcostello@gmail.com. I would love to join virtually or in person, if I can.

about the author

RILEY COSTELLO, an Oregon native, graduated with a degree in psychology from Santa Clara University. Her first novel, *Waiting at Hayden's*, was named one of the best beach reads of 2019.

sincerelyriley.com

instagram: @rileycostello

facebook: @rileycostelloauthor

Made in the USA
Las Vegas, NV
23 December 2022

63994370R00164